W0081385

LEGENDARY FRYBREAD DRIVE-IN

Intertribal Stories

LEGENDARY

Intertribal Stories

FRYBREAD

Edited by CYNTHIA LEITICH SMITH

DRIVE-IN

Heartdrum

An Imprint of HarperCollinsPublishers

HarperCollins Children's Books,
a division of HarperCollins Publishers, 195 Broadway, New York, NY 10007

HarperCollins Publishers, Macken House,
39/40 Mayor Street Upper, Dublin 1, D01 C9W8, Ireland

Heartdrum is an imprint of HarperCollins Publishers.

Legendary Frybread Drive-In: Intertribal Stories © 2025 by Author Consultant CLS, LLC
"Maybe It Starts" © 2025 by Katherine Hart
"House of Stray Cats" © 2025 by Eric Gansworth
"Mvskoke Joy" © 2025 by Marcella Bell
"Game Night" © 2025 by Darcie Little Badger
"Look Away" © 2025 by Karina Iceberg
"Patent Red" © 2025 by Author Consultant CLS, LLC
"Braving the Storm" © 2025 by Kaua Māhoe Adams
"You Had One Job" © 2025 by Andrea L. Rogers
"Heart Berry" © 2025 by C. Isaacs
"Momentum" © 2025 by Christine Hartman Derr
"I Love You, Grandson" © 2025 by Brian Young
"The Rest Will Come" © 2025 by K. A. Cobell
"Language Lesson" © 2025 by Jen Ferguson
"Hearts Aflutter" © 2025 by AJ Eversole
"Love Buzz" © 2025 by Byron Graves
"Jilly Bean and Jessa Jean" © 2025 by Angeline Boulley
"Kathy's Poem" © 2025 by David A. Robertson
"Open Mic at the Drive-In" © 2025 by Author Consultant CLS, LLC
Letter from Cynthia Leitich Smith © 2025 by Author Consultant CLS, LLC

All rights reserved. Manufactured in Harrisonburg, VA, United States of America.
No part of this book may be used or reproduced in any manner whatsoever without written permission
except in the case of brief quotations embodied in critical articles and reviews. Without limiting the
exclusive rights of any author, contributor, or the publisher of this publication, any unauthorized use
of this publication to train generative artificial intelligence (AI) technologies is expressly prohibited.
HarperCollins also exercises their rights under Article 4(3) of the Digital Single Market Directive
2019/790 and expressly reserves this publication from the text and data mining exception.
harpercollins.com

Library of Congress Control Number: 2024947204
ISBN 978-0-06-331426-9

Typography by Molly Fehr
25 26 27 28 29 LBC 7 6 5 4 3
First Edition

For Rosemary, who is legendary, and . . .

for the musicians, gamers, beaders, and fashionistas,
the foodies, romantics, wisecrackers, and time travelers,
the poets, storytellers, language learners, and survivors,
the artists, activists, athletes, and rising readers . . .

That neon sign
at the drive-in
shines for you.

CONTENTS

FOREWORD

Together, seventeen writers imagined Sandy June's Legendary Frybread Drive-In, established by grandparents of various tribal Nations to offer hope, humor, and healing to young heroes of Turtle Island. We imagined the regulars at the drive-in, who might mosey down well-worn paths to its tall neon sign. We theorized visitors might be lured by the sound of rising music or the scent of smoking beef, or they might accidentally stumble through the surrounding trees or even catch a ride through time in Sandy June's food truck.

But all you need to do is turn the page.

MAYBE IT STARTS

Kate Hart

Maybe it starts with the cellar.

Maggie hates the cellar. Not just because it's dark and wet and full of spiders and who knows what else, and not just because it's always scary weather that necessitates entering its depths. She hates the cellar because it almost made her parents get divorced. When they moved out of their apartment into a real house, Dad wanted a smaller, cheaper one that came with a basement, and he told Mom he'd only buy this one if she agreed to use her tribe's assistance program to get a shelter installed. Whether Mom objected more to the help itself or the fact that her non-Native husband called the Chickasaw Nation "her" tribe, her parents didn't speak to each other for days, and even after they bought the beautiful house in the Fayetteville historic district, "the cellar" felt like code for dark, unsettling times.

So Maggie really does not want to go to the cellar.

She could just stay in the house—her parents are gone on a weekend getaway to Kansas City and they'd never know—but the rules have been drilled into her since childhood. Fayetteville is Tornado Alley adjacent, in the Arkansas hills just east of the Oklahoma border, and since her parents are Okies by birth, they take the frequent watches and warnings seriously. The worst systems seem to break up and go around the mountains, but you just never know when the weather will roll a strike, and at the moment it sounds like a wild night at Ozark Lanes all around her. Even a warning doesn't mean she has to go to the cellar, though. The real indicator is the local newscaster. If they name your town, pay attention. Your neighborhood? Put on your shoes. Your street? Get your butt underground.

And they definitely mentioned the Fayetteville historic district, so Maggie takes her butt outside to the cellar, along with her phone, even though it's almost dead. Pausing on the porch steps, she checks one more time to see if Mom has apologized (ha) or sent a text pretending nothing happened (much more likely), but there's no—

"Ow!" She grabs her head. It's hailing.

Muttering profanities, she races across the lawn to open the cellar door, holding it cracked to watch from inside. Hail piles up into ice drifts, growing from pellets to Ping-Pong balls. When a gust yanks the handle out of her grasp, she decides to batten down the hatches, latching it behind her and inspecting her surroundings via phone flashlight. Not much to see, just concrete walls with a built-in bench. It's not a real cellar—no shelves for preserves or rations for nuclear fallout—just a temporary safety pod. Running a hand through her wet hair creates a grim mental picture: emerging from the shelter to find reporters in the neighborhood, trying to interview her while she looks like a bedraggled cat. At least she's dressed and not in her pj's. The same meme makes the rounds every storm: "Tornado season PSA: Bras on, teeth in!"

Crash. She shrieks as something hits the door with bone-rattling impact. The wind wails impossibly louder, throwing debris against the door like a machine gun. This is why Mom used to add "bike helmet" to the storm list when she was little—a mattress over the bathtub only protects so far from blunt force trauma. She hasn't been this scared of a storm since she was a kid. Maggie sits on the hard bench and wraps her arms around her knees. **This storm is bad**, she types, just in case Mom gets a weather alert. **I'm safe in cellar.**

The text won't send. "Crap." Nothing will load at all. She scans the floor for the weather radio, but Dad took it out to replace the batteries and it hasn't made its way back. She should have brought a flashlight. She hopes the damage isn't too bad. She hopes the neighbors got somewhere safe.

In the dark, all alone, she can admit: She's also a little grateful. Mom can't stay mad after a storm like this.

It's not like Maggie went *looking* for a long-lost cousin. It's certainly not her fault a whole family of them turned up, much less that one invited them to meet—and it is 1,000 percent not her fault that the reunion coincides with a big tribal event. It might be a liiiittle bit her fault for buying concert tickets in Oklahoma City for the same weekend without asking, and mayyyybe she was a little dishonest when asked for more details, and perhaaaaps she didn't need to yell, "Damn it, Janet, why are you like this?" knowing that Mom hates to be called anything but Mom.

But didn't Mom react exactly how she expected? Maggie scowls into the dark, mentally counting the weeks until she'll be eighteen. Wait till she gets to college. All the other kids will be going wild at keg parties while Maggie's big rebellion will be getting an Ancestry.com membership and attending family reunions.

Her phone flashlight dies, but thankfully the storm sounds like it's winding down. Sighing, she stands up and stretches, then unlatches the door.

It won't open.

Maggie jiggles the handle and pushes again.

Nothing moves.

Jamming her shoulder against it, she gives it a shove, then a stronger one, but nothing happens. She can't even nudge it enough to let light in, and with dawning horror, she realizes their giant oak tree must have fallen on top of the cellar. Dad is going to be crushed, metaphorically. She's glad she hasn't been, literally. But she's alone in the dark, with no phone, no food, and no bathroom, and her parents are hours away with no idea that she's stuck.

Screaming won't help, but she does it anyway, pounding on the door with both fists. When her throat hurts from yelling, she leans against the wall, buries her face in the crook of her elbow, and tries to swallow a shuddering sob. "I need help," she whispers to herself.

A small crack of light appears.

Maggie steps back, mouth open, then jiggles the handle.

It swings open.

Maybe it starts with the truck.

Janet didn't want to drive a truck. She wanted something small, like a Honda Civic, or something cute, like a Volkswagen Bug, but she did not want the beat-up, two-tone Ford pickup with a cracked windshield and a backfiring tail pipe that made it sound like the vehicle had eaten beans for every meal of its life. She didn't care that it had been her father's, or that it ran like a top, or that it somehow never ran out of gas, or that her mother had saved it all these years just for her.

It drew attention. And Janet didn't want attention.

It was only one of the many ways in which she disappointed her mother. Her rebellious, ethereal, aura-reading, forgetting-she-had-a-daughter-at-all mother didn't just like to be noticed—she demanded it. She wore gauzy skirts and bangle bracelets, anklets that chimed when she walked, patchouli that smelled up the house, dresses made of tablecloths and fishnets sewn together—and a full face of incongruous makeup with a "signature red" lipstick. She refused to answer to any form of "mother" or "mom" or "Mrs.," forcing Janet and any friends she brought home to call her Star, though her name was actually Sharon.

Her mother worked long hours, and when she had free time, she disappeared for days on end. Explanations were rare and disappointing, and she seemed genuinely confused that Janet resented being left alone. She read palms, she read tea leaves, she read *Mother Earth News* and every lurid bodice ripper she could get her hands on, but she could not read her daughter, and so she didn't notice how much it hurt when she missed things like school plays. Birthday parties.

Graduation.

Janet found her impossible to live with, much less emulate, and her only goal was to get the hell out of Tulsa and Oklahoma entirely. "Indian Territory," her mom insisted on calling it, just like she insisted on calling them both Indians. Their shared light skin and hair didn't stop Sharon the Star from telling people it was their "proud Chickasaw heritage" that made her so "spiritual and connected to the earth."

Janet was fairly sure that Reiki was Japanese, Wicca was British, and yoga came from a different kind of Indian, but her mother had no time for such trivialities. She was busy painting a portrait of Jerry Garcia or making dream catchers or trying to launch a restaurant that served nothing but herbal teas.

Janet always wondered what life would have been like if her father had survived Vietnam. Would Mom have been more normal? Would she have spent more time at home? Would she have insisted on pretending to be Indian? She had no grandparents to ask—her father's parents were deceased, and her mother's had disowned them for reasons Janet didn't fully understand. So she decided to forget about the past and concentrate on the future. She studied hard, she drove the beater truck, and she saved the money from her after-school waitressing gig to fund her escape. The University of Arkansas wasn't as far away as she would have liked, but it wasn't Oklahoma, so when they offered her a full scholarship, she got in the truck and took off.

Sharon the Star tried to stay in touch, in her own way. She sent bundles of herbs that Janet wasn't allowed to burn in her dorm room, not that she wanted to. She sent belated birthday cards and random newspaper clippings about people Janet didn't know. She came to visit once or twice, always at an inconvenient time, and after her distracted daughter snapped at her during finals week junior year, she didn't try to visit again.

She missed graduation.

Janet didn't give her a chance to miss the wedding—she just eloped. She bought herself a cute little Volkswagen and sent the truck back to her mother in Oklahoma. Janet considered not even telling Sharon the

Star when she got pregnant, but she had no one else to ask for advice, and to her shock, her mother finally came through. Turned out some of those herbal teas were actually good for nausea. And lo and behold, when Maggie was born, Sharon the Star became a doting, if somewhat flighty, grandmother. Janet appreciated the change, but she couldn't trust it. She couldn't let Maggie get hurt the way she had. So Janet limited their visits and discouraged family trips, and though Sharon had found proof that they were, in fact, Native, Janet just couldn't make herself care. A paper trail to a Chickasaw great-grandfather none of them had ever known was a path into a past she'd spent her whole life escaping. But she did give in and use her tribal citizenship twice: Once to help pay for grad school.

And once to get a cellar.

Maybe it starts with red lipstick.

Star had always been a loud person. She screamed her head off as a baby. She played rowdy games as a little girl. She played that darn rock 'n' roll music at top volume as a teenager, and she liked boys who drove noisy cars. Motorcycles. Shiny new two-tone Ford trucks.

She tried her best to please her parents, but it just seemed impossible. *Lower your voice, tone down your clothes, turn off that music.* It wasn't just that she didn't want to—it was that she couldn't. Loud was part of her, grating against a wrongness she perceived but couldn't identify, something in her family that had no name or face but demanded to make a sound through her. Its volume grew as she did, a swelling crescendo alongside budding hips and breasts, making itself manifest in bell-bottoms. Tie-dye. Platform shoes. Red lipstick.

The night her mother took a Kleenex and forcibly tried to wipe the makeup off her face, Sharon flounced from the house and into her boyfriend's truck. She left with a single mission in mind: get the hell out of Oklahoma and never come back.

They settled down in New Mexico, but the boyfriend was sent to Vietnam and never made it home. He left her with the truck and with Janet, the daughter he never got to meet, both of which came back to Oklahoma with Sharon.

"We were going to get married!" she told her parents—it was the truth!—but the cart had already preceded the horse, the milk had been drunk without the cow's purchase, et cetera, et cetera. There was no saving Sharon's reputation in their eyes, and just as little hope for her future. Of course she could stay, they said. But they had some rules. And their first rule was that they wanted quiet.

And Sharon tried—she tried every way in the world to tamp herself down. But when Janet got bigger and started to blossom, she wouldn't ask her little girl to wilt. Even if that meant making it on their own.

So they got in the truck. Sharon found a shitty job and a shitty place to live, and then better jobs and a better place to live, but not a better vehicle, because the truck somehow kept running. She gave Janet all the freedom she'd never had as a child, and when her daughter proved to be the responsible sort, she gave herself a little freedom, too. She gave herself a whole new name. She found friends and lovers and passions and hobbies, and most importantly, she found answers about her family. When she realized Daddy wasn't her biological dad, several things clicked into place—but several other things swung free and set her spinning for a while.

By the time she'd calmed down, Janet was gone, and Star realized perhaps her daughter had wanted a little less freedom and a little more guidance. Perhaps her own mother had wanted lots of things that Star had never guessed. It was too late to mother her daughter, and too late to be a good daughter to her mother, but she could make amends via her grandchild. And she started with the truth: "My birth father was Native. I have family beyond the parents who failed me. You have family beyond me and the ways I failed you."

But Janet didn't find these truths convincing, much less comforting. And Maggie would have to hurt her mother to seek those truths herself.

So maybe it really starts with the frybread stand.

Maggie steps through the door into fading sunlight. The air is cool, crisper than normal, but the ground isn't wet, and her backyard is . . . not her backyard. Blinking, she tries to make sense of the pockmarked parking lot in front of her. It smells like . . . Sonic? Turning around, she finds a green door labeled Any Gender Restroom. *Sonic isn't green*, her brain helpfully supplies.

She walks toward the front of the building, where coordinating green picnic tables sit beneath a canopy, with vehicles parked on either side. Arkansas doesn't require front license plates, so the number of cars from far-flung origins like Washington, Montana, and Ontario stick out. But most confusing is the big yellow-and-green sign proclaiming "Sandy June's Legendary Frybread Drive-In."

She slows to a stop, and despite the confusion, her spirits lift.

She's always wanted to try frybread, but opportunities have not been forthcoming, despite her knowing for years that she's Chickasaw. Of course there was the cellar debacle, but Grandma Star also sends her books about Native history and culture and let slip that Mom used a tribal scholarship for grad school. Of course Mom would never have told her. The only thing Mom hates more than accepting help is needing it in the first place, and that's what being Native seems to mean to her. Frybread would somehow be an admission of need.

A woman turns the corner and almost crashes into her. "Maggie!"

She steps back, eyes wide. "Hello?"

"Thank goodness." The woman takes both of Maggie's hands in hers. "Come on over here, honey. Are you okay?"

"Um . . ." She looks around, then down at herself. "Yes? I think?"

"Good, good." The woman continues to pat Maggie's hands as she subtly pulls her toward a picnic table. Her gray hair is short, earlobes long, with enormous beaded earrings that sway with her steps. A pin on her shirt says *Legendary Gra* with *Auntie Bernadette* written on masking tape over the rest. She all but forces Maggie to sit down. "Are you hungry? Thirsty?" Before Maggie can answer, she claps her hands together. "Just a minute, sweetness." She heads back the way she's just come.

Maggie grips the wooden table to steady herself and does the anxiety exercise Grandma Star taught her. Five things she can see: Green tables. Order window. Big stage. Mural. Lots of people her age, including a group carrying instruments. *Everyone must be here to see the band.* As if that helps makes sense of anything. She closes her eyes. Four things she can hear: Cars idling. Birds chirping. Mom calling her . . . She opens her eyes, then rubs them and stands up as her mother emerges from a bathroom. Mom gasps and runs over, almost bulldozing Bernadette, who's balancing several baskets. "Are you okay?" Janet asks, throwing her arms around Maggie.

"Yeah, I'm . . . Are *you* okay?" Maggie asks.

Janet squeezes Maggie's arms, then looks around for a long minute. "I think so." She shakes her head. "How did you get here?"

"I was in the cellar." A horrible possibility occurs to her. "Am I still there? Is this a dream? Am I dead?"

"Not unless I'm also dead," Mom says. "Or passed out somewhere in Kansas City."

Maggie can't follow this conversation. She can't even follow her own thoughts. "Okay, so where are we?"

Bernadette clears her throat and nods to the sign, like it's obvious.

"And you are . . . ?" Janet asks.

"Bernadette," the woman replies, like it's obvious, too. "Your great-auntie?" She sets the baskets down and reaches into the pocket of her apron to pull out another name tag. *Legendary Grandparent: Star.* Pressing it into Janet's hand, she says, "Tell your mother she left this here. I'm covering your grandmother's shift," she adds, turning to Maggie.

"Oh," Maggie says. "O . . . kay?"

Auntie Bernadette squints at her. "You look peaked. Have a seat." She slides a basket of fries under Mom's nose. "You want pashofa? Or just a burger?"

"I don't even know what pashofa is," Mom says. "Or where we are."

Maggie knows one answer. "It's like a hominy stew."

"This one also has pork," Bernadette says.

Mom tries not to scowl, but Maggie can see it starting to bend her face. This place may not be real, but Mom's reaction is: Her relief at seeing Maggie is soured just by Maggie knowing a single Chickasaw thing. This is why Maggie didn't tell her about the cousin, or the reunion, or the tribal event. Maggie certainly isn't planning to share that she wants to study tribal law and languages until she's safely in college—and that's if she ever works up the courage to admit she wants to go to the University of Oklahoma in the first place.

Bernadette puts a basket in front of her. "Vegetarian, right? Thought so," she says as Maggie nods. "The pashofa's not really veggie friendly, but that black bean burger is good, and I brought you some frybread to try on the side." She gestures at a dish of purple something. "Grape dumplings for dessert."

"Oh. Wow." Maggie tears off a piece of frybread. "Thank you so much."

Mom pauses, then pushes the fries away. "I don't have my purse. We can't pay for this. I'm so sorry."

Bernadette purses her lips. "Your money's no good here anyway."

"Oh, but—"

"Them's the rules."

Mom shakes her head. "But we—"

Bernadette sits down. "Would you let family pay at your house?"

"Of course not, but this is—"

"What if I let you do some dishes?"

Mom raises an eyebrow. "That would be . . . better, I guess, but I'd rather just pay you back."

"Okay, but what if your time is more valuable to me?"

Mom stares. "Then . . . I guess . . ."

"What if I say *Maggie's* time is more valuable to me? Would Maggie doing the dishes work just as well?"

"I . . ."

"What if I don't need her to do dishes? What if I need her to do something that takes a little more effort? Something with a less obvious reward?"

"Honestly, I . . ." Mom takes a drink, clearly trying to stall.

"It's not a handout if you're giving back," Bernadette says, pushing the ketchup toward Maggie. "And there are lots of ways to do that." She turns to Maggie. "Right, sweetheart?"

"Um . . . yeah." It feels like a trap, but she's starving, so she'll risk getting dish duty. "I suppose."

"Take your momma here. She used a Chickasaw scholarship to get a degree. Was it a handout?" Janet gasps, but Bernadette keeps talking. "No. Because it helped her raise you, and now here you are, set to go to law school and learn Chikashanompa and give back to the people." Maggie and Janet both gape at Bernadette, who steals a french fry. "It's not a handout. It's an investment."

Mom is staring daggers at her. "Law school?"

"Well . . . I . . . yes. I kind of . . . want to go to school." She glances at Bernadette, who motions her on. "In . . . In Norman."

"In Oklahoma." It sounds like she's saying, *In hell.*

"I know you hate . . ." It seems rude to say *Native stuff*, given their surroundings. "Family history and that kind of thing. But it's important to me." Now that the seal has been broken, Maggie's words start to tumble out. "I want to meet our other relatives and have . . . have cousins! And aunties! And, like, learn about our tribe! Go see the cultural center! Be . . . part of things!"

"But we just—" Mom squeezes her eyes shut. "We don't *belong* there, honey! We weren't raised in it, and we don't look right, and we—"

Bernadette puts a hand over Mom's. "Look around this joint." She pats gently and pulls Mom to her feet, leading them around the building. Families have filled up the green picnic tables, and they nod or raise a hand in greeting. Maggie can only identify half of their meals—tamales and burgers are easy, but there are also bowls filled with rice and what might be stew with cornbread. At the back of the property, several girls her age seem to be using the wooden stage for a painting project. One holds up a cardboard sign that says "Not Your Wild West Show!"

Bernadette smiles. "Every skin and hair color," she says. "Every age and shape and size. Lots of different languages and foods and clothes, and they're all *here*." Maggie still wants to know exactly where *here* might be, but Bernadette is gathering steam. "They're modern and adapting and moving forward. It's not about superficial appearances or stereotypes, and it's not about living in the past—it's about honoring that past by building a future. . . ."

That's what I want to be part of, Maggie wants to say, but Mom shakes her head. "You and I both know it's more complicated than that."

Bernadette laughs. "Of course it's more complicated than that!

That's life. Nothing's ever simple." She tugs a lock of Maggie's blond hair. "But the flip side of not 'looking right' means you can walk away from it completely and never ask yourself if that's actually out of respect, or just out of fear." When Mom doesn't answer, Bernadette softens her voice. "Neither of you would be here if you didn't belong, but you can make that choice. It's just not what our girl here wants."

Mom turns to Maggie. "Is that true?"

Maggie blinks back tears. "I'm sorry, but . . . yeah. I know you want me to major in business or something, but this is really important to me. I just . . . I want to find my place, and I feel like my place is here. I mean, not *here* here," she adds, waving a hand. "Wherever the heck this is, but you know, with—"

"Honey. Stop." Mom holds up a hand, and Maggie braces herself for a lecture. Instead, Mom's bottom lip is wobbling. "I never meant to . . . squash your interests or force you into a subject you hate." Her eyes land on the mural behind the stage, where one of the painted dancers is wearing bright red lipstick that clashes with her pink beaded collar. "There's just a lot you don't know about how I grew up. Your grandmother . . ." She glances at Bernadette. "She was a lot different back then."

"But that's the whole point," Maggie says. "She's different from that *now*."

"Yeah." Mom takes her mother's name tag from her pocket and studies it, then sighs and hands it to Maggie. "She is. I guess we all are."

Before Maggie can answer, Bernadette clears her throat. "Well! Janet, you and I have a little more chatting to do, but the two of you will have to finish your own conversation at home. It's time for Maggie to go."

"Go where?" Maggie can't even hug her mom goodbye as Bernadette hustles her toward the building. The sound of a horn blaring gets louder with every step they take, but it's not coming from the cars—it's coming from the bathroom.

Auntie Bernadette hands her a foil-wrapped package. "Dinner to go, since you didn't get to finish." She squeezes Maggie's shoulders. "Don't worry, help has already arrived, and I'm gonna work on your momma a little more. But it's going to be okay."

"Okay?" Maggie echoes.

"Okay." Bernadette smiles, then pulls the door open and pushes her into the dark stall.

Maggie fumbles one-handed for a light switch, but the screech of metal on metal opens a gap behind her, illuminating the concrete walls of the cellar.

The end of a crowbar appears as a voice calls over the blaring horn. "Maggie!"

It sounds like . . . She shakes her head. "I'm here! Help!"

"She's there!" The voice comes closer. "Maggie, can you hear me?"

"I can, I—" Maybe this was all a dream and she's still stuck in it. "Grandma?"

Someone jimmies the door open a little wider, and half of her next-door neighbor's face appears. "You all right?"

"Yeah, I'm—" Is she fine? "I'm not hurt."

"Glory be," someone says behind him.

"Is that my grandma?" she demands.

He's not listening. "You just hang tight," he says. "There's a truck on top of the cellar that we gotta move, but don't worry. Damnedest thing—it landed right side up, not a scratch on it, keys in the ignition."

"Looks pretty old, though," someone else says. "You think it'll start, or we need a tow?"

"Don't worry," Grandma Star says, loud and clear. "It'll start."

HOUSE OF STRAY CATS

Eric Gansworth

I was not even a little surprised at the stack of linens and clothes on the couch when I got home from my summer job at Sandy June's Legendary Frybread Drive-In. Yes, as far as I can tell, everyone used the full name, at least the first time they spoke it in a conversation. You might eventually shorten it to Sandy June's.

If you were Indian, you knew all about Sandy June's, eventually—and if you're Indian from around here, how to find the Bench Tree opening, a nearly invisible entrance. But good luck, Mr. Anthropologist, Mr. Ethnographer. A sign out front said "You Need to Be This Red to Ride This Ride (though we might make an exception this time)." If you weren't Indian and you laughed, you could come in. If you stomped off, well, you stomped off, didn't you?

I was fifteen and finally had a real room of my own, one that even included a window. But there were occasional costs—mostly temporary dispossession. I often had some say in giving up my room when someone's meteor had crashed on the rez. Our house had a no-questions-asked privacy policy. We were sort of a House of Second Chances. Really, more than that, and sometimes with repeaters who couldn't get their lives straight. My mom grumbled it was like the House of Stray Cats, folks using their nine lives.

My siblings' straggly friends who got booted from home for selling Gramma's Sunday roast right out of the freezer for a quick buck moved right in until things cooled down for them. Somehow, my mom still trusted them and never did install that fridge lock she'd threatened.

"What's up with all this?" I asked, pointing to my clothes. I'd put in eight hours at work, part of Sandy June's early-morning prep crew before we opened at eleven. I'd showered at work and wanted nothing more than to catch a nap in my bedroom, in a pair of shorts and nothing else.

"Really, Jackson? You don't know what that means?" My dad raised one Spock eyebrow.

"Who?" I started to ask. On National Picnic Weekend, a ton of Indians came home. Somebody was bound to stay with us, but I didn't usually get dispossessed. Something must have been up if we had only one returning stray and I was still being booted.

"Uncle Max," my dad said finally, giving a look I didn't understand. "Solo."

"Cosplaying *Star Wars* or *Empire*?" I asked, trying to get him to crack. "Makes a difference." I held my palms in front of me and snarled my lips like I was frozen in carbonite.

"How did I raise such a dorky kid?" He sighed.

"In your own likeness, maybe?" We side-eyed each other. "Something more?"

"You wanna ask Max, plenty of opportunity. He's on vacation. Two weeks." Two weeks was a serious cramping of the lifestyle I enjoyed as the last kid at home.

"I know he's my actual uncle, but why can't he stay where the other strays do?"

"Your room used to be his room. Your bed was his bed," my mom said, wandering in. Since Max was her brother, she'd be the formal authority. "And right now, Max needs some connection to home." We lived in the house they'd been raised in.

Our house looked large from the road, making it the target for strays. Inside, it had evolved as each of my siblings felt that sharing a room wasn't fun anymore. My parents added flimsy privacy walls, cutting a big room in twos or threes, each the size of a walk-in closet. My mom's best friend, Sadie, a.k.a. my current boss, politely called it "ill-arranged."

As my parents booted me from their tiny rooms, they said I'd understand when the time came. And at fifteen, you knew the ins and outs of wanting privacy. I maintained my private domain by welcoming the strays whenever my mom informed me of a new one. I'd strip my bed, putting fresh sheets and blankets on it, then make up a narrow "private room" for myself. Then I was supposed to leave a fresh towel and washcloth on my newly made bed for the invader.

"Maybe you'll take your uncle to Sandy June's tonight," my dad added. "Hear that band's pretty good. Maybe stay for the midnight movies."

"I just got home," I said. "And I'm clean. For the first time in hours, I don't smell like a giant walking frybread." We didn't have a real bathroom, an annoying situation my mom insisted on calling *tradish*. Sandy June's had showers for the camping area, which was also an employee perk, so I officially had a right. I liked Sandy June's, particularly summer night activities. It was cool to belong in a meaningful way. This year, they resurrected the midnight movies. My mom and Uncle Max used to hustle rides for the Late Night Cult Movies when they were my age. I could stream most of those flicks, but I missed the adventures they'd had.

"Does Uncle Max know about Fireball?" I asked. My dad wanted Max occupied deep into the evening.

"Have to ask him when he gets here," he responded. None of us wanted to tell Max about this change, but I was apparently chosen. No one knows when or how Fireball arrived. Many people said it was like lacrosse, a gift from the Creator. But it was only played here? It was older than anyone currently alive. Indians came home and others made purposeful trips for the two nights of the year it was played. The one thing we knew for sure—the new generation of chiefs had decided it was time for Fireball to die, and nothing I, or anyone else, said was going to have any impact.

"You two want a fifteen-year-old to tell his uncle that Fireball— the one thing he comes home for every year—has suddenly gone the way of the dinosaur?" It was a huge ask, something you might try to trick a stranger into and hope for the best rather than deal with yourself. But my parents generally requested so little of me, how could I say no?

"Gotta become a man sometime, isn't it, though?" my dad responded. "Since you won't be playing, and we won't have that handy marker to know when you're all grown up." At fifteen, I would have been sort of eligible to play, though no one really enforced the rules. You were left to your better judgment. Fireball was a fierce game, and some guys had permanent damage from putting their bodies through it. I was not exactly a fierce guy. Uncle Max wasn't fierce, either, but like others, he saved vacation days, crossed state lines, and came home for National Picnic. We usually watched together in our lack of fierceness.

We were also usually accompanied by his wife, Angelina. She was Indian. I was always afraid to say her tribe's name out loud, because it seemed like they went by two or three different names simultaneously, depending on who you were talking to.

It was very easy to use the wrong one and have everyone hissing at you like a car with four slashed tires. At first, I thought people were joking when they said he'd married a Winnebago. I was picturing Uncle Max hooking up with a large camper on wheels. What I'm saying? I was unsophisticated and tried to use nosiness only when it counted the most. Anyway, her community was in Wisconsin, maybe? That's where they now lived. They'd met at the Indian dorm in some college, maybe there.

No one really talked details when people went away to college. They were just "off at school." When they got married, Uncle Max chose to be a "real old-time Indian" and relocate to the territory of his wife's people. It was impossible to think of young Max spending nights in the same bed I did, dreaming about the future, wondering about the past, debating about whether he was going to play Fireball the next July. He hadn't lived here since before I was born.

"Deal?" my dad asked. Max and Angelina always stayed in town, so I agreed, for Max.

"One condition," I said. "This stays untouched in the fridge until I can be here. Maybe we'll have it for breakfast." I revealed a perfect wheel of tradish cornbread. Sadie, ever loyal to my mom, had slipped it into my bag, neatly wrapped in foil, saying it was for the three of us.

Sadie had negotiated for her cornbread debut with the legendary grandparents who made the big decisions at Sandy June's. Her brand name was Sovereignty Sadie's Wheels of Fate. This was not cornbread the way you think. It's made of a hulled and cooked meal (an epic process) that's been ground and shaped, taking forever to float to the surface of the bubbling kettle. She claimed her favorite seasoning was a Hint of Mystery.

Sadie's Sandy June's debut was a plan to soothe brokenhearted people who'd just heard about National Picnic's new rules. No one could know how fast word of the cancellation had spread. Like Sandy June's location, Fireball news was all word of mouth, divulged with the greatest of discretion.

For those in the know, Sandy June's campground was the perfect option. The rez had no accommodations, so a lot of people selected the camping area. It was a five-minute walk to Picnic. On Picnic weekend, Sandy June's business picked up as soon as the neon kicked on, and my lunch-bussing demanded more hustle. I'd been looking forward to a break between my Sandy June's shift and the start of Picnic at six tonight.

"Well?" I said, sliding the new wheel, still warm, in the fridge.

"Hard bargain," my dad said, just as we heard Uncle Max pulling in. "Okay, deal."

Max entered and set his bags next to my clothes and linens, acting like it was totally normal to show up alone with only his luggage. He slid a sweating cold six of bottled iced tea in the fridge, staying tradish by bringing food to the family home he'd entered. His gaze paused over the foil-wrapped wheel.

"Uncle Max, why don't we head down to Sandy June's Legendary?" I said, trying to sound perky and excited. He smiled, looking up.

"Your uncle just got here after driving for hours and hours," my mom scolded, while my dad made disappointed clicks and hisses with his tongue, like this hadn't been their idea.

"I'm working there, so you could use my shower privileges."

"You saying I stink, kid?" he said, leaning over me with fake menace. One of the worst rez insults was suggesting someone smelled bad.

"No, no, no, no," I said. "I just know that I like a shower on a hot summer day, and there ain't one inside the five thousand walls in this house." He gripped the top of my head and shook it. Then he grabbed a change of clothes from his bag, tossed them in his backpack. "Sounds good," he said. "You ready?"

"Not yet," I said. I hadn't done Stray Cat prep, since his appearance was a surprise. But there was no way to strip the room of my sheets without it seeming awkward. My mom had protocols to go overboard with the Stray Cats but also be very subtle in our generosity.

"You're fine," my mom said, which meant that she'd take care of those things.

"Why don't we take your car?" I asked. It was almost a ridiculous suggestion, since the walk to Sandy June's was ten minutes tops, even if you were being lazy. "That way, we can stay for the midnight movies and not have to worry about walking through the dark so late at night."

"Tell ya what," Uncle Max added, staring out at the stretch of our property. "Why don't we go through the back paths? Save us some steps."

"You can't get there from here cross-lots," I said, and his face immediately blossomed like a flower emerging from a big tree's shade.

"Haven't heard that word in a long, long time." He grinned. "Cross-lots off the rez is called trespassing. Other people's property requires provable permission and you better be able to present that proof at a moment's notice."

"Even if all you're doing is walking through the woods?"

"No such thing as just *the woods* where I live. Except maybe patches in public parks, and those close at sundown."

The Tuscarora rez was small, according to a lot of people. It was the only one I'd ever really spent time on, so I had nothing to compare it to. Parents passed family land to their kids, and whole stretches just belonged to the Nation. It was supposed to be for the Future, but I never knew why the Future needed it. We stepped through an opening in the bush line and entered the back paths, following the bare earth created by generations of rez feet, doing the cross-lots drift. The deep areas held no houses, no buildings, just some woods, occasional planted fields, meadows, and paths. Even if you wanted to build a house back there, how would you get to it in the winter?

This stretch mostly saw use from hunters, or guys with ATVs and snowmobiles. Max made his way easily, aside from a couple of pauses to stay on track. The trees and bush lines all looked the same to me.

But he found traces of paths whenever the one we were on disappeared.

"Let's say we hang back here for a minute," Max said as we neared a thick patch of overgrowth. He stepped in, almost disappeared immediately, and then encouraged me to follow. I found him at a treehouse, weirdly polished and fancy, like the treehouses you saw on TV shows but never did in real life. It was a tiny one-room shack wedged into the crotch of a maple, with firm boards nailed into the trunk as a ladder. "Go on up, and I'll follow right behind." The inside was weatherproof enough to keep out rain. Two vinyl cushions perched on benches so you could even sleep there. Under them, sealed bins held blankets and more outdoor cushions. I propped open one of the hinge-mounted windows. Waves of laughter crested the trees. We were just a bush line away from Sandy June's Legendary campgrounds.

"Nice to know about this place, right?" he asked after we sat quietly for a little while. I nodded and he asked if I thought I could find it again. I admitted I wasn't sure. "We'll have to make that a goal to accomplish." After a while, he closed the window and showed me how to secure the latch tight. We headed for an obvious clearing I somehow hadn't seen before, and we crossed into the back of Sandy June's, where both food lines were long but went fast and orderly, lubricated by a million jokes and laughs.

"So, is there someone at Picnic your mom doesn't want me to see?" Max asked as he studied the big menu board. I raised my eyebrows like I hadn't understood him. "Kid, no one wants to go to work on their time off. Someone's liable to put you to work, whether you're on the clock or not. I know your ma thinks it's weird that Angelina didn't come. And maybe it is." My mom knew awkward opinions were like gasoline rags in a summertime barn, but I knew what he was talking about. "But Picnic is something—well, Angelina didn't grow up here, so it don't mean the same thing to her. And she always felt people were staring at her." When they were in college, Angelina had offers to be a greeting card model, but only if she dressed up in one of those Sexy Indian Halloween costumes. She declined, of course. Wherever she went, people noticed. When she had come to Picnic, *everyone* noticed. She had maybe misinterpreted the notice. "Don't you have friends from off the rez?"

"Sure," I said, recognizing that I already kept the two sides of my life neatly separated. I'd never mentioned Sandy June's to any of my non-rez friends. It felt like it was supposed to stay legendary *and* invisible unless your bones resonated with the same songs. And if I went anywhere with new guys I'd met in school, I didn't ask rez friends to join us.

"Probably you started to live on both sides when your voice lowered and you started needing deodorant," Max said. "When you discovered the usefulness of showers."

"I guess that's true." I hadn't put those facts together. We were moved from the rez elementary school to the big central junior high at the same time most of us hit puberty, around eleven or twelve years old. "But Angelina's Indian, right?" I wasn't sure what I was asking Max, but I wanted to get it right. Maybe I was worried she thought her rez was fancier?

"You got Indian friends from other places yet?" he asked, nodding.

You might see cousins of friends at Picnic or regional powwows. But my rez friends were the kids I went to school with and maybe a few of their cousins who liked Star Wars or comics. About a year ago, a group of us started holding bonfires at dedicated clearings in the woods, nowhere near enough to houses for parents to come nosing around our flickering flames. "Seems like Sandy June's hires Indians from all over, but what's weird is . . ." I didn't know how to describe this to Max without sounding totally bonkers.

"But whenever they claimed their communities were nearby, they described places you've never heard of," he said. "Is that it?" I nodded reluctantly. Life was confusing enough at fifteen, so I never pursued it when people mentioned these nonexistent places, and now here was my own uncle saying the same nonsense. "The Indian dorms in most universities feel like that, too. I ever tell you I met Angelina at Sandy June's?"

"Nuh-uh!" I laughed. I was positive Sandy June's hadn't been around that long. But then again, it did have a sort of mid-twentieth-century look, and its history always seemed clouded, like no one's stories about the place ever matched your own, so you stopped offering others your details. "Are you and Angelina . . ." I thought about how to put it. "Are you both gonna still have the same favorite places?" I finally settled on.

"Maybe," Uncle Max said after a while. "Maybe we'll go to them at a different time. Know what I mean?" Part of my new understanding of life was there would always be two sides to everything. "So you're old enough for me to tell you that truth. Now, you gonna return the favor? Does your mom think there's someone at Picnic I won't want to see?" he asked again, slightly rearranged. "I'm gonna go shower. You think about your answer while I'm busy." He vanished, and I considered making a break for it.

"Well, if it ain't Maxon and Jackson!" Sadie shouted, leaping out from around the corner. "Where'd Maxon go? Didn't I just see him?" Was Max's real name Maxon?

"Showering." I gestured to the building in the distance. I had to repeat myself, because someone was trying out Morse code with their car horn in the parking lot. "He'll be right back. Sadie, how am I going to tell him about the new chiefs canceling Fireball?"

"Your mom stick you with that job?"

"And she's booted me out of my room so Max can have it while he's staying here." Sadie definitely heard every word of that, including Max's current accommodations and Angelina's absence.

"My Wheel of Fate couldn't even get you better odds than that?"

"To be fair, they don't know how magical your cornbread tastes."

"They most certainly do. I taught your dad how to make it for their wedding day!" One of our eight thousand *traditions* (a.k.a. rules) was that a groom had to learn to make cornbread and serve a piece to every guest at the wedding, to show he's a good provider. If you didn't do it, you couldn't have a tradish marriage, and not everyone was up to the task.

Sadie always respected the choices of others and only offered to teach you if you were ready. She might even tell you that you weren't ready. Life with her was a little complex. What with her being my mom's best friend, you'd think she was maybe spying for my parents, but more often, her presence was like wearing a life preserver. Today, she'd slipped me a piece of that cornbread for lunch. It was so hot the chunk of cold butter was almost fully melted by the time I'd salted it.

She'd given me that piece so I'd share the full wheel at home.

"Hey, it's Skatey Sadie!" Max somehow tossed this insult while appearing right behind me, casually lubricating it with a *tsssss* to note he was joking and she *tsssss*'d back to accept the joke, another couple of slashed tires exchanging greetings, another couple of cats claiming the boundaries of their territories.

"Maxon Action." She laughed, embracing him as she shrugged off her SJLFDI apron like it was made of fog. Max had never been the hugging type, effectively dodging my mom's, but this man next to me was an entirely different Max. Like a brand-new model.

"Sometimes guilty as charged," he said, grinning, as we walked to the main building.

"Jackson, take over for a bit, eh?" Sadie said to me, her apron magically appearing in my hands, feeling alive, trying to tie itself around me. "Don't worry, I'll see you get overtime," she added, pulling a wheel from her cauldron as we stepped in, placing it on a tray prepared with butter, salt, a sharp knife, and two plates. Between the other bussers side-eyeing my sudden elevated status and the sad-faced out-of-towners asking if the rumor about Fireball was true, I couldn't hear a word of what Sadie and Max had to say.

I told all my customers the same thing. "Would we offer you cornbread this amazing if your heart wasn't a little bit broken?" Not quite a confirmation, but an invitation to join my journey on the road to acceptance. Since Fireball had always been a community word-of-mouth event, we should have anticipated the future and the changes it brings. The last few years, people had begun posting clips online, and immediately you noticed a different mix: a bunch of people who thought they were auditioning for a reboot of *Jackass* showed up. For longer than I'd been alive, only the right people ever seemed to know about it. As I said, Fireball was always fierce, but our community had made their own choices, and now that its existence was announced online, it was also out of our hands.

Fortunately, Sandy June's existed in some zone of its own. You could take pictures of Legendary events and keep them, but if you tried posting them online, something always went wrong and sometimes you lost your pics entirely. Someone added a little joke poster to the message board where people left notes for each other: "Sandy June's Legendary Is a No-Selfie Zone. Enforced by Elf on the Shelf. He Comes to the Rez for Summer Work." People who could read that message understood. After that, they just kept their phones pocketed.

The sky was turning dark, and the Legendary house band had come on.

Normally, Pink Floyd's "Dogs" would be a weird party band choice, but Dog Street divided the rez's north side from its south. It was a natural. Probably a request from one of the cousins, and it had been on their song list for years. Down to the last two wheels, I was about to put up a sign that we were sold out when Sadie and Max surfaced. Sadie revealed a tub she'd kept back, asking Max to help her dump the breads in her cauldron. In those few minutes, the sun had gone down, and over at Picnic, cars would be peeling out. A stubborn group of people might try starting an unsanctioned game. Max and I stepped out of the building, and the cool night temperatures were beginning to settle. "Did you and Sadie finish that whole wheel? Just the two of you?"

"You ever see cornbread go begging?" I shook my head. It was a Nation crime to leave even a few crumbs behind. Cornbread was a labor of love, and you had to acknowledge all the work that went into it, and somehow, you were never too full on it, unless you took more than your share, leaving someone else out in the cold. "Kept this back for you," he added, passing me a paper towel–wrapped slice. "Figured you wouldn't have much time to eat, serving on your own like that, with no prep."

"People were cool. And there was always enough floating to the cauldron top that I never had to wrestle or worry about a wheel not being done enough."

"Then you're a natural." Max had already buttered and salted it. "So we gonna watch the band and stick around for the movie?" He didn't seem antsy to rush over to the Picnic, hoping to catch the nonexistent Fireball game.

"I'm all sweaty from being in the kitchen," I said, noting how drenched my shirt was, and I sniffed it. "I really don't think anyone's gonna want to be in the seat next to me."

"You knew I was taking up your evening after you'd been working here since early this morning, but you still came anyway." Max paused and studied the sky, like you looked to the classroom ceiling for hope during a math pop quiz. "You even suggested we come here. And you never answered my question."

"Didn't I?" I asked, studying the new sprinkling of stars. "Did I need to?"

"No, I can follow the Dog Street Online News myself. I knew, even living where I do, that there wasn't going to be any Fireball. Something that dangerous to play would attract a certain kind of tough guy wanting to show how big his . . . how brave he is."

"I'm not a kid anymore, Max. You can say balls."

"Let me pretend a little while longer. I don't get to see you that often. But once people started posting video of a private rez activity, I knew it was just a matter of time. Suppose I wanted to see for myself, but now I don't need to for real. People are pouring in here, so they're not waiting at the Picnic for the ball to be sparked. Confirmation enough."

"Mom thought you might get mad, if you were there."

"Did she think I was gonna stomp around like a baby if I got there and people were leaving?" he asked, shaking his head. "Your ma thinks I'm the same kid who went to another state for college. She couldn't understand why none of the local ones was good enough. I wanted a chance to meet Indians from other parts of the country. And I did. I met Angelina here at Legendary, but I got to really know her at college." Was I supposed to say that was a good thing or bad?

"You're not mad about Fireball?"

"Well, sure. This place looks less like the home I moved away from every time I come back. But what happens here, what leaders say are the best things for the community? They know better than I do. I gave up my right to an opinion fifteen years ago."

"Just like that? You just accept that's true?"

"Nah, like I said, once Fireball got posted online, it was gonna attract people who played for the wrong reasons. And the community has no rules in place about who can and can't play, so the only way to stop—"

"Is to stop the game. Why do you think they come? The ones who screwed it up?"

"Who screwed it up?" Max flipped it back out to me as Sadie was finishing with the last of her customers and the people coming in for the midnight movies began to snag their seats. "The strangers showing up to play, thinking everything should belong to them? The people who posted video online? The people who didn't ask them to stop recording? The players getting tougher and riskier every year? All of them? None of them? Things change, kid. Most things. Can't believe my old treehouse stays untouched every year. If someone else uses it while I'm away, they always put it back the way it was."

"It's yours?"

"It has been. It'll be yours before I leave this time. I'll make the arrangements with your mom. If you wanna put a house there some-day, if you decide to stay, the land'll be there for you. And if not, well, maybe you'll keep the treehouse tradition up. I usually do some main-tenance every year. I always said I came back for Fireball, but really it was for the House of Stray Cats."

"That's what my mom calls our house whenever someone wanders in with their lives on fire. It's a joke we say when she boots me to the couch."

"Is that what she says? She knows that's what I named the tree-house. It's for anyone who needs to just get away, to just be themselves and not have to worry about their community responsibilities, even if just for a little while."

"She usually says, 'This is like the House of Stray Cats,' because a stray cat's territory is way bigger than people understand. Anyone who ever lost a cat never understood the cat was probably still around, just prowling in another part of its territory. It's the way she lets our unexpected visitors know it's okay. I never knew she was referring to a real place."

Max nodded, pleased that his sister had not boosted the name he'd given to his place. "Do you feel that way? Really?" I asked. "That you sometimes need to just be yourself instead of a part of the bigger community?"

"It's a lot of pressure, living up to everyone else's expectations of you. Guess that's why Angelina's moving west for a while. Said she'd tried life in the middle and here in the east and she wanted to see life at the other end. Said she lived most of her life trying to be the person everyone else wanted. Can't begrudge her. Didn't mean to be, but I'm probably one of those people expecting things she didn't feel she could give. I wanted to try something else, too, a different life, but she saw that every year, like clockwork, I was drawn back here. I'll always be a part of this community whether I'm here or not, but I did lose my place to have a voice. So she and I, we put our stuff in storage till we decide what we're doing. And I came back."

"Sadie always makes fun of Mom and her House of Stray Cats, taking in all the people who need a little space."

"And the whole time she's making room for others, your mom's making you give up your space. You ever call her on that?"

"She wants me to never forget what it means to be a part of a community. To have to sacrifice sometimes."

"She always did have a narrow definition of community," Max said, digging in his backpack. "Here, go shower and change into these." He'd picked up some of my clothes from the stack when he'd entered the house. "Never know who you might meet and want to impress. I'll go save us three seats. Sadie's joining us." Sadie had hinted that she and Max had history I didn't know about. "Any idea what the movie is?"

"Not sure," I said. "Last weekend it was *Cat People*." *Cat People* was about shape-shifters, moving back and forth between human form and big cats, especially when they wanted to be with each other. Then they'd switch to human form and go about their business unnoticed. But trouble always followed them. They only found connection with each other.

"Pretty tough to be a Cat Person living here so close to Dog Street," Max said, and I suspected that might be true for any number of people. I was the last of my mom's kids, and the only one still living on the rez. My brothers and sisters had all considered their territory to be larger than our plot. The house was likely to become mine by default and nothing else.

"I don't suppose Sadie knows her way to the Real House of Stray Cats," I said.

"I don't suppose you need to know that, do you?" he said.

"I don't suppose any of that cornbread is gonna be left when we get home," I said.

"I don't suppose we'll be able to scrounge up some more by morning," he said.

I understood he was saying that either one of us might see Sadie tomorrow, each for different reasons. I took the clothes and headed to the showers, just in case I met someone in a nearby seat. Maybe I'd get some popcorn, just in case I had an opportunity to share. You never know whose territory might cross your own, whose mystery might begin to unfold in front of you, at just the right moment.

MVSKOKE JOY
Marcella Bell

She was walking alone, just like the morning Chitto had almost accidentally run her over with his truck.

Petite and Black, with hundreds of tiny braids cascading down her back, she walked with unexpectedly long strides, eating up the pavement while looking straight ahead, body framed by late-afternoon summer sunlight.

She was *always* freaking alone.

She was in the Mvskoke Audio Visual Society (MAVS), the Indigenous web content creation group he'd founded at the beginning of the school year, but every time he saw her outside of their meetups, she was by herself.

How was that even possible?

Drumming his fingers on his steering wheel as he came to her, Chitto made an irritated sound in the back of his throat and pulled over. He pressed down the sidewalk-side window button. "Get in, Harry," he said. "I'm giving you a ride. You're going home, right?"

"Hey, Chitto," she said, coming to a stop. "I am," she went on. "But you don't need to take me. It's not far."

"I know how far it is, Harry. I've been to your house." *A lot*, he didn't add, since back in September she had volunteered her place to be HQ for MAVS's weekly meetings. They'd kind of made her house famous. "Hop in. The distance is even shorter on wheels."

"I don't think that's how distance works," she said, "but sure. Thanks."

Before, she might have smiled at him as she said it, but not today. She hadn't smiled at him a lot since the day they'd kissed and then he'd told her he didn't want a girlfriend.

He pulled the handle to open the door for her and she climbed in. "Where're you coming from?" He'd just finished lacrosse conditioning. Monday through Friday, nine to four. He'd be at it most of the summer. Pulling his arm back as Harry got in, Chitto was glad he'd showered. He wished he'd taken the time to braid his hair, though, rather than putting it up. Braids were a little more deadly with his long hair than the man bun he was currently rocking.

"Drum lesson with Cat," Harry said, sitting straight-backed as she settled herself, backpack in her lap, body centered in her space on the other end of the pickup bench.

"Oh, cool," he said. "Your grandpa would've been happy." Immediately, he wished he'd said anything else.

But Harry smiled for the first time since he'd picked her up. "You're right," she said. "And I wouldn't have gone back to my lessons with her without you guys. I'll owe the gang for that for a long time."

"It's not a debt, Harry," he said, hands tight on the wheel. "It's family. You're Mvskoke. We're going to take care of you."

"That's what my grandpa was trying to tell me all along," she said. "I was just too sad to get it." She turned toward him fully, and Chitto's stomach did a funny flip—like it did every time their eyes met since that night. . . . They didn't need to date. It was a thrill enough to just hang out with her. "Without you guys and this past year . . ." She shook her head before looking away again. She spoke quietly, always, but he never missed a word she said. "I don't think I would have reconnected with Cat at all, and if I hadn't done that, I wouldn't have gotten the message my grandpa left for me. . . ." She drew a deep breath and then let it out slowly. "And *that* would have been an actual tragedy."

Her eyes were glisteny. That didn't happen as often anymore, but he knew she still got sad about her grandpa. He wanted to make her happy. Shooting her a grin, he joked, "Not as tragic as my engagement. It's been nearly a year since we started Mvskoke AV, and everybody else has officially gone viral while I continue to languish in low-view hell. It's starting to look like the problem might just be me."

"Your content is great," she said, laughing a little. Heat warmed his cheeks. A little laugh was enough. "It's educational."

"Don't patronize me," he said, still grinning as he took the turn toward her house. "Engagement tanks when I post." Harry was the only person he could talk to about it and keep a smile. She could patronize him all she wanted.

"You'll find your groo—wait, what in the . . . ?" Harry leaned forward to look through the windshield. An enormous wooden sign rested at an angle opposite Harry's turnoff. Propped up by a wooden frame, edged with show lights, it read "Sandy June's Legendary Frybread Drive-In" in loopy neon. *Legendary* stood out in yellow, while the rest of the words buzzed in green, all against a black backdrop.

"When did that get there?" Chitto asked.

Harry shook her head. "After I left for my lesson today? It wasn't there before."

A new frybread drive-in? This close to the school? Chitto's mouth watered at the thought. It was exactly the kind of progress he was hungry for. A huge sign, prominent and loud, that reminded everyone that Oklahoma was Indian Country—not like some PSA or historical marker about the Trail of Tears, but something alive and modern—neon and grease and a huge sign in the middle of town.

"Want to go?" he asked, the words tumbling out.

"Oh," Harry said. "Uh—"

Chitto noted her arrested expression and faltered. *Had he just asked her on a date?*

"Yes," she said.

Taking a quick right (instead of the left he normally took to get to her house), they entered new territory.

But Sandy June's was not the new restaurant he'd expected. It was a squat, humble box of a building with a big rectangular service window nestled at the end of a long row of covered parking spots and green picnic tables, mostly occupied.

The lot extended a long way back, and people, in pairs and small groups, clustered and milled about everywhere. Many of them were Indigenous—long- and short-haired, light- and dark-complected, dressed like punks and clean girls and mob wives and everything else that had ever become an aesthetic. Like him, they belonged here. This was *their* place. *His* place. Shivers lifted the hairs on his arms.

Sandy June's looked like it'd been here for decades and needed a fresh coat of trim. But that couldn't be possible. He'd lived in the city of Muskogee his whole life and had never heard of it. And there was no way he would have missed that sign before.

Parking his truck in an open spot near the middle of the row, he flipped the key in the ignition and turned to Harry. "Ready? Have you ever had frybread?"

Harry might be an established member of MAVS, but she wasn't tribally enrolled, and her grandfather had been her only connection to the culture before he died. Chitto never knew what she would be familiar with and what she wouldn't.

Scoffing, she opened her door and said, "I wasn't born under a rock, Chitto. Plus, even though *you* missed Mel's filming, *I* thought I was going to explode from eating it after how many takes it took Mel to be satisfied with her cooking video." Sliding down from the truck, Harry added, "It was worth it, though. Her frybread was delicious and the video is still one of her most viral."

Chitto laughed. Ten months into MAVS and the way Harry carried herself had changed—even if she didn't realize it. She belonged here, too. "I remember that one now," he said with a smirk, angling his chin up. "And that's good. I didn't want to have to try to explain one of the greatest things in the world. Shall we?"

They arrived at the counter, its frosted-glass window taped with a smattering of flyers, some with print faded in the sun, the corners of their paper curling with age. The two most prominent sheets, however, were so fresh that the Sharpie ink was practically bleeding. They read "Coke" and "Pepsi," indicating that folks should line up to order according to preference. Wooden condiment baskets sat in a row on the counter.

An older Black woman, somewhere between typical auntie and typical grandma age—hair braided along the edges of her face and pinned into a low bun—greeted them, smiling broadly. She wore a blue apron with green ribbons in multiple shades sewn across it over a dress with a blueberry print. "Hesci and welcome!"

"Thanks," Chitto said, glancing around her to see if there was anyone else behind the counter. With Indigenous people from seemingly all over the place—repping hints of their different tribal affiliations in subtle ways—he had hoped to catch someone on staff who was also Native. "Great place!" he said. "Who owns it?"

At his side, Harry scanned the tables, her attention catching on a table of people so engrossed in their game that they didn't notice the girl staring at them just a few feet away.

Behind the counter, the woman's eyes narrowed a fraction. "You might say it's a sort of cooperative, of which I'm a founding member. My name is Sarah R. *R* stands for Rector, if you ever look me up." She tapped her beaded name tag.

"Sarah Rector? Just like—" Harry began.

Sarah cut her off. "Just," she said, the word heavy, reminding Chitto of when his mom and aunties switched into code to talk about things he wasn't supposed to hear. "'The world's richest colored girl,' right here at Sandy June's," Sarah added.

Harry frowned. "Not one and the same, though," she said, the higher pitch of her voice making her sound younger, turning her statement into a question. "That wouldn't be possible. She died a long time ago."

Sarah smiled, her eyes so gleeful they sparkled like water in sunlight. "Certainly did. Time moves a little different here at Sandy June's. Think of it as an Elder's pace in a technologically accelerated world."

Rubbing her arms like she was suddenly cold, Harry smiled the fake smile that she'd used a lot earlier in the school year. Back then, it'd been because of losing her grandfather. Today, though, with her mouth curved into a stiff upward bow and her eyes wide, she looked more like she was meeting a ghost.

"I've never seen this place before," Chitto said, giving Harry a chance to settle down from whatever was happening in her head.

"You look pretty young yet," Sarah replied, her voice flat as she turned his way. "Give yourself some more time before you've seen everything." At his side Harry snorted and Sarah sent her a quick smile before turning back to Chitto. "You're not the first person to say that, though. We've been here forever, but like you, we're still trying to be seen."

Like me? Chitto wondered. *Trying to be seen?*

"Well, now that you've got that mega sign out there, I don't think anyone will miss it," Harry said.

Clapping her hands together, Sarah brightened. "I absolutely agree, of course. I put that one out there today myself, in fact, and look how it worked. Brought you two in real quick."

"You put the sign out?" Chitto asked. That sign weighed more than he did. Sarah couldn't be more than five foot seven and was approaching the age where she would start getting her plate first at gatherings. She nodded. Unwilling to believe, yet smart enough not to say so, Chitto replied, "Good thinking."

"Mvto. The acknowledgment means a lot, coming from you." She spoke the Mvskoke word for *thank you* easily, gratitude flowing out. "So. What can I get you? Need a minute with the menu, or are you ready?"

Harry shook her head, wide-eyeing the menu. As soon as they entered Sandy June's driveway, the sounds of horns and screeching brakes had disappeared. In their place, birdsong and breeze and the gentle hum of muffled conversations floated all around them.

The menu had everything Chitto expected from a place like Sandy June's—french fries, milkshakes, burgers, and NDN tacos, of course—but also the kinds of things he craved, like Native teas and Indigenous specialties like pashofa.

"Maybe basic is best the first time?" he said. Harry nodded. "We'll take one plain frybread and one with powdered sugar and honey."

"Excellent choices," Sarah said. "I'll go get the ingredients."

"Thank you," Chitto replied, but her back was already turned.

A girl with a Star of David necklace had come up to the other line beside them while they chatted with Sarah, and at the table behind them, the gamers' volume peaked then fell again, drawing their attention. When Harry turned back to Chitto, her eyebrows were pulled together. "Did she say 'get the ingredients'?"

Chitto squinted back in the direction Sarah R. had gone. "I'm pretty sure she did."

Reappearing as if summoned, Sarah pushed a rolling cart up to her side of the window. It was loaded with a big bag of flour, a huge silver mixing bowl, salt, buttermilk, and baking powder.

She *had* said she was getting the ingredients.

Looking at the cart, the first words that bubbled out of Chitto's mouth were, "You put buttermilk in it?"

With an ageless dark brown stare, Sarah R. lifted an eyebrow. "I do." She began opening containers. "There's a door right there around the other side of where you're standing." She nodded in the direction she meant while getting ready. "Come on through there."

"What?"

"Come on around through there," Sarah repeated. "You obviously need to be put to work." By habit, he obeyed the Elder's instruction.

Harry took a step to follow as well but then stopped, her hands coming to her abdomen at the same time as a funny look crossed her face. "I'm sorry. I need to use a restroom. Can you point me in that direction?"

"Certainly, my dear," Sarah said warmly. "And no sorry necessary. You'll find the facilities right around the corner. Everything you need will be there."

"Thank you," Harry said, starting in that direction.

Watching her go, Chitto walked into the drive-in and Sarah R. gestured to an apron hanging on the wall near the door. From the employee side of the window, the outside world looked fluid, all the people on the other side wavy, like an impressionist watercolor. Chitto washed his hands. Then they got to work.

Or, more accurately, Sarah did. Her hands moved at a normal pace sometimes, but at others, a blur. Soon she was flapping a piece of rounded dough between her hands, placing it in the large silver skillet of hot oil on the stove in front of her. Handing Chitto a ball of dough, she watched him attempt to replicate her motions.

Had he never made frybread before? He could retrieve years' worth of memories of eating it—making it, he came up blank.

"You've really got it down," he said.

"I should. It's my momma's recipe."

"I'm sorry," he said. "That was rude of me to assume you'd learned it here."

Sarah shrugged. "Well, of course I had to learn it at some point. I didn't come into this world knowing how to make frybread. That wasn't what you meant, though, was it? You assumed I had to learn it on the job because I'm Black. From the moment you saw me, you assumed I wasn't Native."

Chitto's mouth dropped. Kitchen sounds drifted around them from the drive-in's recesses. He shook his head. "No. No way. That's not what I meant, at all. I know there are Black Natives. One of my best friends is—" Hearing himself, he cut the words short.

"See? You notice Blackness first and let that affect everything you think thereafter. You don't seem to have the same problems when it comes to white- or brown-looking folk meeting your expectations of who is or is not a Native person, though. Might be something to consider about yourself."

"What?" he asked. *Something to consider about himself?* Hadn't he been promoting the diversity of the modern Native experience through his content for the better part of a year now? That's exactly what MAVS was all about—showing the world that Natives weren't just one thing.

"But what about Black people, Chitto?" Sarah R. asked, like she could read his mind. "Do you maybe secretly think that Black people are *just one thing*?"

The dough he had been poorly flattening to that point tore at a thin spot, splitting in half before it fell between the grates of the stovetop—straight onto the open flame. "Whoa!"

The dough burst into flame. He looked around for something to put it out with. *Was it salt for grease fires?*

Sarah R. lifted her arm, moving as if she was going to reach right over the flame. Chitto reached his own arm out, shielding hers from the fire below. Heat singed his arm. Sarah snatched a small box of baking soda and poured it over the small flame until it went out. Chitto examined his arm.

It was unscathed.

"Remember," Sarah R. said, giving his arm a pat. "It's baking soda, not salt, when there's oil involved in a fire."

"Everything all right up there?" someone called from the back. Outside, another patron stepped into the line. Sarah R. was going to have to return to the counter soon.

"Sure is!" she hollered. "Everything's going according to plan!"

"I'm sorry I dropped the dough," Chitto said when she turned around.

"You made your reparations," Sarah R. replied, nodding to the arm he'd used to shield her. "And better still, all is never lost." She pulled two plates from behind her back, frybread on each. "Here you go," she said. "One plain, one sugar. Just as ordered. Don't wait for your darling friend, though—just save her a bite. She's going to need a bit more time." The frybread on each plate—bright, golden, and fluffy—looked too good to resist so, once again, Chitto obeyed. He first took a bite of the plain.

Salt, cloudy substance, and filling heat. It was the taste that filled his mouth every time his friends went viral around him—salty because it wasn't his triumph, but at the same time, comfort food. It filled him up to see each one of them succeed. Their wins *were* his wins, especially when what they were doing was for their people.

He took a bite of the sweet.

Harry filled his mind—her braids, the deep warm glow of her skin, her smile—all of it coming together like a mist until she was the only thing he could picture. She was more than talent and a pretty face. She'd volunteered her house as a place for MAVS to meet up when they needed a home. She'd come up with the idea for their first post and later been integral to their first efforts going viral. She wasn't loud, but she showed up. When she spoke, her words enhanced the efforts of those around her. Without her, none of the success that MAVS had built would have been possible. And when she'd been introduced to him, he'd taken her as a Black girl who didn't know the first thing about being Mvskoke.

"Just like me," Sarah R. said, again addressing words he hadn't spoken.

It hit Chitto as he chewed, turning his bite rubbery: he didn't just need to consider something about himself. He was the problem. That was almost enough to rob his tongue of the sweetness of the frybread—it had almost robbed him of Harry.

The relationship between the Freedmen and the Nation was a big issue. No people, not even his, he realized, could participate in chattel slavery and not feel the effects of dehumanizing another group of people lingering in the minds of people into the next generations. When he'd first met Harry, he hadn't thought that MAVS was equipped to deal with that. MAVS was about celebrating reasons for Mvskoke pride.

"Indeed, there is a lot to address," Sarah said, nodding. "Remarkably, it's possible to celebrate *and* address, though." Outside, somebody laughed, and a dog barked. "Take me, for example," she added. "I am one of Sandy June's legendary grandparents. I'm a leader of this community and in many of our most important conversations. And I am also Freedmen. Our Nation has not always been on the right side of history because we are real human beings, both heroes and villains and everyone in between. Isn't that better than being Hollywood Native sidekicks?"

Chitto straightened his spine. "Yes, ma'am."

"Whether our history becomes a legacy we uphold or one we untangle depends on who we want to be and the world we want to live in. Southeastern Native folks reconciling with Freedmen is just one of the things that needs taking care of, you know." She squinted against the burning midsummer late-afternoon sun that glinted in at a hard angle through the window. "The planet is getting hot out there."

Chitto nodded, sensing she was talking about more than just the day.

"All of us here at Sandy June's believe in you. It's important that you know that."

A figure approached the window outside.

The Freedmen were a Muscogee Nation–level issue and climate change was a global one—bigger than the scope of a group of teenagers working together to create short-format video content. But seeing the sign for Sandy June's, seeing Native people abundant and at ease, tasting the frybread, salty and sweet, had reminded him of what it felt like to look into the future and believe his actions could make a difference.

And the sweet frybread had reminded him of something else, too. Harry.

Where was she? Stepping outside the drive-in, hands filled with frybread plates, he scanned past the line for her. There! Harry was looking back over her shoulder, rounding the far corner of the drive-in hut.

"Harry!" he called.

Flipping around, Harry smiled, the expression big, stretching across her face. Harry's eyes were magnetic, like firelight in the dark. Whatever had happened while she'd been gone had been good.

Was the way forward with Freedmen as simple as acknowledgment and reconciliation? Could their future be united, but this time in a good way, joined not by bondage but by loving hearts and shared Mvskoke values?

The sweet frybread—*Harry*—made it seem worth trying.

"Hey," she said. "Sorry I took so long. I . . . met some people."

"You find everything you needed?" Sarah R. called with a smile, leaning through the order window.

"And then some," Harry said. "A girl gave me a pa—" Stopping mid-sentence, Harry pivoted verbally and physically, eyeing Chitto as she added, "and then I met another woman who worked here. Willa.

She was . . ." Harry sighed as if she couldn't find the words. "She was amazing. I don't know how she knew what she knew. Maybe she overheard us earlier? She checked on me and introduced me to this guy named Levi. He's a documentary filmmaker." Harry reached down to pet the little white and brown, beagle-y-eared-looking dog that'd come up to sniff her leg. "Oh! There's a stage back there, too. Maybe we could film something here? The place is huge."

"Bigger than you even realize," Sarah said, drawing their attention back to the service window. "Sounds like it was a productive trek."

"Definitely," Harry said. "Levi was great."

Chitto's neck tensed every time she'd said Levi's name. "Always good to connect with other creators. . . ."

Sarah R. burst out with the kind of auntie laugh that could probably be heard way back in the wings of the stage. Wiping tears, she caught her breath and said, "You're a good boy, Campbell, so I'm going to give you a little extra help."

Had he told her his last name? "What's that?"

"Your little online content problem."

Had he mentioned his content problem?

"Try to have fun," she said. "Don't worry about educating, being funny, looking deadly . . . none of it. Just enjoy yourself. Do the things you love, *with people you love*." She paused, tilting her head in Harry's direction. "And share that. Go to places you're curious about. Talk about things that make you smile. Give the world something they've hardly seen, *Native boy joy*. You'll never outdo your ancestors when it comes to suffering. They don't want you to try. Show the world that

Native people are still here, living rich lives."

Mouth full of frybread, Harry clapped and swallowed hard. "This! So much! We've been *trying* to tell him!"

For a moment, Chitto couldn't speak. Sarah was right. He'd been trying too hard. *Native kid talks about Native history. Native kid dances traditional dance. Native kid makes impassioned pleas and cultural jokes.* In all of that, he hadn't tried just sharing what he liked.

But Sarah hadn't just said that. *People you love . . .*

Harry. Surrounded by strangers on a late summer afternoon in front of the service window at Sandy June's, his heart full of frybread and his mind clear, he realized it. He'd been overthinking his future at the expense of his joy. Having a girlfriend didn't have to doom his chances to get into college or make him go broke. He liked Harry in the here and now. And he was going to have to make up a lot of ground if he wanted a chance with her.

"Ding, ding, ding," Sarah said, clapping her hands together. "Well, young people, it has been a pleasure getting to know you, but it's time to move along now. You go on out there and get back to it. You're making us proud."

"Oh, here. Let me pay first," Chitto said, reaching for his wallet. "How much?"

"And me, too," Harry said, to Chitto's annoyance.

Sarah R. waved them both away. "No, no, no. We're family. Family eats free."

"I couldn't," he insisted.

"Me either," Harry added.

But Sarah was adamant. "Pay it forward. Seven generations." She winked at them. "Your work is out there, and you've got a lot of it. Now get."

Raising his palms in defeat, Chitto said, "All right. All right. We'll go. But Sarah?"

"What is it?"

"Mvto."

GAME NIGHT

Darcie Little Badger

SATURDAY

KingDM 2:16 PM

@Timber @WhateverCore @Picnic_ant

Don't forget to level up before tonight's DnD session.

Timber

ok. check your dms. I need spell suggestions.

WhateverCore

How much gold did we get from the mind flayer encounter?

KingDM

50 gp 10 copper

My brother in games, do you ever take notes?

WhateverCore

Notes? Never. Thanks, King!

Picnic_ant

I'm set. <3

NEW

Timber 6:05 PM
had to do chores. sry i'm late.

KingDM
No worries. We're still waiting for @Picnic_ant

WhateverCore
Bruh. I AM worried. Picnic's never late.

KingDM
Life happens. Give her another 10 min.

KingDM
Anyone have Picnic_ant's phone number?
@Timber didn't you meet Picnic_ant last year at summer camp?

Timber
yea. I can text her.
no response.
calling.
oh went to voicemail.
maybe she's sleeping.

WhateverCore
Can you knock on her door or something?

Drive past her house.
Throw pebbles at her window.

Timber
picnic lives 12 hrs away.

WhateverCore
W H A T.
You're in the same state.

Timber
everything's bigger in texas.
including texas.

KingDM
OK game postponed. Let's regroup next week.
@Picnic_ant when you see this, leave a note so we know
you're ok.

SUNDAY
Timber 3:58 PM
hey, anyone hear from picnic?
she never got back to me.

WhateverCore
No.

KingDM

Weird. Picnic_ant hasn't logged into Steam since Thursday evening.

Her last post on YourPlace was Friday morning.

WhateverCore

@Picnic_ant @Picnic_ant @Picnic_ant

Timber

she's not beetlejuice. you can't summon her that way.

KingDM

Should we call somebody?

WhateverCore

And say what? "911, our friend from the internet missed a game. Please do a welfare check."

KingDM

Bro, I'm serious. If she never responds, how do we report it? Do we even know her real name?

Timber

it's cora.

her apartment building is run-down.

maybe power went out?

WhateverCore

No phone or computer for over 24 hrs?

If she's gone tomorrow, I'm taking emergency actions.

Timber

what are those?

WhateverCore

Don't know yet. Gotta sleep on it.

Timber

i feel helpless.

KingDM

It won't be easy, but we'll check on her. Maybe family can help. Or people in different gaming groups? There's options. I'll reach out to mutuals.

Timber

just wish she wasn't so far away.

MONDAY

Timber 3:01 AM

ilu @Picnic_ant.

please be ok.

NEW

Picnic_ant 7:42 AM
Hi everybody. I'm alive. Sorry for making you worry.

KingDM
@Picnic_ant!!! What happened???

Picnic_ant
It's been a hard week, and my phone's in a ditch somewhere. Finally got my laptop.
Last minute, but can I run Saturday's game? Wanna try a new one-shot campaign.

Timber
omg @Picnic_ant you're here!!

Picnic_ant
Hi @Timber. <3 Did you get any sleep last night?

Timber
not really.

Picnic_ant
Please take a nap and ilu too.

KingDM
@Picnic_ant you can absolutely test your one-shot. Let me

know if you need help with setup.

PS I agree that naps are good, @Timber.

NEW

WhateverCore 2:14 PM

OK I'm awake. What did I miss?

@Picnic_ant!!!!!!!!!!!!

SATURDAY

Picnic_ant 6:00 PM

Welcome, players. Tonight, our game unfolds on Earth, present day. First, describe your character. They can be anyone or anything. There's just one rule: they represent you.

KingDM

Do our characters have stats like wisdom, strength, dexterity, etc?

Picnic_ant

If you want. It's not required, though.

KingDM

I am an apprentice wizard named King. My former master was corrupted by dark forces, so I turned against him to save our realm. Unfortunately, during battle, our magic tore a hole in reality, and we fell through a portal to Earth. I landed in New

York with nothing but the robes on my back and my ancient Staff of Dragonfire, which does not work in this mundane realm. My goals are twofold: destroy my former master, and then return home.

WhateverCore
I'm an alien named Bob and am observing humanity as a science project. To avoid detection, I can shape-shift into a human teenager or a cow. There's a spaceship in my garage, and I own a multipurpose ray gun disguised as a laser pointer.

Timber
my character is me.
i'm a yaqui girl named timber who likes ttrpgs and does ok in school. except in the game, i got my own car and don't have to borrow my cousin's truck.

Picnic_ant
What kind of car do you have?

Timber
it's a 1969 ford mustang mach 1 i restored for fun.

Picnic_ant
Your characters are all perfect. Let's begin.
Every Saturday, Timber, King, Bob, and a girl named

Picnic_ant gather at a local restaurant or cafe to eat and play games. Y'all may be from different worlds, but the love of adventure unites you in friendship. Timber, as the only person with a car (spaceships aren't road-certified), you usually drive everyone to the meeting spot.

This Saturday, you pick up King and Bob without any trouble. However, when you reach Picnic_ant's address, she isn't waiting on the curb. She lives in an apartment with her mother and older brother (who are at work). The apartment windows are dark, and nobody answers the door when you knock. What now?

Timber
I text her and ask what's happening.

Picnic_ant
You contact Picnic_ant using text and the group DMs, but there's no response. It's been a day since her last message.

KingDM
What does the last message say?

Picnic_ant
The message is: "I found a good place for our game. Have you ever been to Sandy June's Legendary Frybread Drive-In? It's on Kindcreek Road. Or at least it is for me. Usually."

WhateverCore

Bob uses teleportation to go through the apartment door to look for Picnic_ant.

KingDM

Bob can do that?

WhateverCore

Yes. With the alien tech in his ray gun. Bro, his species invented faster-than-light travel. They're OP.

Picnic_ant

The apartment is empty. There's no sign of trouble. However, there's also no indication that Picnic_ant has been home recently.

KingDM

Unless Bob's ray gun has a "detect friend" setting, King suggests that they visit the Sandy June place and look for Picnic_ant. Maybe somebody else dropped her off.

WhateverCore

No "detect friend" settings. Just teleport, stun, evaporate, levitate, and shrink.

Picnic_ant

Timber, you follow the directions in Picnic_ant's last message.

You've been up Kindcreek Road before; it cuts through a wild patch of hill country, flanked by fruiting prickly pears and disheveled oak. People live here, between the trees. Their small houses blend in with the land. Children play on porches with scraggly cats and sun-faded plastic toys. Adults cook dinner over bowl-shaped barbecues or chat with neighbors across their low fences. Last time you checked, there's no drive-in on Kindcreek, but as the road becomes rough, its asphalt splitting, you look to the right and see an island of activity and light. A neon sign advertises SANDY JUNE'S LEGENDARY FRYBREAD DRIVE-IN. Patrons—families with young children, groups of chattering friends, couples on dates, and solo diners—sit at green picnic tables, their plates piled with food. Timber, you park and look around. There's no sign of Picnic_ant.

Timber
I have a photo of her on my phone. It's from summer camp a year ago. I'm going to ask employees if they've seen her lately.

KingDM
Does King know about the drive-in? Can I make a roll for knowledge?

Picnic_ant
Go for it.

KingDM

I roll a 20-sided die. It lands on 15.

Picnic_ant

King's heard stories about this drive-in before. According
to the lore, Sandy June's is more than an ordinary building.
It appears to Indigenous people across the vast continent,
nourishing them with food and community, serving frybread
and traditional fare of the homeland, plus typical drive-in
choices, all of which change based on its unfathomable
whims. Indeed! Sandy June's breaks the laws of space-time.
Or perhaps it breaks nothing. Perhaps it's invited within
space-time, where it swims like a salmon against the current.
At first, you can't believe that the stories are real in a place
without magic, but it's hard to deny your own eyes. For
Kindcreek Road passes through a neighborhood that's been
known as an "Apache rancheria" for over 150 years. In fact,
it's where Picnic_ant was born, before her father got sick.
Picnic_ant's momma had to sell their little plot of land. It was
the only way to afford his treatment.
The cancer still killed him.

KingDM

Picnic? Is that real or is it just part of the game?

Picnic_ant

Maybe both.

KingDM

I'm really sorry.

WhateverCore

Me too. Shit. I didn't know. Is there anything we can do to make things easier?

Picnic_ant

Thanks. Don't worry. It's been four years. My family's getting by. What's Bob's next move, @WhateverCore?

WhateverCore

Bob asks Timber to send him a copy of the photo. Then he questions the people at the picnic tables. "Have you seen this girl?"

Picnic_ant

Timber, you go to the walk-up window, where people order their meals if they don't have a car. A middle-aged auntie in a bead-brimmed snap-back hat (with the phrase "roll for initiative" embroidered on the front) and a white apron stands there, smiling. Her graying hair is in a low ponytail, and she doesn't wear makeup. Not even lip gloss. However, black-and-white tattoo roses cascade down her neck and arms, Carolina roses with delicate petals. When you show her the picture of Picnic_ant, she snaps her fingers and says, "I know that kid, all right. She used to eat here all the time, but it's been four years. Whatever happened to Picnic_ant?"

You explain the situation, that you're trying to learn the same thing.

The woman's eyes go distant, and then she unties her apron, saying, "Hang on. I'll be right out." After that, she calls over her shoulder, "Frank, can you watch the register?"

A booming voice answers, "Sure, SJ!" SJ must be her name, but what does it stand for? You wonder if she's the legendary Sandy June or just an employee with coincidental initials.

SJ exits the drive-in through a side door. Up close, she's shorter than you expected—just five feet tall, in tennis shoes—and she carries the scents of a kitchen. Spiced masa, rich stew, and solé flowers. There's even a hint of fried dough. "What do you think happened?" she asks you, Timber. How do you respond?

Meanwhile, Bob and King: You walk from table to table, sharing Picnic_ant's photo and asking customers, "Do you know this girl?" No, they say. No, no, no. Until! A scruffy young man with a calculus textbook glances up from his homework and says, "Uh-huh. She used to live next to my cousin. What's the problem?"

Timber

I tell SJ that me and Picnic_ant are friends, and even though we only met one time irl I know her. I really know her, and she's never late. She also usually messages me all day, but she's been quiet, and I'm scared because I don't understand what's happening, but I'm sure that something's wrong.

KingDM

King asks the scruffy student, "When's the last time you saw her?"

WhateverCore

Also, Bob explains that they were supposed to meet Picnic_ant for games and dinner, but she never showed, which is really odd.

Picnic_ant

Timber, as SJ listens to your concerns, she nods and frowns, increasingly serious. Clearly, you've convinced her that the situation is dire. "Have you tried calling her ma?" she asks. "Is she still working at the offices downtown?"
Unfortunately, Picnic's mom lost that job a couple of years ago; in the last economic dip, the offices—several gray, joyless buildings filled with cubicles and meeting rooms—laid off half their cleaning staff. Currently, Picnic's mom is a private housekeeper, and she works in dozens of addresses across the county. There's no way to call her work, and you don't have her personal number.

Timber

What about Picnic's big brother? Where's he work?

Picnic_ant
At the movie theater. Only multiplex in town.

Timber
I tell SJ, "Hey, Picnic_ant's brother is doing the late shift at the movies, so we can call there."

Picnic_ant
"Even better," says SJ. "We can go there!" She leans close and whispers, "The Sandy June's Mobile Frybread Food Truck doesn't run on gasoline or electricity. It's a machine of space-time. Let me explain. All machines exist within space-time. But the food truck goes off-road. We can be at the movie theater in a heartbeat."
Meanwhile, King and Bob receive answers, too. The scruffy student explains, "I saw Picnic_ant at the grocery store a couple of weeks ago. She bagged my food. Actually, she's there every Friday afternoon, so." He shrugs. "Maybe work ran late." You remember that Picnic_ant sometimes refers to a new part-time job, though she rarely goes into details during game night. She's always worried about complaining or bringing too much real life into the escapism.

WhateverCore
Yeah, well, Bob wishes that she never worried about stuff like that.

KingDM

King enjoys talking to friends. That's the whole point of game night, actually.

Timber

@Picnic_ant i tell you my problems. you can tell me yours. it's always ok.

Picnic_ant

Thanks, everyone. I'll remember that.

But your characters have to make a decision now. Do you go to the movie theater or the grocery store?

WhateverCore

Grocery, right? They're the last people who saw her, and if the food truck has a teleportation mode, we can always visit the movie place afterward.

Timber

I agree.

KingDM

Make that three votes for the grocery store.

Picnic_ant

After everyone reaches a consensus, SJ leads them to a food truck parked on the edge of the asphalt lot. The boxy vehicle

has a yellow paint base with the name "Sandy June's Mobile Frybread Food Truck" elegantly lettered across its long side. A metal sign hangs under the currently shut order window:
TODAY'S MENU
Nopales + solé salsa + chips or frybread
Tacos
Tamales (bean or potato)
Veggie roast (local assortment)
Mesquite bread + honey
Drinks = cota tea, yaupon holly tea, lemonade, milkshakes
"It's a new concept," SJ explains as she opens the back doors to reveal the truck's gleaming kitchen setup. "The truck offers a subset of the day's drive-in menu." Only the 20-lb molcajete, which is secured with straps on the food-prep counter, shows any signs of use; fine particles of corn are embedded between the basalt grain in the molcajete's bowl. The powder is residue from a century of grinding corn into flour against the heavy volcanic rock. "My father was a mechanic, and I learned a thing or two about cars. Enough to invent a space-time engine. Thought it'd be nice to take Sandy June's on the road, especially after kids like your friend Picnic_ant kept losing their homes." As she speaks, SJ shows you where to sit; there's a couple of side-facing seats in the kitchen area, and somebody can sit up front, too.

WhateverCore
Bob calls shotgun!

Picnic_ant

Sure.

After everybody climbs aboard, SJ slides onto the driver's seat. "We'll find her," she promises while flipping a silver switch beside the wheel. The dash resembles something from a retro sci-fi movie, a spaceship's control panels or Doc Brown's modified DeLorean. As SJ's stout fingers zip across the controls, a soft blue light envelops you; there's no roar of fuel combustion or electrical hum. Just a soft, unfelt whoosh of wind, and then the blue light fades. Through the front window, Bob can see the grocery storefront, a rectangle of brightness in the dark. You're idling on the street between the parking lot and the front entrance.

"I'll stay with the transportation, kids," SJ says apologetically. "Can't let them tow my food truck. Its engine is programmed to self-disassemble if a stranger gets ahold of it."

Timber

I get out and sprint inside the grocery store to ask one of the employees if Picnic_ant is still working.

KingDM

King follows as backup.

WhateverCore

Bob teleports inside with his ray gun, so by the time Timber and King arrive, he's already asked the front checkout lady about Picnic_ant.

Picnic_ant

The checkout lady says, "Picnic_ant left after her shift ended. That was hours ago." She might've left, but you three know that she never got home.

KingDM

How does Picnic_ant get to and from work? I make a roll for knowledge. My d20 lands on 11.

Picnic_ant

I'm allowing King a plus-four knowledge modifier for friendship because he's tight with Picnic_ant. So, 11 + 4 = 15, which is a success. He knows that the grocery store is just six miles from Picnic_ant's apartment, and she usually takes her bike. The shortest path goes past a field of wildflowers and through two different neighborhoods.

Timber

Maybe her bike broke, and she's stuck. I say we should check.

WhateverCore

Bob teleports back into the food truck and asks SJ, "Can you actually drive this truck, or does it just randomly appear places? My friends and I want to retrace Picnic_ant's route home."

Picnic_ant

"Of course it can be driven," SJ replies, tapping the wheel sharply. "What do you think my steering's for? Decoration? Hop in!"

SJ waits until everyone is settled before she pulls out of the parking lot. As it moves, the truck is quiet, aside from the clinking of pans and cutlery. Bob, you're tasked with navigation while Timber and King keep lookout. There are two large windows at the back of the truck (one per rear door).

KingDM

King rolls a d20 for perception.
Dang.
It's a 3.

Picnic_ant

King, you don't see anything suspicious, but fortunately Timber's eyes are peeled. As the truck turns onto Flores Road, which goes between two fields of yellow wildflowers and squat oak trees, there's a flash of light in the ditch. The reflective spokes of a bicycle wheel glint in the headlights.

Timber

I shout, "Stop!" and point and say, "Bob, teleport to that bike in the ditch."

WhateverCore

Which Bob does, by the way. Plus, he takes everyone with him since his ray gun has multi-person mode.

KingDM

You've never mentioned a multi-person mode before.

Picnic_ant

I'll allow it.

There's a red bicycle twisted in the brush. Its hind wheel is bent in half, like a folded pizza. In the ditch, a person in a bike helmet lies facedown in the ditch, with her leg bent wrong at the knee. Cactus spines cover her clothes like lint on a wool shirt. She must've tumbled through a prickly pear plant. There are several in the area, near the road.

Timber, even without seeing her face, you recognize the girl immediately.

Timber

stop.

pause game.

@Picnic_ant, were you hit by a car last week?

Picnic_ant

That part of the game is based on reality.

WhateverCore

Bruh

That's CONCERNING.

KingDM

Are you hurt??? Why didn't you tell us earlier?

Picnic_ant

I didn't want to make game night all about me and my
problems.

WhateverCore

We are BEGGING you to make it about yourself. You got hit
by a CAR.

Timber

it's ok, picnic. we're here for you.

Picnic_ant

Ok.

Yeah.

The last few days have been bad.

I was just trying to get home.

It's hard to remember what happened after the car hit me.

I get flashes of flying, rolling, and stopping. One moment,
it was afternoon, and the next, it was sunset, so I probably

passed out. I tried to flip over, but the pain in my right leg was too much, and the rest of my body stung because a cactus had left its points in me.

KingDM

They left you there???

Picnic_ant

Yes. I was alone.

When I couldn't find my phone, I crawled out of the ditch, using my arms instead of my legs. It hurt like hell, but I wanted to be seen by a passing car. Refused to die alone like roadkill. Thirty minutes later, a woman in a food truck found me there. She raced me to the hospital, and I spent a couple of days recovering. Got a cast on my right leg, but it could've been worse. No brain injury, no internal damage. I'll be fine.

Timber

i'm so glad you're doing better.

WhateverCore

Did they catch the person who hit you???

Picnic_ant

No. They probably never will.

KingDM

@Picnic_ant, do you have any food allergies? I'm sending a
care package from Dad's trading post.

Timber

oh same! i'll send one.

WhateverCore

We should collab on a gigantic care package for @Picnic_ant.
Let's GO.

Picnic_ant

Aw, that's kind, but you don't have to. <3

Timber

we want to tho.
i wish i could have been there for you.
in the hospital.

KingDM

Seriously, me too.

WhateverCore

Whatever you need, let us know.

Picnic_ant

I will.

<3

Timber

<3

KingDM

<3

WhateverCore

<3

TUESDAY

WhateverCore 3:10 PM

Hey. Random question. Is Sandy June's Legendary Frybread Drive-In real? Because Mom and I just drove past one. I'd never seen it before, but it's literally on our rez.

KingDM

That's a strange coincidence, @WhateverCore. I saw a Sandy June's yesterday. Yellow and green color scheme, just like @Picnic_ant described. Maybe it's a chain restaurant.

Timber

yea i spotted one this week too wtf.

a chain of frybread?

no way. it takes forever to cook.

no such thing as mass market frybread.

wait @KingDM you're tongva and @WhateverCore you're

mescalero.

isn't the frybread supposed to appear to indigenous ppl

like us?

Picnic_ant

That's the lore 100%

Let's meet at Sandy June's Saturday.

SJ says it's OK to use a table for our TTRPGs. Maybe she can

be DM someday. She's been playing for over 40 years.

WhateverCore

You're joking. I'm in New Mexico. The space-time thing was

just part of your game.

Right?

RIGHT?

Picnic_ant

See y'all soon <3

LOOK AWAY

Karina Iceberg

Up. Down. Back and forth.

That's how our game goes. It's called Look Away.

The rules:

1. There are two players—Boat Boy and Fish Girl (that's me).

2. We look away from each other.

Every day, all summer, we do the same thing.

I go up and down the ramp, taking fish off the charter boats, then dropping them off at the top to be filleted for the tourists. He goes back and forth on the docks, hosing down the charter boats, once the tourists and fish are gone. But that's not the game.

This is the game: my gaze rises to his, and he finds somewhere else to look. Then he glances back up at me, and I look down at the fish.

There is one minor problem with our game. . . . I might be the only one playing it. At the beginning of the summer, I was pretty sure we both were. I don't know how. I just felt it, certain that when his eyes went down, they were a bit crinkled, or that his lips tipped up just a tiny bit.

It happens now, when he looks up to find that, once again, I can't stop myself from staring at him, and he suddenly glances down at the hose in his hand. But what if it's all just in my head? What if the eye crinkles and the almost smiles are just him with something in his eye, or something stuck in his teeth? And I'm just the high school freshman—amendment, *almost* freshman—who thinks that for the first time a guy might be noticing her, when he's just had a pleasant summer looking wherever he wants, and it just happens to be *not* at this Fish Girl.

It seems like the rockfish on top of the load is laughing at me.

Ugh. At the beginning of the summer, I felt giddy. Our grandparents introduced us. Grandmary runs one of his grandpa Joe's charter boats down here in Sitka every summer when Grandpa Joe needs help during the tourist season. Says it gets her out of the village right when she's tired of everyone, at the end of a long winter. This year she brought me along, so I could get to know the town before I start at the Mount, the Native boarding school for kids from villages too small to have a high school.

At the time Grandmary introduced us, "Mary, Elliott," I'd thought it was the beginning of something. My first crush, way too late at fourteen! I mean, it's not my fault, growing up in the middle of Nowhere, Alaska, in a village of about a hundred people, give or take. It's not like there are a lot of potential crushes running around right under my nose. But there were a few moments, when we went into town, at powwow, or just around, when I noticed someone.

I thought that was a crush. It was nice.

Now I understand the true meaning of the word.

As my gaze finds its way to him, to find him *maybe* looking, but then looking away immediately, I feel crushed. *Crushed.* No one explains that a crush isn't fun but is actually named for its ability to destroy. Summer's almost over now, and nothing happened. Except a lot of longing on my part.

Last winter break, I read a book hiding in Grandmary's closet that laid out "the rules" of dating. They basically boiled down to:

1. Don't make the first move with a guy.

2. Be amazing.

3. Really, don't make the first move.

I've already got number two down, but following number one and three haven't gone so well. Waiting for Boat Boy to ask me out has been torture. At first, it was perfect: I'd see him sitting there reading one of my favorite books of poetry by Joy Harjo, and I'd bring my copy to read the next day and I'd see his almost smile and look away—then nothing. Then out on one of my trail runs, I spotted him up ahead, so I started running every day just to glimpse him—but once again, just look-aways.

At first, I figured he's kinda shy, like me. But a whole summer of shyness?

I wish for the wind to shift, to pull the fresh ocean air inland, instead of wafting the smell of rotting fish from the barrels down the ramp over me. It's been a long, hot day, and I know I smell just like the fish guts being picked at by the gulls. I push my hair out of my face with my arm, sweaty and covered in slime. No wonder Boat Boy looks away. Then I spot my favorite cousin.

"Mary!" Dara calls, looking for me on the docks as I drop off the last load of fish, yelling it at the top of her lungs. Because that's her usual volume. Her only other option is a whisper.

As I come back down the ramp, I notice that Boat Boy is looking at Dara— my beautiful cousin, voted both Miss Nuchalawoyya and Miss World Eskimo-Indian Olympics this year. He's looking at her and not looking away.

She walks right up to him and says, "Ell! What are you doing here?"

Ell. He has a nickname.

"Hey, Dara," he says in a voice as calm as the evening water. "Working for my grandpa again this summer. I thought you went down to the Lower Forty-Eight for the summer?"

He not only has words but many. I want to melt through the slats in the dock. So much for him being shy and Look Away being real. He has no problem looking and smiling at Dara.

Dara smiles back, flipping her hair. "Back to catch Grandmary and Mini Mary before school starts." I cringe at my nickname and the fact that she finally remembers my existence. "You know my little cousin, Mary? She's starting at the Mount this fall!"

His eyes flick to me for a moment—the longest moment all summer—but they're back on Dara by his next breath. He nods but says nothing . . . because what else could he say? *Sure, I know your cousin. I've been industriously ignoring her pushing fish and tossing fish guts all summer long.*

Dara says, "Mary, this is Ell. He'll be a sophomore this year. He's one more person you can ask about the classes. I was his mentor last year, and you'll get paired up with someone, too."

I mumble something about needing a shower and offer a half-hearted wave. Walking away, I overhear Dara ask *my* Boat Boy out to SJ's tonight. Even worse, he says yes.

How to lose a boyfriend you never had:

1. Read some book about the "rules of dating."

2. Fall for the rules, hook, line, and sinker!

3. Watch as your cousin ignores "the rules" and gets *your* date.

4. Gape, openmouthed, like the rockfish and halibut you stare at all day.

Looks like it's time to wash off my crush.

I come back from my run and shower a second time, but my misery is still stickier than fish slime. I try to prepare myself for Dara's date with Elliott—you know, motivational words like, "You don't hate your fave cousin" and "Who needs boys anyway?" But when the moment appears, it's worse than I imagined.

Grandmary, in a tone one doesn't argue with, tells me she expects me to be at Sandy June's, where she'll be making the best frybread ever. (I mean, she's not wrong.) Dara tells Grandmary that we'll catch a ride with Ell, to which Grandmary nods, saying she's getting a ride there early with Auntie. (The traitor—Grandmary even winks at me! After I even told her about my now unrequited crush!)

Fine, whatever. It's just one night; I'll disappear and hide in the background of their date and leave them alone as soon as I can. But then Ell pulls up in his grandpa's old green truck, the kind with the giant wheel wells and a single bench. A single bench for the three of us?

Ugh.

He gets out and comes around to open the passenger door for Dara.

"Mary"—she points, gesturing at her full hips—"there's no way

I'm going to squeeze into the middle. Up you go, Stringbean."

Ell offers me a hand up. A strong, gentle hand. *Groan*. I scoot to the middle of the bench. The cab is small, and to make enough room for Dara, I have no choice but to put one leg on each side of the stick shift. Could this get any more awkward?

After closing the door for Dara (*sigh*), Ell moves to the driver's side as I fantasize about better places to be:

1. Gutting fish.
2. Cleaning out garbage.
3. Picking up the sled dog poop.
4. Scraping the mildew off the fish deck.
5. Digging my own grave with my bare hands.

I start to panic as he opens the door and slides in, and suddenly, his leg is pressed against mine. Kill me now.

I try to fold over myself, kicking the stick shift and somehow managing both to knee myself in the chin and whack my foot against Dara's arm. Shaking her head, she pushes it back toward the other side of the shift. "Not a chance," she says.

Ell leans in, voice soft, breath smelling of mint. "You're not in my way." His first words to me, and they're sadly true. Not in the way of his date with Dara, not in the way as he reaches over my leg and shifts into gear, pulling the truck out toward the road.

Because it's just me:

1. Who feels this rush, touching him.
2. Who feels my heart pounding in my chest.
3. Who feels heat up my arm and leg pressing against his.
4. Who wonders how an arm and leg could feel this good.

5. Who's been playing an imaginary game of Look Away.

6. Who feels the enormous weight of this crush crushing me.

But I'm on his date with *my cousin*—and not just any cousin, but my favorite cousin. The one I've been missing for two years all school year long, dreaming of the day I'd follow her to the Mount. The cousin who always looks out for me, who always calls, always has my back.

And here I am, between Dara and her date. She's gazing out the window, and I . . . I'm the world's worst cousin. It's not her fault that we like the same guy. I take a deep breath, trying to exhale every thought, every feeling I've ever had about Boat Boy. Especially as she launches into this story I've never heard before about how our grand-parents fell in love at SJ's—how Grandmary jammed a nail into her own tire near curfew just so she could ask for a ride home.

Just when I am sure we must be lost, we finally arrive under the fluo-rescent lights of the drive-in, which looks eerie as the sun disappears into the edges of the forest of big Sitka spruce pressing in from all sides. My legs are wobbly, and Dara grabs my hand to steady me. "Walk much?" She laughs, then makes a beeline for the lawn in front of the stage, the blanket grasped tight in her arms as she runs to find a spot near the front.

Who knew Dara was this into music? Before I can wonder for long, she calls back to me, "Mary, the usual, please!" And I realize that she's stuck me with ordering. With her date.

Some days, you just can't catch a break. The silence stretches between us, long and awkward. So long and so awkward that I give in to the fact that it's just one more part of the endless torture that is today. In the silence, I draft my funeral procession:

1. Give Fish Girl a crush on Boat Boy.

2. Make sure Boat Boy has absolutely zero interest in her.

3. Instead, give Boat Boy a crush on Fish Girl's favorite cousin.

4. Make Fish Girl watch said crush unfold right in front of her eyes.

5. Put her smack-dab in the middle of a tiny truck cab with the lovebirds.

6. Squish her against the aforementioned crush, leading to *all the feelings*.

7. Starve her with silence in the line for food, next to an utterly beautiful Boat Boy.

It's poetic, really, the cruelty of the universe.

After eons of waiting, we get to the front and Grandmary hooks us up with Indian tacos, and as she winks at me again, I try to let it all go. To give up this crush. To not let my love of my favorite food get tangled up in the memory of this day.

I take a perverse satisfaction in rushing off toward Dara, planning to drop her food and finally find my escape route.

Only to find Dara right in front of the stage, practically drooling all over some dude, laughing, her hand plastered against his arm, leaning into him, and with a face that might as well have heart emojis as her eyes.

What to do when your cousin has clearly been abducted by an alien:

1. Gape.

2. Stare.

3. Wonder.

4. Celebrate.

5. Feel guilty.

6. Do something?

7. But what exactly?

8. Panic at approaching Boat Boy!

Ell finally catches up, almost running into me as he sees them.

"Don't look!" I yell.

At this, he steps back and obviously looks, because how else are you supposed to respond to such a ridiculous thing?

"I'll find out what's going on!" I screech and run down the lovers.

"What are you doing?" I whisper-shout at Dara.

Dara looks surprised. "What are you talking about?"

"One minute, you're on a date with Ell, and the next you're over here making googly eyes at this lothario!"

At this the (admittedly beautiful) singer laughs, but lucky for him, he is polite enough to turn it into a cough at my death glare.

Dara has the nerve to pull said lothario aside for a whisper, and he nods and says, "See you after the show."

"Not if I have anything to say about it!" I quip.

He nods at me as he walks away. "Good luck, kid."

Then Dara is in my face, full Concerned Cousin look. "What is going on?"

"Why were you off with him"—I gesture at the singer—"when you came here with Ell?"

"Mary," she says, pulling me away from the stage. "That is the lead singer of Not Your Wild West Show. They're not only rez famous, but almost *actually* famous!" The name of the band she's been talking about all summer starts to ring a bell. "They're having their last show, and I promised him I'd be here. He's the guy I've been calling you about *all summer long*."

At this, I feel the chagrin on my face. Okay, she had been telling me about a crush. We'd both been talking about our crushes. Hers sounded a bit more promising whereas mine was unrequited. It had made me feel like I had a kindred spirit—until she asked out my crush! "But you asked out Ell?" I push.

"I didn't ask out Ell for me! I asked him out for you—because clearly you didn't take my advice when I told you that silly dating book was something Grandmary confiscated from one of the aunties back in the day, because it was leading them astray way back then. She didn't even know it was still in her closet." Dara has both hands on her full hips, but she has a half smile as she looks down at me.

Some of this . . . sounds like maybe she did say all of that. But I'd been so in my head, I'm not sure I actually heard any of it.

"Wait, did you say you asked him out for *me*?" I panic, looking over in horror to see Elliott laughing with a friend. "He doesn't know that, does he?" I deathgrip Dara's hands, hoping that she hasn't given me away.

She laughs, giving my hands a squeeze. "No, I just invited him with us. He knows I wanted to see his cousin, the singer." She nods back to the stage. Then she smirks. "But he is probably wondering why you yelled at him when he saw us."

I groan at the realization that I'll have to explain this, crumpling into Dara, who is nice enough to give me a hug. Suddenly, I understand the singer wishing me good luck.

"How am I going to explain this?" I ask Dara.

"You could try the truth." She laughs as she gives me a nudge, then heads toward Elliott to grab her tacos on the table, before waving to some friends. Then she's off, and I'm suddenly cold in my tank top, in the shade of one of the big spruce trees.

The wind has finally picked up, followed by big, fat drops of rain, and a full downpour begins. I run toward the building, only to realize that it's too packed, and people are rushing for cars and trees to hide under.

A hand swoops in to grab mine, pulling me toward one of the giant spruces, and we get under just as hail starts pelting down.

I look up to see Elliott, holding up an arm with half of his blanket to share.

I climb under, feeling the warmth of the material, and of him, as he wraps both his arm and the woven cotton around me. "Thanks," I say.

He nods, giving me a side-eye. "So . . . earlier?"

"Sorry I yelled. I . . . I got some things mixed up." I'm mumbling by the end.

"Like what?" he prods.

"I thought you were here on a date with Dara," I say, not sure how to say the rest.

"Why?" he asks, turning toward me, and I feel his breath on my cheek.

"Well, you saw Dara and smiled at her . . . and I thought . . ." I take a deep breath, accepting that I'll just have to live with my embarrassment. "I thought there was something between us, with the game, but then you looked at her and smiled and talked, so I figured that you were into her." Now I'm wishing for the imaginary grave I dug in my head.

"What game?" he asks.

"Well, I called it Look Away, and I thought we kind of had a thing, but then you never asked me out, and the book said that the guy always makes the first move, so it just kind of took me a while to realize that you weren't that into me." I'm rambling, and my face is flushed, and I hope he can't see it, but at the same time, I'm still leaning into the arm he has wrapped around me. And when I feel him wrap that arm a little bit tighter at my words, I feel brave enough to glance up, to see him smiling.

"What if I'm more of a second-move guy?" he asks.

I feel lighter than I've ever felt. My heart pounds even faster than the hail all around us as I try out a new game: I press up on my toes, wrap my arms around him, and slowly, slowly, slowly, I lean in as we both look right into each other's eyes until our lips meet.

PATENT RED

Cynthia Leitich Smith

No way I'm letting last night get me down. It was nothing, nada, a blip. On the whole, my experience was a blast. Santa Fe? Gorgeous. The camp food? Shockingly tasty. I came. I saw. I walked away with an embossed certificate that reads "National Student Leader." I made friends, held hands in a circle, mumbled along to "Kumbaya," and now here I am in the cramped aisle of a commercial jet, traveling by myself like a fancy, mature young woman.

Via the speakers, a feminine voice says, "Once again, this is a totally full flight. Please place personal items under your seat and use the first available overhead space for your larger carry-on." A baby is wailing. Somebody just sneezed. Bags are being stowed, seats taken, earpieces inserted, travel pillows positioned. My oversize backpack is bumping a few passengers in aisle seats. Window shades are down because of the heat.

I reach my row, where a guy—whose hair is longer, prettier, and darker than mine—is folded into the window seat, reading a tattered paperback about modern Indigenous music. That doesn't guarantee he's Native, but I'd bet my beadwork on it.

"Hey," I say in a remarkably (for me) understated act of articulation.

"Hey," he replies with a glance at my turquoise backpack. "Need help with that?"

Hesci, chivalry! Or fine, it could be sexism. Too early to say, but I'm an optimist. He looks to be about my age. Potentially my type. Oh, how I appreciate a pretty boy who reads! Hmm, maybe I'm the one who's sexist. "Nah, I'm good."

With those lanky legs, he can't be comfortable folded into that spot like a cricket. Air travel is obviously torture for the tall. "You want the aisle?"

"Nah, I'm good," he says.

"That makes one of us," I reply.

"Ahem," comes a salty, southern-tinged, vaguely familiar voice from behind me. "You can flirt *after* you sit down." As if we won't all arrive at the same time. Besides, I was *not* flirting, at least not yet. The closest overhead bins are filled with roller bags, so I contort myself to shove my backpack beneath the seat in front of mine. Realizing my booty has already landed on my cushion, I sit up.

"Ahem," the salty woman says again, nudging one of my backpack straps with the pointed toe of her red patent high heel. Wait, I recognize those shoes! A glance at her pinched face confirms it. It's her—the special closing-night speaker from leadership camp, acting condescending to me for the *second* time in less than twenty-four hours. I catch the stray backpack strap with the sole of my decidedly less glamorous sneaker and drag it out of the aisle.

Does *she* recognize *me*? I don't think so. No reaction to my retreat logo T-shirt, either.

Home is the Muscogee rez, which means my community is Muscogee and intertribal and interracial, and, yeah, it was kind of odd for me this past week, being the only Indigenous person at the leadership camp. But not in a terrible way.

The group was mostly white, probably because mostly white school districts have the moola for airfare to send their young leaders to summer development programs at popular vacation destinations. Anyway, my heritage didn't come up in conversation. But when I'd glanced over the program schedule, I'd appreciated that a Native businesswoman had been highlighted as our closing-night speaker.

Whatshername is polished and professional and probably ten years older than my grandma. Of course she ends up seated in the row right behind mine. I use the camera function on my cell phone to watch her get situated and slip on her earbuds.

Go ahead. Cancel the sound. Cancel the world, like you canceled my voice in front of the whole retreat community.

"You okay?" asks the boy beside me.

"Good, good." I realize I'm lightly kicking the top of my over-stuffed backpack and stop. "I'm fine." I don't sound convincing. "How're you?"

"Good," he says, returning his attention to his book.

I put my phone on airplane mode. So what if she embarrassed me during the Q and A session? As the flight attendants secure the plane, I click my seat belt, pulling the slack tighter, and reach to dig in my purse—not yet safely stowed—for a packet of motion-sickness pills and try to rip it open.

The air on the plane is stuffy, uncomfortable. Outside, it's over ninety degrees. At least when we get up in the clouds, the cabin temperature should cool. The guy next to me adjusts his overhead fan and gestures at the medicine packet in my fingers. "Need help with that?"

"Nah, I'm good," I reply as the plane taxis to the runway. After struggling another minute, I surrender the packet and find myself briefly mesmerized by the sight of him tearing open the package with his teeth. For a half second, it dangles from his lips, a sight so much more compelling than Whatshername behind us, who, when I asked how #LandBack fit into what she was saying about socioeconomic development, replied, "Young lady, I'm looking for more than performative hashtag questions. If you're going to invoke a Native American movement in a conversation, you should first do your homework and learn what it's all about."

I mean, really? Did it ever occur to her that my uncle is a federal Indian law attorney and that we've had plenty of conversations about #LandBack?

With a huff, I whisper, "Do I look like some clueless, idealistic brat who doesn't understand that I'm never going to have all the power in the world . . . even though if I had all the power in a room—like a rustic retreat meeting room—I wouldn't use it to strut in like a badass and then talk down to a younger Indigenous person and make her feel sad and small, especially in front of a whole crowd of non-Native people?"

Given that my rant is disguised as a question, it takes him a moment to decode. Is the plane slowing down? It shouldn't be slowing down. "Did you introduce yourself to her?" my neighbor asks, wiping off the packet on his T-shirt before returning it to me.

Before I can respond, there's another announcement. "Sorry, folks. Due to a mechanical issue, we're going to return to the gate and change planes." A groan fills the cabin. "It might take a while. Make sure you've downloaded our app for updates. . . ." The voice keeps talking. I stop listening, fold over the top of the chewable medication packet, and tuck it back into my purse. It's not only that the trip is delayed and that will cause havoc with my connection in Denver. It's also that Santa Fe's regional airport is under construction, mostly gutted and boarded off.

As the plane turns, the boy asks again, "Did you introduce yourself to the speaker?"

"I would've." My voice stays low, quiet. "But I didn't get a chance before her presentation, and afterward, I made a beeline for the marshmallow roast." My forearm brushes his, and I exhale, suddenly feeling more philosophical. "I shouldn't let her get to me. I mean, we're talking about someone who felt the need to prove she was a badass at the expense of a random teenager asking a completely valid question."

He leans closer and whispers, "Why are we whispering?"

"Because she's sitting right behind us."

"She is?" he asks at full volume, craning his neck for a look.

I playfully elbow him and sink in my seat, not sure why *I'm* the one who's embarrassed. When my new friend chuckles, I join in. He adds, "I'm Ben. Like the clock in London. Menominee-Apache."

"Charlotte," I reply. "Like the spider in the book. Muscogee-Caddo."

"Hyphenated NDNs for the win," he replies, and we bump fists.

Waiting to disembark, we make small talk. Fill in introductions.

He's a junior. I'm a senior. He's traveling to Chicago to visit his cousin Jonah, and I admit to attending the national student-leadership camp. "So, you're a dork," he teases. At my pretend-indignant jaw drop, he says, "I'm a dork, too." He tucks his book in a duffel bag. "Music dork."

"You play an instrument?" I ask.

"I sing." At my brightening expression, he qualifies that. "In the shower. Along with the radio. To my rubber duckies. Not out loud, not in public, not for other people. Someday, if I get ambitious, I might try the tambourine."

Somehow, I get the feeling he's being modest.

By then, we're gathering our bags, and the cabin is noisy with everyone else doing the same. A lot of families with kids are traveling— summer vacation and all that. A few passengers are wearing face masks. Because of how tightly my backpack is wedged, Ben waves the people behind us to go on ahead. With one manicured hand on the top of the across-the-aisle seat in front of her, the haughty speaker from my conference pivots to address us. "I heard you two laughing at me, and young lady, I had no idea you were Muscogee Creek. Where I come from, we raise our children to be more respectful than that. But I understand that Oklahoma Indians are a diluted bunch."

"Ouch," Ben breathes.

I bite my lip at the insult, unsure whether—beyond me—her crack was supposed to be about culture, quantum, or the nearly forty tribal Nations within what's currently called Oklahoma. I'm on the light-skinned side. One of my granddads was Irish American. I got my complexion and freckles from his side of the family, but, sure as hell, I'm Native enough to make Custer nervous.

I don't say any of that. Sourpuss has moved farther forward. The middle-aged South Asian couple who had been seated across the aisle is standing between her and us. Besides, we're on a crowded plane and the last thing I need is for some jackass to post a video of me in a more-NDN-than-thou shouting match. My mom raised me to know when to keep my sometimes-sassy mouth shut. So I do, mostly.

The regional airport is probably cozy under the best of circumstances, and this is far from that. Around the gate, every chair is full, and passengers for the next outgoing flight are standing shoulder to shoulder as those deplaning from mine grumble into the makeshift lounge. The airline service agent raises his mic to point out that there's not enough room in the lounge and we're going to have to wait outside security, and then he reminds us—again—to download the airline app. Taking out my phone to update my mom, I trail after Ben through the exit.

For a split second, I'm caught in a silent shimmer. No signal. A cool breeze. No shuffling chatter of the other passengers. We're outside. Only Ben is still here.

"We're . . ." I spin around. "What happened to the airport?" I stagger backward. "What happened to New Mexico?"

"First timer, eh?" he asks, offering me the crook of his elbow. I grab it, grateful for someone steady to hang on to. With his other hand, Ben pushes aside leafy branches blocking our gravel path, and we step into a grassy clearing. He asks, "You hungry?"

"Usually." I breathe in the array of cars—several vintage—parked in the service stalls of a bustling drive-in, the sixtysomething bellhop on roller skates, a trio of girls in ribbon skirts getting out of a wood-paneled station wagon, a scruffy guy playing a fiddle on the bed of a pickup. Beside him, seven-foot-tall twins strum hologram guitars and sing a song of gratitude for safe sisters and two-spirit relatives. A song of land returned, of sky scrubbed and water protected. Ben, who's humming along, pauses to take my backpack as if it weighs nothing. That settles it—chivalrous. I ask, "Did you bring me here somehow?"

He shrugs. "Welcome to Sandy June's Legendary Frybread Drive-In." At my baffled expression, he adds, "Some say 'June' is a last name. Others say it's a middle name. I've heard that Sandy and June were two different people—sisters or brothers or lovebirds. Bingo buddies or rival aunties who made peace over bison burgers." He gestures toward the tables. "A lot has happened under that awning. Storytelling, marriage proposals, intertribal negotiations."

Sandy June's. The name sounds vaguely beachy. Or like a summer oasis tucked into space and time. The boy on the fiddle turns a knob on an oversize boom box, cranks up the volume, and starts strumming. I have no signal on my phone. Nothing. Not even a dot. Normally, I'd be worried that the airline was trying to message me, that I'd miss the flight, but with every step forward, I feel lighter on my feet. Like my everyday burdens are floating away.

"You're not just type A." He chuckles. "You're type triple A."

Navigating the cracked asphalt, I reply, "Part of my charm."

He grins. "It's been theorized that you're more likely to find your way here if the drive-in is part of your family history, your clan history, or if a regular brings you. But it's my belief that, day to day, any Native person may come across that neon sign, especially if they need it."

"Any Native person?" I stiffen, wondering if you-know-who is somewhere nearby. As we weave through the picnic tables, it's ridiculous to feel as though she has no right to be in a place where I've barely set foot. Of course, it's also ridiculous how much it already feels like home.

"Ben!" comes a boisterous voice from the order window, bordered by flyers announcing next weekend's Battle of the Bands. "Hey, man. Good to see you." A guy sporting a 2S T-shirt with boot-cut jeans rings a cowbell. "It's lunchtime for the legendary grandparents. Could you and"—he gestures to me—"your friend here give us a hand?"

Ben leads the way again, this time around the building. "Not every Elder here runs the drive-in. A few regular customers show up in the mornings with their gear to fish off the dock. A romance-novel book club meets once a month on foldout chairs in the campground, and of course it's a popular destination for food, company, and people-watching."

Inside, we drop off our bags as legendary grandparents wearing beaded name tags are streaming toward picnic tables out front. Meanwhile, the existing diners—mostly teens with a sprinkle of middle-aged folks and their kiddos—are rushing to clean up and clear out to make room. A girl with fading pink hair is ladling up bowls of elk soup to serve with cornbread.

I say, "Hesci, I'm Charlotte."

"Like the spider in the book?" asks the pink-haired girl.

We're destined to be friends. Maybe not today, but it'll happen. I don't have to be told that this is a routine flip in the drive-in dynamic, that these legendary grandparents may run Sandy June's, but it's on us as the young folks to serve them, too. Their orders are already in, and the thick stew is popular. I sneak a warm, savory spoonful while loading up a tray.

Outside, as I'm dropping off the food, the grandparents' jokes and laughter rise, along with grumbling about medical dietary recommendations. I navigate around a walker and a couple of canes. At a crowded table, legendary grandmother Sarah R. asks for cota tea with her bison burger. We strike up a conversation, and, come to find out, she's Muscogee Freedmen. She tears off a bite of burger and tosses it to a brown-and-white mutt with oversize ears. "I don't have my glasses on. What's that your T-shirt says?"

"Uh . . ." I'd forgotten I was wearing it. I glance down at the stylized font. "National Student Government Leadership Gathering. Shining Stars of Today and Tomorrow."

"Good for you, honey!" she exclaims. "There are few things I enjoy more than watching a young person succeed in this world, whatever that means to them." Another toss of the burger flies to the pup. "Today, tomorrow . . . What about yesterday?"

"Yesterday?" I echo. I'm charmed by Grandma Sarah, by all the loving Elders here. Maybe this place is good medicine. Maybe people come here to heal.

Ben taps my shoulder. "There's a customer off by herself on the dock behind those trees. Could you run this Navajo taco to her?"

"Sure," I say, trading my empty tray for his. "If you can get Grandma Sarah's tea." Meanwhile, my phone is still out of commission, and I take a moment to reconfirm the fact that that means the airline app is useless, too. No updates or other notifications. Then a food truck rambles onto the grounds and dazed-looking teens hop out in bell-bottoms; tie-dye shirts; long, flowing dresses; and fringed ponchos. "Retro," I say.

Ben runs a hand through his longer, prettier, darker hair. "Uh . . ."

Grandma Sarah pipes up. "Not where they come from. Or should I say *when?*"

I inhale the spicy smoke of the taco and glance up at Ben. "You won't leave without me?"

He leans in to whisper in my ear. "Charlotte, we've got all the time in the world." Which, at face value, may not sound like the most romantic thing anyone has ever said, but trust me when I swear to you that it *was*. It was *the most romantic thing anyone has ever said*. What's more, he means it—literally, and I believe him. I stop fretting about my phone signal and the flight from Santa Fe. As I carry Ben's tray toward the whispering trees, Grandma Sarah calls, "Good luck!"

Rippling water sparkles. The sky glows cottony white and cornflower blue. The birds—well, they're some kind of duck . . . or loon? I don't know. For a girl who half grew up on Lake Tenkiller, I'm no expert on waterfowl. But it looks peaceful and feels peaceful . . . until I spot my new archnemesis. With her back to me, she's seated on the edge of the dock. Her killer red high heels are set to one side. Her bare feet dangle over the water.

I approach, mindful of my footsteps, pause—her shoes between us—and make a half-hearted attempt to bend down and offer the meal. My voice is flat. "Here's your lunch."

"I'm not hungry."

Fine, I tried.

As I move to retreat, she adds, "Don't you go anywhere, Charlotte. Sit."

Sit, like a dog. I sit, realizing she must've been eavesdropping on my conversation with Ben on the plane. Or at least overheard my name spoken since we were seated only one row in front of her. I wait. And wait. Sometimes I hate being a good girl.

I'll say one thing for this woman: Her shoes are freaking gorgeous. Shiny. I swear I can almost see myself in the reflection—me, her, the sky. I kick off my sneakers, pull off my socks, and let my bare feet hang, swinging slowly next to hers.

Meanwhile, the rejected taco is getting cold, and I'm hungry. No reason to let good food go to waste. As I chew my first oniony-greasy-spicy-cheesy-crunchy bite, she says, "I'm sorry. I shouldn't have spoken to you that way. Before I left Alabama for Santa Fe, this smug asshat I work with—or, well, work against—put me down hard, and it's still burning my gut. Last night I shoved that hurt onto you and did it again today after I overheard you telling that young man—Ben—on the flight about my behavior. I . . . I suppose I felt ashamed and defensive and overreacted and . . . never mind. That's no excuse."

No, it's not. I should be gracious and accept her apology. But I'm not feeling it.

"I'm Evelyn. My people are the Eastern Band of Cherokees."

My mom says to always look for the good in people. Evelyn is a pretty name, and her Cherokee cousins in Oklahoma are my neighbors. Counting the shoes, that's three things I like about her.

Evelyn extends her hand as if to touch my shoulder but stops short. "You know, our feet look to be about the same size." She lifts her heels. "Wanna try 'em on?"

The red is bright, alluring. The toes so pointy they could double as torture devices. I've never worn high heels before, just kitten heels to church and school dances. These must be four-inchers. Evelyn says, "My feet are seven and a half wides."

"Mine, too." The apology is sinking in. Somebody got in her head. I guess sometimes I let people get to me, too. Maybe we're more alike than I wanted to admit. Besides, forgiveness is divine. I set down my plate, hop up, and wiggle my feet into the irresistible shoes.

"Head up," she says. "Shoulders back." Thankfully, the dock is in better shape than the drive-in. It's not wobbling, I am. Evelyn adds, "Deep breaths, focus, take your time. One step, then another." It's harder than it looks. I throw my palms out to catch myself if I fall.

Evelyn chuckles. "Come on, Charlotte! If I can do it, so can you. Besides, if you're going to grow up to be a badass like me, you've got to learn how to strut."

I laugh. Good thing neither of us is holding grudges. I exhale, head up, shoulders back, projecting confidence. "I've got it. I'm walking." Steady, strong. "I'm doing it!"

"Yes, sweet girl!" she crows. "Yes, you are!"

We both cackle. I feel glamorous, empowered, and so freaking tall.

BRAVING THE STORM

Kaua Māhoe Adams

I was born scared

that's just how I came out
crying, screaming, and absolutely terrified

and I've been scared of
everything   ever since

but Papa?

he is the bravest person I know—

               well

he was

Papa is—
was

my grandfather

my mother's father

and my favorite person
in this big, terrifying world

things I am scared of

clowns

roller coasters

white-water rafting

spiders

snakes

horror movies

horror books

horror

precalculus tests

getting onto a ski lift

getting off a ski lift

swimming in lakes

swimming in rivers

swimming in the ocean

swimming

walking into the lunchroom by myself

talking to Andrew Lau, hottest guy in the tenth grade

taking things out of the oven

really steep hills

caves

caverns

tunnels of any sort

bridges

heights

whales

cavities

gingivitis

every dentist I've ever gone to

I am scared of a lot

but Papa

he has—had—a way of making me   not so scared

                    at least not
                              all the time

Mom and I spend
every summer in Hawai'i

while Dad stays home
on the mainland

because someone needs
to

walk the dog
water the plants
and check the mail

but also because Dad
is not Hawaiian

like me and Mom
and Papa

and summers in Hawai'i
are—were—just for

us

that's why summer
is my favorite season

not because of
>   no school
>   no homework
>   no responsibility

though I like those things too

summer is my favorite because
that means—it used to mean—spending every day

with Papa

back home in Seattle

I am
>   boring
>   awkward
>   kind of smart but not *that* smart

I am Marley Scaredy-Cat McKinnon

but in Waimea
with Papa by my side

I am—was—

     wild

     exciting

     even   brave sometimes

brave enough to dive under a wave

brave enough to let a moʻo rest in my palm

brave enough to catch a fish on my line and reel it in all the way

I am—was was was—Nohealani

Papa never calls me—*called* me—Marley

because Marley is scared

all the time

but Nohealani?

that girl was brave

one time when I was little
maybe five or six or seven

we were in Waimea
and a summer storm started to roll in

the sky churning and rumbling
threatening something big

saying *I'll do it, you know!*

taunting, goading, talking trash until

ba-BOOM

thunder beat so hard
I felt it in my chest

everything opened up all at once
rain pounding heavy into the earth

the roar of the storm shook the house
grabbing it by the sides

saying *how do you like this, huh?*

sure

Waimea has blue skies
and sunny days but

it does rain here
and when it rains

it pours

every crack of thunder
sent me deeper under the covers

ba-BOOM!

       ba-BOOM!

ba-BOOM!

I didn't move
I couldn't move

until

a pair of soft brown hands
worn from years of

      fixing
      holding
      tanning in the sun

ushered me out from my hiding spot

come, Nohealani   Papa said, leading me out
                     to the lanai

I held on to his arm

scared that if I were to let go

the whistling wind would sweep me up
and away

ba-BOOM!

ba-BOOM!

ba-BOOM!

I gripped harder
tucking my face into the soft fabric of his T-shirt

but he forced me to look out onto the landscape

to watch the horizon
           where the ʻaʻā rose up to meet
the trembling sky

a storm is nothing to fear
look, it's almost done anyway he said
             pointing to something in the distance

a sliver of blue

cutting

through

the gray

see? he smiled
Papa had the best smile
the kind that could light up
                    the world
every storm passes eventually

so it's ironic
that today of all days

the day we laid Papa to rest

a summer storm is rolling in
        and there's no one here

to hold my hand
        to point out slivers of blue
to tell me   there is nothing to fear

because when he left
he took every little bit of bravery I had
        with him

Mom comes flying into the living room

we're staying at Papa's
for the summer

like we always do

but this time is different

> because a home without its heart
> is just a house

Marley, honey? Mom tosses me the car keys
they land in my lap
I need you to go to the store

outside
the storm is in full swing

I swallow hard

but—?

she pinches the bridge of her nose
she's been doing that a lot
usually at me   always at me

we have fifty people
who are going to be here in two hours

she says this as she throws off her shoes
        ties up her long hair into a messy bun

we barely just got back from the church

I need you to get a few things for me

       she's already walking away
              her back toward me

it's going to be fine she says over her shoulder
get yourself a treat or something

and
don't
freak
out

it's just a little rain

I got my license
six months ago

but unlike my friends
who counted down the days

until they could finally
take the test

Mom had to drag me
into the DMV

and make me promise
I wouldn't fail on purpose

add

freeways
one-way streets

bike lanes
flat tires
parallel parking

all to the list
of things I'm scared of

oh, and don't forget

driving in a storm

Waimea

is nestled against the Kohala Mountains
toward the northern tip of Hawaiʻi island

it isn't a big town
in fact, it's categorically small

small enough to fit in my open palm
small enough that I know every light, turn, and road
          like every line and crease of my hand

this place is a part of me

like the freckles that dot my nose
like all thirty-two teeth in my mouth
like every soft, dark hair on my arm

but the rain is coming down hard
harder than the pounding of my heart

even with the windshield wipers
going as fast as they can

I can barely see
and it doesn't take long

until I take a wrong turn
and I am officially   lost

walls of green monstera

rise on either side of me
as fear

bubbles up
my throat

turning bitter
on my tongue

the radio goes static

I hit the dash with the heel of my palm

bang!
      bang!
            bang!

but the radio
just goes

craccckkk   cracckkk   crack

POP!

then

silence

I search for a place to turn around

eyes scanning
for just a few feet of space to pull a U-turn

but I'm so focused
I don't even notice

when the rain lightens
when it stops altogether

when the road turns to dirt

     then to gravel

          and finally to asphalt

I only look up
    really look when

    suddenly

       everything

     o   p   e   n   s

to light

        light

  light

green and gray
gives way to

        blue white   yellow yellow yellow

and a massive wooden sign

SANDY JUNE'S LEGENDARY FRYBREAD DRIVE-IN

lit up in neon lights
green against black
the only exception being the word *legendary*
      in bright yellow

the windshield wipers squeal
against the glass

      eeee! eeee! eeee! eeee!
making me jump in my seat

I flick the wipers off
and follow the asphalt driveway
      past the sign

into a parking lot that's long overdue
for repairs

the car goes
ba-doom ba-doom ba-doom

      over dips and cracks
in the asphalt

as I roll to a stop
in a free spot at the end

I get out
look to the sky

and try to figure out
where this sunny day came from

and when Waimea got a drive-in?

it doesn't take me long

to realize that I am not
in Waimea anymore

but there's something
about this place

that feels safe
that feels like home

Someone opens the door
to the restaurant

letting out
a rush of voices

and a delicious
smell that's

almost
enticing enough

to draw me
inside

when a group of kids
around my age

exit the restaurant
wide grins on all their faces

laughter rolling
like thunder

I'm too nervous to go in

add

walking into restaurants by myself

to the list

because restaurants and lunchrooms
are basically the same thing

so I decide to walk around outside
instead

the food truck sits

in the back

I make note of the menu
my mouth watering

when I notice
a little cardboard sign

handwritten in curvy script
that feels so familiar it pinches

Papa's Friday Special

laulau plate lunch
            comes with one scoop rice
            and one scoop mac salad

memories of making laulau
memories I've purposely kept down

rise up to the surface
demanding to be seen
                        heard

                        felt

we always made laulaus

the last night of our
summer stay

it started as a way
to distract me from the fact

that Mom and I would be on a plane
first thing the next morning

back to Seattle
back to boring
back to awkward
back to smart but not *that* smart

back to Marley McKinnon
back to being scared   all the time

at first I didn't like laulaus

                    they used to be
                    on the list   too

I was intimidated by the green color
and the earthy fragrance they gave off
          when pulled out of the pot

then Papa showed me how to make them
how to fill them with my favorite things

salty beef
white fish
tender 'uala

how to roll them with care
how to break the stem of the ti leaf to act as a string
        so they didn't fall apart while cooking

something about making them myself
made me realize they weren't scary at all

that I love laulaus
that every time I taste one I hear Papa's laugh
        see his light-up-the-world smile

that's why I took them off
        the list

someone's voice

yanks me out of the memory
like a puppet pulled violently by its strings

      but

wait

     I

           know

that

voice

I would know that voice

anywhere
anytime

      under a wave
      up a mountain in the wind

caught in a storm

I would follow that voice

because that's not just *someone's* voice

that's Papa's voice

my papa's voice and he's calling out to me

Nohealani, my girl

Papa stands illuminated

by the late-afternoon light
looking like a guardian angel

sent just for me

but he is not some unearthly being
he's Papa

a dish towel hangs limp over his shoulder
sweat darkens the places where his T-shirt sticks to his skin
a beaded name tag sits proudly over his heart
    it reads *Sandy June's Legendary Frybread Drive-In*
    above *Papa Kaleo*

Papa?

       he smiles
       holding out his arms

next thing I know my feet are pounding the earth
       I'm running as fast as I can
       the world melting away
       until it's just   Papa and me

he's catching me

holding me
hugging me
patting down my hair
smiling, saying *don't cry don't cry don't cry*
laughing, saying *my girl my girl*

my Nohealani

I have a million things

that I want to say
that I need to tell him
that I should ask him

I hated your funeral
you would have hated it too
no trust me
Mom made me wear pantyhose
we had to sing hymns
I hate driving
especially driving in the rain
I'll be a junior soon
I'm supposed to start thinking about college
well everyone has been already
I've been putting it off
I'm scared to get rejected
I'm scared to leave home
I'm scared to grow up
I'm scared no one will ever call me Nohealani again
I'm scared to live in a world without you
I'm scared you are the only reason I was ever brave
I'm scared all the time
I miss you
you've only been gone for two weeks but I miss you
is this a dream

is this heaven
oh, jeez, did I die in that storm
is this a simulation
how did I get here
what is this place

but all that comes out is

how is this possible?

papa pulls away
leaving just an arm around my shoulders

I'm here every Friday

he says it like it's nothing new
like it's a fact

> like telling me the sky is blue
> like telling me the ocean is wet
> like telling me the sun rises every day

but how are you here?

right now?

when you're—

he stops me

none of that is my business
all you need to know is
this food truck is special
and I'm not just talking about the food

but do get a tamale before you go he adds

he flashes me another smile

they're 'ono

that's when I realize

his hair isn't all white, but
streaked with strands of black

the lines around his mouth are there
but not as prominent

this is the Papa from my childhood

and now, a million new questions
sit at the tip of my tongue

but before I can get one out

he's leading me around to the other side
of the food truck

to a setup that is achingly familiar

two foldout tables
arranged in an L shape

covered with plastic tablecloths
patterned with red blooms of hibiscus

large silver pots sit at the center
bubbling and steaming

stacks of luʻau and ti
leaves sit washed and ready

foil containers of neatly cubed
meat, fish, and ʻuala covered with plastic
to ward off bugs, taking up most of the space

want to help me? he asks

all I can do is nod

Papa hums

soft nameless tunes
while we work

standing side by side
with him

I am transported

to every last night
of summer

in his backyard
surrounded by

aunties uncles
and cousins

Mom at my right
Papa at the left

all of us working
with quick hands

to fill and roll
laulaus

the stacks growing
taller into mounds

of precious emerald

glossy ti leaves
shining like jewels

when the last laulau is rolled

dread drops heavy
like a stone in my stomach

I need to get back

  to Mom
  to Marley McKinnon
  to being scared all the time

because I don't totally get it
the magic of this place

but I know Papa
isn't coming back with me

Papa glances at me

my little rain cloud he pats my cheek
what troubles you?

I speak to the ground
to the grass beneath my sneakers

I don't want to leave you
I'm—I'm scared
I'm scared all the time I admit

though I think he already knows that

how do you do it? I lift my chin to look at him
how are you brave all the time?

he's still for a moment before
breaking into riotous laughter

Papa! I'm serious!

he hooks his arm around me
I know, my girl, I know he says
before kissing my cheek

I am scared all the time too

but I am many things
I am happy
I get embarrassed
I worry

I am human
just like you *and that means I get to feel*
                                    everything

which can feel like a burden, yes

but ultimately it's a gift

Papa makes me face him
makes me look in his hazel eyes

hazel like Mom's
hazel like mine

everything passes he begins

days
weeks
months
years
time can be strange like that
        it can do a lot of things we don't understand
            but it never stops
sad moments
pain
hurt
grief he pauses
to wipe away a tear from my cheek
fear too   especially fear
but even the biggest storms break at some point

but how do you make it through the storm? I ask

he smiles
like he was hoping I would ask that

grabbing both of my hands in his
and squeezing

you got to hold on to these moments

the happy
the peaceful
the beautiful
the safe

moments

as tight as you can
until they are a part of you

until even time can't take them away

Papa walks me back to the car

with two plastic bags
packed tight with laulaus

and a tamale
just for me

he shuts the door for me
waits for me to roll down the window

takes my face in both hands
smiling his light-up-the-world smile

how do I get back? I ask

the way you came he says
as simple as that

I love you, Papa
I manage to choke out
around the growing lump in my throat

I love you too, Nohealani

now go be brave

I follow the road

past the sign

over asphalt
over gravel
over dirt

through the tunnel of monstera

and back out into
        the storm

by the time
I find my way back into town

stop at the store for Mom's list
and return to Papa's house

people have already started to arrive

I'm sorry I'm late I say
                running into the kitchen
with full arms

Mom looks ready to yell when

I stop her
holding out the laulaus

and ask
where's Papa's big silver pot?

everyone loves the laulaus

so 'ono!

taste just like your papa's!

where did you get these?

I shrug
          smiling to myself

just a new spot I found
but it's a little off the beaten path

I find Mom sitting by herself
on the lanai

even though it is still raining
even though the clouds still rage above

I take her a plate with laulau
hand her a fork

she smiles
pats the porch chair next to her
inviting me to sit

she takes a bite
her eyes go wide
then teary

where did you get these?

local guy I say

she goes *hmmm* thoughtfully
takes a few more quiet bites
looks up to the sky

I really wish this rain would stop already
she mutters

I scan the sky with her
pause
feel the smile spread wide across my face

take her hand
hold tight   as tight as I can
use the other to point out

a sliver of blue
            peeking through the gray
                        just over the horizon

what? she asks

it's almost over, see?
the storm is already starting to pass

YOU HAD ONE JOB

Andrea L. Rogers

The bison weren't going anywhere, and Maggie was lost again. Well, not lost. She was on a road that existed on a map. Probably. She just didn't know this route. But the road was blocked by these big, beautiful animals busy being bison. She was at the top of a hill and waiting for the bison as if they were a long train because there's nothing you can do. Trains are going to be trains and the same is true of bison. They're going to do what they're gonna do. They're going to take care of their babies. They're gonna eat tall grass, and they're gonna move when they feel like it, and we get to live with that.

"All who wander . . ." Maggie muttered. Her window was down. Several bison turned and looked at her. Then, wary, they moved away.

Maggie picked up her phone and scrolled through the pictures she had just taken of E. That was the reason she was late. She had stuck around while E's aunties and mom and family friends dressed her in her Osage clothes. As soon as she was ready, Maggie drug her out to stand in front of another Osage family's cornfield so she could shoot a few portraits.

In the first, E stood alone, in clothes made for her and passed down from family. She wore earrings and jewelry and moccasins and ribbons pieced together with love and care. In the second, E stood with a cousin. In another she was surrounded by her aunties. In one, E's parents stood behind her. Their faces were brighter than the sunlight bouncing off the beautiful cornstalks behind them. Finally, she had taken one of E lined up with her whole family behind her. Then they had gone to dance in her tribe's dances, E for the first time.

Maggie glanced to the passenger side of the truck at the heavy ceramic bowl holding twenty-five-pound bags of self-rising flour. Her aunt Mabel's bowl had once belonged to her grandmother. It was the family bread bowl, a dark yellow glaze over red-pink clay. You could tell the clay's color from a small chip on one side. Maggie's gaze returned to the truck's digital clock. The vehicle was old enough that the clock wasn't very bright. She had to squint.

It was 1:30 p.m. Three and a half hours. She had three and a half hours to make one hundred pieces of frybread. Aunt Mabel could make that much in forty-five minutes, but she was an expert. Maggie had been headed to her aunt and uncle's house to use their outdoor cooking setup. It was a propane tank turkey fryer and worked great for frybread. At least in the shade.

She had to fry enough bread so that up to fifty people could have at least two pieces of frybread that evening at E's surprise birthday party.

What had she been thinking when she planned this party? Maybe she should have just ordered pizza.

She hadn't been thinking. She had been feeling. Her best friend's family was in town from all over and her best friend was dancing for the first time, and it was, almost, her birthday! Maggie had met E when she really needed a friend. Maggie's father had recently passed, and she and her little sister, Virginia, were temporarily living with their aunt Mabel and uncle Roy in Michigan while her mom finished nursing school back in Oklahoma. When would Maggie ever have an opportunity to do something like this for E again?

Maggie pondered the bison. Were they watching her? Suddenly, as if one body, the bison turned and stared across the field of big bluestem—the way she was supposed to go, according to her fickle map app.

The GPS was now suggesting she follow this sort of Jeep rut. Of all the days for the main road in town to be covered with nacho cheese. Maggie was in her uncle's old blue two-tone F-150, and the truck could handle the rough dirt road, not that the bison were giving her much choice.

She took a deep breath. She didn't check the clock again. She did not check the clock. She was definitely not going to look at the clock again.

She could read it out of the corner of her eye.

Man, she had only three hours now.

How had she been stuck here for thirty minutes?

Because bison are gonna bison. She counted at least a hundred in the herd. Maggie smiled as the baby bison skipped—no, hopped. Too cute. Then the bison all turned and regarded the four-wheel-drive road leading to a dust storm in the distance. Then they were all running along past her, the truck was bouncing, being bumped by this huge herd, this family of bison, this clan. And they left nothing behind but the road and dust. Now Maggie could drive forward, follow them slowly. She had a choice. Maggie checked her phone screen for ETAs.

The directions she had been following were gone.

The makeshift Jeep road was now the only AI-informed option. Maggie put the truck in drive. Moments later, she found herself at the top of a hill parked within sight of Sandy June's Legendary Frybread Drive-In, according to the neon sign. She also found herself perplexed.

She had never seen this place, though it sounded familiar.

Where was she? It was Osage land, but was she in Pawhuska or Barnsdall or maybe even in Bartlesville?

Maggie was the most geographically challenged person she knew, but she associated the general area with the Osage and Delaware. She checked her GPS, but it had gone completely squirrelly. "Saloli," she muttered, because that was the Cherokee word for *squirrel*.

"And I'm Dagsi," she muttered. A turtle. A slow, lost turtle. She would never make it back in time to cook fifty pieces of frybread, let alone one hundred. Maggie took a deep breath. She ran her tongue over her teeth. There was grit there. She considered the outdoor market and drive-in stand. Maggie didn't think she had ever visited it before, but it poked at her heart, as if it were a place she had once called home. How did she not know about a place like this in the middle of the tall grass prairie?

Maggie needed to rinse the dust from her mouth. Maybe she could get a Pepsi, or better yet, some iced tea. She parked. A local could tell her how to get back on the road and get to her aunt and uncle's house and get to frying.

All Maggie had to do was mix the dough, let it rest, mold it into plate-sized pieces, drop the dough in hot grease, watch it, turn it, watch it, drop it into an ice chest on top of newspaper to stay hot. Not burn herself or set fire to anything. That's all she had to do. It was a super super super important job. But it was only one job.

Couldn't she do this? Couldn't she do this one thing by herself while her friend danced for the first time in the Osage dances? Maggie was Cherokee, but she understood how important these dances were. It was E's homecoming, really. Something the whole family was honoring. Maggie wanted E to know she understood.

Now, here she was setting everyone up for disappointment. And hunger. She should have had the oil hot and at least ten pieces of bread made by now. That wasn't a lot, but it would have been a good start. Better than what she had.

She took a deep breath.

Maybe between the heat and the stress her brain was misfiring entirely.

Maggie parked in the drive-in's somewhat empty lot and walked up to the ordering window of Sandy June's. It was closed. Not abandoned, but seemingly empty. A handwritten sign—black marker on cardboard—read "Frybread Fryer Wanted!!!!" Was everybody on break?

"Hello? Osiyo!" Were they napping? I mean, you know, all the crap that colonization brought us? Couldn't we have gotten a siesta? Maybe the workers were on a siesta. It was two o'clock in the afternoon. It was hot. And there was nobody around.

She looked at the menu. There were the usual soda choices, including Pepsi, but even better, there was yaupon holly tea. Iced or hot. That's what she needed. Yaupon holly was the only plant indigenous to this land that contained caffeine. It was the first plant she, Virginia, and their mom had planted when they moved into their small house in Tulsa. Her mother would pick the leaves and dry and roast them to make tea. It never failed to cheer Maggie. Yaupon tea would cool and clear her head.

She knocked on the glass window and before you could say "Osiyo," it slid open. And there was Sandy June herself. The airbrushed apron said so in a neon-yellow-and-green font against a black background that matched the sign. Or maybe all the aprons said so? Maggie couldn't know for sure.

"Are you here to apply for the frybread-frying job?"

Maggie blinked. Holy, this auntie cut to the chase. "No. Well, I mean, I don't think so." Am I, she thought? "No? I would like a glass of iced yaupon holly tea and, well, actually, I need directions. I have to find my way back to my auntie's to make one hundred pieces of frybread."

Silence. A pin on the woman's shirt said *Auntie Bernadette* in black marker, covering something that began with *Legendary Gra*. So, she wasn't June.

"I mean, it's for my best friend's surprise birthday. I have the flour and the ice chests and my auntie's bread bowl in the truck." Maggie was babbling. Bernadette's long beaded earrings swayed.

"Your friend doesn't know it's their birthday?"

"No. I mean, yes. Well, we are a few weeks early. So, it's a super surprise party." Maggie wiped the sweat from her brow.

More silence.

"By five o'clock. Guests are supposed to start arriving by five o'clock, so I am, kind of, in a hurry." Babbling. Babbling was happening.

"Who are you?"

"Maggie Wilson."

"Maggie Wilson? Cherokee? I knew your daddy. He came here a time or two. Was real proud of you and your little sister. And smitten with your mom. Wait there." The window slid closed.

Maggie didn't know what to say. Her father had been here? Where was here?

The side door of the drive-in opened. "Well, get in here," a voice called. "Are you waiting for an invitation? Or maybe you want to bring in a bunch of flies, too?"

Maggie came around and strolled in. As she stepped inside, she heard the sound of someone somewhere playing a fiddle.

The woman held out a glass of iced tea. Maggie tried not to appear too eager, but she took a big drink.

"There's more in the coffeepot and ice under the counter there." She gestured with her chin. "You help yourself. I'm Auntie Bernadette. Here's my proposition: Over the next two hours, with my help, you can fry up nearly three hundred pieces of frybread. You need a hundred for your party. I need a hundred, too. And then I need at least fifty small pieces for people who just want a snack." Maggie's eyes went wide as the auntie continued, "Now don't get excited. We'll both make the dough. If you can do that, you and I will both be better off. We'll both have what we need."

Maggie thought a moment. The disappointment of her friend and the judgment of family flashed before her eyes. Bernadette held out an apron. Maggie stepped into it and turned around. "Auntie?"

"Don't worry. You can do this. You can feed your friend's family. It's in your DNA."

Maggie felt emotional. She had missed E so badly since she moved. She wished she hadn't had to trade getting to be with her mother for losing proximity to her best friend. When they had seen each other nearly every day it had been so easy to do thoughtful things for each other, the kind of things that showed you were paying attention, to have inside jokes only they got. She had been grateful Aunt Mabel and Uncle Roy followed them back to Oklahoma. But E was her best friend.

Bernadette grinned mischievously. "Smile, sister. You want to be happy when you cook for your people. Otherwise, your bread will be tough on the outside and gooey on the inside." The auntie made a face.

Maggie waved in the general direction of the truck. "I've got ice chests and flour in the back seat."

"Go get one chest and the flour. And don't forget that bread bowl."

On her way to her truck a girl stopped her. "Siyo! I'm Lucy. Do you know where the paints and brushes are supposed to be stored?"

Maggie looked at her blankly, wondering why she was asking her, forgetting she was wearing an apron that seemed to indicate she worked here.

"For the mural," Lucy said slowly.

"Oh! I'm sorry. I don't really work here—or, well, I just got here, too. I'm Maggie. Auntie Bernadette probably knows. Let me grab my stuff and I'll take you to her."

Lucy followed Maggie and offered to carry the ice chest, so Maggie didn't have to juggle it along with her auntie's ceramic bowl and the bags of flour. By the time they got back, Auntie Bernadette was up to her wrists in dough. Lucy and Auntie Bernadette talked while Maggie washed her hands. She watched Bernadette talk and turn the bowl with one hand and mix with the other. The woman was more impressive than any machine.

"Come by when you're on break," Lucy hollered at Maggie when she turned to leave, to which Maggie responded with a "Hawa."

Maggie knew she wouldn't quite be able to mimic Bernadette's motions. It was like watching her own auntie. Her auntie said her secret was warm water and letting the dough rest. Maggie hoped it would work for her. Or that at least she wouldn't dump it on the floor.

Maggie cut open a twenty-five-pound bag of flour. She poured it into her bowl, squinting against the airborne flour dust. She turned the water on and tested it with her hand. It needed to be warm, not hot. She got it to the right temperature and then reduced the flow. She set the bowl into the sink beneath the faucet. She rotated the bowl with her left hand and stirred with her right, reaching down to the bottom of the bowl, her fingers massaging the water in. She glanced up to see Auntie Bernadette watching her. She looked back down at her bowl and turned off the water, then snuck another look at Bernadette, who raised an eyebrow. Maggie turned the water back on for a moment. Then off. She looked at Bernadette. Auntie nodded. Maggie mixed the water into the flour. Auntie Bernadette had finished mixing her large bowl and washed her hands. She placed her bowl on a high shelf and covered it with dishcloths. She set a few more out on the counter for Maggie.

"Once it's good and mixed it needs a little rest. Kind of like you and me. But you don't want to mix it after it rests. Makes it tough."

Maggie nodded. The dough felt soft, no lumps. A nice pillowy consistency that would fluff up more while it rested. Maggie stopped kneading, washed her hands, then covered her bowl with the cloths.

"Why don't you have a look around the place?"

Maggie reached back to untie her apron.

"Here, give me your hand." Auntie Bernadette placed something that felt like stiff paper in Maggie's hand. "You probably won't need it, but it's nice to have some walking-around money." Maggie put it in her pocket without looking at it.

"Wado."

"Ho'mi. See you in thirty minutes. And refill your tea glass. My tea is on social media." All the relatives were on social media.

Maggie laughed. When she opened the door, she saw the place had come alive. Everyone seemed to have woken up from siesta. Men and women wore pins that said *Legendary Grandparent* next to their name and escorted other confused teens around. She noticed Lucy at a Rock the Native Vote table talking to a woman with a stylized image of a muskrat on her T-shirt and some Cherokee syllabary.

Lucy looked up and waved Maggie over.

"Maggie, this is Ruth Muskrat Bronson. She's raising money and signing up volunteers to canvass neighborhoods and drive Elders to their polling places."

Ruth held out an empty giant nacho cheese can. *Weird*, thought Maggie.

"Buy some raffle tickets?"

Maggie reached into her pocket and pulled out her "walking-around money." Her walk had been pretty short, she thought.

"Wado," said Ruth, handing Maggie a ribbon of blue raffle tickets.

Ruth began her spiel. "Many people don't realize that their local elections can impact their community in very serious ways. Did you know some elections are decided by one or two votes? Sometimes older people find themselves without a ride at the last minute to their tribal or local elections. Where do you live?"

"Tulsa."

Ruth had already handed her the sign-up clipboard. "I have a lot of Elders who will need rides in November. Your help will be appreciated." Ruth took the clipboard back after Maggie signed it with her details.

"Hawa," said Maggie.

"Wado, Wegi." Maggie smiled. It was nice to hear her nickname in Cherokee.

"Come back later for the bands. Raffle ticket will be drawn then. Need not be present to win!" She laughed.

Lucy and Maggie walked the grounds. Lucy showed Maggie the mural she was going to restore. Maggie promised to come back and see it. When it was time to wake up the bread dough, Maggie rushed back to the stand.

"Donadagohvi, Wegi," Lucy hollered.

"Donadagohvi," Maggie replied.

"Time to make the doughnuts!" announced Auntie Bernadette while handing Maggie her apron.

"Doughnuts?"

"Never mind. It's a joke. We planned it just right. Serving starts in ten minutes. Make me ten big pieces and ten small pieces. Then start on your batch until I ask for more."

"I have another ice chest in the truck," Maggie said. Hesitating.

"Good to know," Auntie Bernadette said. "Now get to frying!"

Maggie turned toward the big fryer. The temperature of the frybread oil was already where it needed to be. It wasn't smoking. It was perfect.

"Oh, and bring me the first little one you fry. I need some bread and honey with my tea!" Bernadette cackled, gesturing toward her phone. "And you have a piece, too." Reader, Bernadette's bread would be delicious.

Maggie reached into Bernadette's bowl and started pulling apart pieces of dough. She had never made frybread on her own before for other people. Now here she was frying ten pieces at a time. Before long she had twenty plate-sized pieces for the party, while steadily keeping up with the orders that were pouring in. Then a hundred. Ninety pieces for the party. Before long, Maggie realized she was already making the last big plate-sizes of bread she needed.

As Maggie finished the last of the bread, Auntie returned. "Beautiful. You're doing a great job. Let me go grab your other ice chest. I'll line it with paper bags. Also, you're off duty. Blackfeet kid just showed up who needs the job. Gotta make money for ACT testing."

Maggie looked outside. A tall kid with long black hair wearing a sheepskin-lined jean jacket, big silver belt buckle, and a black cowboy hat was looking around the grounds, obviously befuddled. A copy of *Where the Red Fern Grows* poked out of his back jeans pocket. He looked vaguely familiar. A cousin, maybe?

While the auntie filled the second fancy stainless-steel cooler, Maggie glanced at the clock on the kitchen wall. Four o'clock. She was good. Better than good. Back on schedule.

Then the auntie asked, "How does it taste?"

Maggie froze. How had she made a hundred pieces of frybread and not even tasted it? What if it wasn't any good? What if it was terrible? What if it was hard? What if it was doughy in the middle? She had been so caught up in her work she had totally forgotten the first rule of frybread.

Somebody's got to taste the frybread.

Maggie swallowed hard and reached into the cooler. She picked up a piece cool enough to eat. She bit into it.

Perfect. The outside, crispy. The inside, cooked all the way. The best frybread, next to her aunt Mabel's and her new auntie Bernadette's, that she had ever eaten. The auntie picked up a larger piece that Maggie had fried for Indian tacos. She broke it apart. Again, perfect.

Maggie had turned it when it needed turning. She had given her complete attention to the food she was making, and what was attention but love in action?

Auntie Bernadette cut a piece of brown paper bag into a large square and drew a map on it. "All right, you see this? Go that way." She used the black marker as a pointer. "And then when you spot this bison, the one who looks like he's winking at you with his three sassy friends by the pond, then you take the road that goes left. That will lead you to the highway, and before long, you'll make it where you're going."

Maggie folded the map in half, set it on the insulated chests of frybread, and carried it all back to the truck. Once she'd loaded everything into the back seat and shut the door, Maggie and her new auntie gave each other a hug full of gratitude.

Legendary grandmother Ruth Muskrat Bronson opened the driver's door for Maggie. "If you ever need me, I'm here."

Maggie felt a relief she hadn't known she was missing. She climbed in and glanced at her phone. Fifteen minutes to get home and celebrate E and family and friends and tribal community and food made with love!

The grandmother pointed with her chin in the direction Maggie needed to go. And Maggie didn't get lost at all.

That day.

HEART BERRY
Cheryl Isaacs

Sela Green had the best hair in school. Ask anyone and they'd tell you, because it was a fact. Dawn Peters—me—had very average hair. Also a fact. The huge difference between us was in my face every Friday evening, when I had Kanyen'kéha class, which she taught.

I knew I should tighten my sad, limp ponytail and move on with my life, but the thing was, Sela's hair supremacy was a new thing. She'd left school in June with ho-hum hair and returned in September with Oh My Goddess! without layers or fancy highlights. Something major had happened to those strands over the summer, but now April had arrived with me no closer to solving the mystery.

Sela's hair had made her into a new person. This new Sela was confident and effortlessly cool. I wanted that, to have all my self-doubt and insecurity gone. I desperately wanted to know what she'd done, but if it were possible to ask, I would have done it long ago.

Sela and I weren't enemies, but we weren't exactly friends. In seventh grade, our mothers had decided *we* should be friends because *they* were. They found ways to throw us together, hoping we would stick like they had. They set up freaking playdates, like we were toddlers, and that was the last straw. Sela and I agreed, without speaking a word, that the friendship would never happen, simply because our moms wanted it. That was a long time ago, but somehow our not-friendship . . . stuck. We'd lived with it so long that even after our moms had given up, it was too late to change course. It had become a habit. And since we were not-friends, I couldn't ask for the secret to her hair sorcery and put an end to my suffering. Her hair had a choke hold on me, and I couldn't get past it.

I stomped down the sidewalk, my Friday night ruined by my own jealousy. Four blocks from home, I stopped on the corner and made a decision. Sandy June's was the only cure for a mood this crappy.

And sweet potato fries.

A quick text to my mom, then I pocketed my phone and crossed against the light—dodging taxis, cars, and a bus that didn't even slow down—before passing through the fancy iron gate and heading straight into the heart of the park.

Like an island in the city, the massive park held secrets that only a few of us knew. I left the concrete path and shimmied through an opening in the dense bushes that led to deeper green—tall elm, fir, and birch standing together.

Seven steps into the trees, I closed my eyes and filtered out the noise of the birds and breeze, and the city beyond that, until a distant but steady thump came to me. Once I heard it, I latched on like a lifeline and started walking through the brush. The only path was the one I heard, the one that pulled me on, deeper into the trees.

Left, then right, then right again, and after that the turns seemed endless. I couldn't explain how to get through, I just followed the strengthening drumbeat and turned where it felt right—and it always was. This was my way to Sandy June's and why the place was a haven.

There were always people from the rez there—every rez—but some of us needed it even more. My cousins on the rez had each other, aunts, uncles, and grandparents. I had language class Friday evenings, one powwow in the summer, and whatever community my parents cobbled together.

Just when I thought I'd be wandering in the trees forever, I popped out on the other side, and the thumping became actual drums, blasting from car radios. A short dirt path took me to a small field, and there it was: Sandy June's Legendary Frybread Drive-In. The air was warm and soft here, already feeling like midsummer, the skyscrapers replaced by sunset-tinted trees.

In line at the pickup window, I saw license plates from every corner of Turtle Island. Sandy June's was hopping, typical for a Friday evening, and as I waited for my order in the shade of the awning, I drank in the chatter in far more tribal languages than I could identify, laughter twining in the air with the sweet smell of frybread. I felt my jaw relax and a soft smile settle over my face. My jealousy about Sela's hair receded. I was at Sandy June's and sweet potato fries were coming my way. Life was good. But when I picked up my tray, I turned to find every single picnic table taken.

Seeing no one I knew, nowhere I could squeeze in, my mood threatened to dive again. No room for me. I walked to the corner of the awning, looking doubtfully toward the back of the building. I could sit on the stage, but the band would start setting up soon.

"Right here." At the farthest table, a woman sitting alone slapped the tabletop. "Right here, niece."

I looked around uncertainly. Was she talking to me?

She slapped the wooden picnic table again, a little impatiently, so I took my tray on over.

"Are you sure?" The table was littered with containers of beads and lengths of thread.

"Yup." She squinted at her needle and swept a place clear for me with one hand.

"Thanks." New people—that was part of why I loved this place. "I'm Dawn."

"Ihstá." Holding the needle at arm's length and squinting.

Mystery auntie. Cool.

Mystery Auntie, sporting a bright floral, flowy, sleeveless top and green cargo shorts, had come from a warmer place. She reminded me of my grandma, solid build with intense eyes, except Mystery Auntie had a very chill, welcoming vibe.

"Those fries." Pulling the thread, Auntie shook her head.

"Please have some." I held out my paper cup, but she lifted her chin at the crumpled-up cup on her own tray.

"They never had a chance," she said, eulogizing her own short-lived fries. She continued threading beads and stitching in silence but just when my mouth was full of salty-sweet goodness, decided to be chatty. "What's up?"

"My life sucks." I dispensed that fact and kept chewing.

She nodded as if it made sense and slid some purple and dark blue beads onto her needle. "I'm waiting for the band. Last time, I got stuck way at the back and couldn't see hardly anything. Blues tonight."

Blues. How appropriate for me.

"You bead?" Auntie asked without looking up.

"Nope." Apparently my great-grandma had, but she'd taken the skill with her. I couldn't bead, didn't dance, could barely speak my language or grow decent hair. There were a lot of things I couldn't do.

"What's wrong with your hair?" Auntie stopped stitching long enough to look up at me, frowning.

Had I said all that out loud? I shrugged. "It's just not . . ." How could I explain? But then I didn't have to, because the explanation stepped out of the trees and onto the grass beside us, sunlight bouncing off her perfect strands, and looking like a freaking goddess. "Crap," I muttered.

Mystery Auntie followed my eyes, broke into a big grin, and waved her arms like she was landing a jet. "Sela!"

The fries flipped in my stomach at the same time that Sela spotted me, her steps slowing for a fraction of a second, just enough for me to know that finding me here wasn't making her night, either.

"Didn't expect to see you here tonight!" Mystery Auntie shifted over to make room. "Sit a minute?"

"I'm filling in a shift, but no reason to go into a hot kitchen before I have to. Thanks." Ignoring me, Sela sat next to Auntie, a curtain of dark hair glowing red around the edges briefly blocking her face as she set her canvas bag on the ground.

I sipped my strawberry juice, the sweetness suddenly gone.

"This is gorgeous." Sela turned over the elaborate floral hair tie Auntie had been working on, running her fingertips over the swirl of blue, purple, and pink.

"My niece is a fancy dancer," Auntie said proudly. "What are you working on?"

Sela reached into her bag and took out a small oval piece of hide, a strawberry in red and shades of pink just beginning to take shape. Every time I saw her, whatever creation Sela wore in her hair featured a strawberry. Today there were three small berries nestled together at the back of her head. What was up with all those berries?

"You two stay put. I need a sweetgrass tea refill." Auntie gave her cup a shake, nothing but ice cubes answering, the tea long gone. "Keep an eye on my stuff. Ravens love beads," she said darkly, casting a wary eye toward the tree line before hiking up her shorts and shuffling to the pickup window. Sela and I sat together, the awkward silence broken only when three little kids ran by the table, chattering in a language that sounded like music. Sela sifted through her beads while I picked green flakes of paint from the table in a pointless attempt to keep my mouth shut. Some people are comfortable with silence, viewing it as a place to rest. Not me. Silence is dangerous because it encourages thinking, and thinking leads to . . . thoughts. Give me silence and I'll fill it with any random fluff that pops into my brain and flies out of my mouth. I lasted a whole seven seconds before I broke. "You know her?"

"We bead on my breaks." Sela shrugged and poked through a round tin of beads with her fingertip.

More silence, and the thoughts saw their opportunity and pounced. Sela beaded and spoke Kanyen'kéha well enough to teach. Did all that mean she belonged at Sandy June's more than me? Did she get through the forest path, hear the drums more clearly because of it?

See? Thoughts. But my mouth wasn't finished. "Is that all you bead—strawberries? You have so many." Instant cringe, because now she knew she lived rent-free in my head.

"Heart berries," Sela murmured, focused on threading a needle.

"Yeah. Heart berries," I corrected myself.

Mystery Auntie was still at the pickup window, leaning on one elbow and laughing. The other people waiting for orders milled around, reuniting with old friends and making new ones, a party within a party. Mystery Auntie glanced over and waved at me, but then continued talking. Was she leaving us alone on purpose?

Sela finally looked up. "Heart berries grow out back there." Lifting her chin toward the field behind the band stage.

I followed her gaze. "Really? I've never seen them."

"You have to go looking. They're small and wild, but supersweet."

"Heart berries." I drummed my fingers on the table. I wanted that hair, I wanted to feel the way she felt, so I just blurted it out. "What did you do to your hair?"

Sela raised her eyes, but they skated over my face and flitted off. "What do you mean?"

"Your. Hair." I squeezed my hands into fists because admitting this was going to suck, but I had to know. "Since the summer, your hair . . . Seriously, it's killing me. You started working here and now you have—" I gestured at her glorious mane. "With your barrettes and stuff."

"It looks different to you?" Sela wound a strand around her finger, peering at it.

Wait. If *she* hadn't done anything . . .

"Your barrettes. And bands." Something I hadn't considered. Magical barrettes?

"I make them here," Sela said, frowning.

We were both silent, stumped for a minute because yeah, Sandy June's was definitely a special place, but was it . . . magical? Honestly, I wouldn't be surprised. People came because whatever they needed, Sandy June's delivered. When we were in need, the ancestors called us here.

"So, what—the ancestors give your hair great volume?" I squinted up at the pink sky.

"I don't think it's really my hair," Sela said.

"Oh, yes, it is," I insisted.

"It hasn't changed, Dawn." She dipped her chin.

So what was giving me hair envy? If it wasn't her actual hair, what did she have that I wanted?

"Maybe it's the way I feel," Sela mused. "When I started working here, I talked to Auntie on break, got back into beading. I don't know, I just started thinking about things differently. Like how my ancestors would be pretty happy that I'm here at all, so maybe I should be, too. Konorónkhwa. That's what they'd say to me, so I should say it to myself."

I love you. I'd never thought of that. But from the few stories Mom had quietly told me about my grandma's time in residential school, there must have been many times for many of those kids when they thought they would be the last.

"Huh." I frowned at the tabletop, which was etched with initials. A personal transformation—that was right up the ancestors' alley.

"But yeah, whatever," Sela said quickly, as if she'd shown too much of herself to a not-friend like me.

"So that's why all the heart berries?" I leaned forward, elbows on the table and chin resting on my hands. Love, sweetness. It made more sense now. I'd been way off course, theorizing jealous secrets, when Sela's actual truth was another thing I'd always sucked at: self-love.

Behind me, Auntie's laugh was a clap of thunder. The drums that had led me here blasted from one of the cars in the lot and my heartbeat fell into rhythm with them. I drew in a deep breath of the sweet-scented air and let it out, letting go of all the frustration and the dark mood that had been hanging over me. This was why I'd come here, for this feeling, this lightness. One way or another, Sandy June's never failed.

I looked up to find Sela with a small smile and holding out the piece of hide.

"Want to try?"

Our eyes met for the first time since she'd sat down.

"Just so you know," I warned, "if you think my Kanyen'kéha is bad, I know even less about beading."

Sela shrugged. "I had to learn, too. Try."

I turned the oval over in my hands, looking at the work she'd already done, each stitch tiny and regular on the back, but the colors on the front were wild and fluid.

The beads felt even smaller than they looked, but I managed to thread five—cherry red and two shades of pink. I started the stitch three times and then pushed the needle through the hide and slowly pulled, snugging up the beads almost like Sela had.

Sela nodded. "Nice."

"Good eye for color, I think." A voice at my shoulder made me jump, almost launching every loose bead on the table into the air. Mystery Auntie grabbed a striped orange folding chair from her pile of belongings beside the table. "I'm going to stake out a good spot." She lifted her tea in the direction of the stage, where amps and piles of cables had appeared. "You should keep going with that. Sela's good." She nodded at the oval in my hand and then leaned down, putting her head close to mine to loud-whisper. "She had a great teacher." She strode off with a cackle, to claim her spot front and center.

In the quiet void that Mystery Auntie left, I remembered that Sela and I weren't actually friends. "Thanks." I handed the oval back to her, suddenly shy as she packed up her supplies, the unfinished heart berry going in the bag last. Sela opened her mouth and closed it, put down the bag, and reached up to the back of her head.

"Here." She unclipped the barrette and held it out to me, over the table. "My hair has to be up in a net anyway. So glamorous."

My fingers itched to take the three little berries, but I hesitated. "Are you sure?"

Sela nodded. "Help me finish the new one as a replacement."

A gift I couldn't turn down. Not because I thought I would magically change; I already knew the secret.

"Thank you." I gathered up a section of hair and clipped the berries into place. Sela and I looked at each other, shy smiles on both sides, my hair pinned up and hers loose and flowing over her shoulders. Even without the barrette, her hair was beautiful. She was beautiful. The drumbeats from the parking lot came to a stop, allowing a moment of quiet to settle over the drive-in—a peaceful pocket of rest where one song ended, and another began.

"Fry?" I tipped my cup toward Sela, where most of my fries still waited. They had gone cold, but I wanted to offer something in return, and not just for the barrette.

Sela glanced at her watch. "Time for my shift. Come to the side door—I'll make a fresh batch."

"That's okay. I should go." I rose, surprised at how dark the sky had become, but time passed differently here.

"You should stay." Our eyes met across the table once more, not that I was keeping count. "The band tonight's really good. I'll come out on my break."

The breeze played with the ends of Sela's hair. I'd been sickeningly jealous, but she'd shared her unexpected secret so freely. She'd complimented my first shaky stitch and made me feel like I did belong here, no matter how long it took me to get through the forest path or how many verb charts I needed.

Konorónkhwa. Fact.

"My mom'll kill me." Also true.

"Come on." Sela rose, a gentle smile tugging at the corner of her mouth. "It'll be that playdate they always wanted."

We joined the stream of people making their way to the stage area, trucks backing up as close as they could get for tailgate seating.

I laughed, struck by a sudden memory. "Remember that time they tried to get us to braid corn?"

Sela giggled. "Worst corn braid ever!"

"They had no idea what they were doing." I shook my head. That particular playdate had left us with something more like a corn octopus that was far too heavy to be hung. The whole afternoon had been a ridiculous disaster.

And also kind of fun.

Our laughter died down. "I guess no one taught them how to do things like braid corn."

Sela nodded.

I understood now why our moms had tried so hard to grow a friendship between Sela and me—to give us what they'd never had.

"Well, we're here now," Sela said quietly as we reached the side door. She touched my wrist. "I'll bring out your secret fries."

Secret fries. The smile that lit her eyes sparked an answer in me, and I couldn't say we were not-friends anymore.

The screen door clapped shut, followed by a chorus of "Sela!" from inside the kitchen. I strolled to watch the stage being set up. In the corners of the back wall mural, I spied tiny bursts of red nestled in the painted blades of grass. I'd never noticed them before, but I guess they'd been there all along—tiny and wild but supersweet. I leaned back against the mural, becoming part of the scene, waiting for my secret fries with a smile on my face for no reason. The first stars were glittering in the sky and on the warm breeze, the scent of earth and heart berries came to me.

MOMENTUM

Christine Hartman Derr

A carpenter bee flies into your classroom window.

Tap.

Tap.

Tap.

It is the worst kind of distraction.

Your physics teacher clears his throat. He glances from the window to your test. He has perfected nonverbal communication. Not so great at the verbal kind, though. Last time you asked for help, he told you to reread the chapter. Like you hadn't already done that five times before asking. As if asking for help comes easily for you.

You go back to your test, a copy of a copy of a copy. You're thrown by the wavy line of print on the fourth question. Your last physics teacher believed in you. You smile, hear her voice say, *You can do this, Mariah.* Visualizing the problem in your head, you straighten the text, bold the faded equation, connect it to the page in the textbook.

There. Got it.

Your pencil—mechanical, size .7 mm graphite only—glides across the paper. The math comes easy. Conservation of angular momentum is your best friend. You apply the problem to the place you implement it—the trapeze bar that lets you *feel* the way the physics equations work. It gives you an understanding that is distinctly, wholly yours.

Your paper lands on the teacher's desk with plenty of time to spare. You return to your desk, lay your head on the cool surface. You picture your favorite place. It comes together, like the equation. Unassuming house. Unkempt yard. You'd never know it was there from the street. The backyard trees shade and encircle it, keep it tucked away. Keep it safe. A gate that squeaks when it pushes against the high grass. Wildflowers everywhere, even under the trampoline. Bees buzzing, no windows in their way. The trapeze bar, shining, waiting. Always ready.

The trapeze doesn't hold a grudge. It isn't mad about how much you talk or how little you say. It doesn't feel sad if you've been away. The bar won't blame you if your grip slips. You won't blame the bar. The freedom of testing your limits draws you back, even when the mosquitoes bite, even when the clouds roll in, even when you feel like the world is ending.

One night when the moon is extra bright, the trapeze calls to you. You sneak out for a starlit solo practice. The trampoline's squeaks make you wince, pause. The trapeze sways as if waving hello. *Welcome back. Welcome home.* You'd never have thought a place so far from family could be home. But the trapeze makes Florida home, even if it's so humid the air is sticky. The night birds chirp; you stretch, jump, reach, grab. The cold from the metal bar seeps through the tape wrapped around it. You adjust your shoulders, swing back, lift your legs, hook on the bar. You hang from your knees, arms spread wide, opening yourself to the place that feels most like home. With the world upside down, the trees dip into a velvety expanse of stars. You arch back, that moment of your knees on the bar making your breath catch just like always, but then you're up, sitting on the bar. The ropes are rough against your arms in the best way, like too-tight hugs. The night wind breezes by, saying siyo—this isn't a place it usually sees you. The crickets and cicadas continue their symphony, music for your routine. You do all your favorite skills, with names like "angel" and "ankle drop," names that sometimes frighten you when you're on the ground.

But you aren't on the ground.

You're in the air.

The only place you feel graceful.

The only place you're meant to be.

When you finally drop down, the trampoline mat sinking, it's like you're underwater. Up there is where you can breathe. Up there is where you can *be*. The trapeze shines in the moonlight. You hate to leave.

You hop off the trampoline. The moon casts the shadow of the trapeze rig away from you. You walk toward the gate, the too-high grass tickling your calves.

Before leaving, you turn back once more. Still the bar waits, still the bar sings with possibility, still the bar lets you be the You that you most want to be: the You who does hard things, the You who pushes outside your comfort zone, the trapeze-artist you. The You-est you.

You whisper before the gate clicks closed, "Galiheliga. Wado."

This is the night that plays in your mind on a loop, even in physics on finals day.

But there's no going back. Your family left that town weeks ago, cardboard boxes stuffed in the back of the Camry.

Everyone else in your family found where they fit in this new town right away. But not you.

Cassie handed you a pile of pamphlets describing community clubs and teams. She was trying to encourage you to find your place. She smiled, teasing, "There's gotta be something here for you, Mariah. Besides, you can't have only one defining personality trait."

Your older sister's throwaway comment sliced right to your center. She saw the hurt, apologized, brought you an ice cream sundae later. Her words still haunt you.

You tried watercolor to chase away those ghostly words. But the paintbrush rubbing against the calluses on your palms calls you back to the bar. Now, it's the last day of junior year. You have two personality traits: no friends here, no trapeze.

The bell rings. You lift your head, gather your notebook, head to your locker. One by one, you take items out. Your last locker clean-out took longer. There were photos, notes, library books, your best friend Shana's borrowed sweater, that one beaded earring. You still haven't found its missing partner. This time, it's a few papers. The freshly printed schedule with crease lines from where it lived in your back pocket for a week. A planner, notebook, Beyond Buckskin pencil pouch. The metal locker door closes with a clang.

You stop by the bathroom, and *of course* your period shows up today. You dig through your backpack for the beaded bag that holds your supplies—the one Auntie Maggie gave you when you were eleven—get sorted. A nagging thought: What time does the bus leave here? You wash your hands, bypassing the paper towel dispenser, shaking the water off. You dodge friends hugging goodbye (not your friends, not your goodbyes), flying footballs, stepping carefully to avoid what's left of the thousand bouncy balls dropped down the stairs as the senior class prank.

You step outside right as your bus pulls away, leaving a black cloud suspended in the air. You pull out your phone to call your sister, even if Cassie will be annoyed, but the screen doesn't light up. With a groan, you remember the low battery warning during your lunchtime video chat with Shana.

Fine. You'll walk home.

Heat rises off the road, turning the landscape hazy. Your sandals slap against the sidewalk as cars whoosh by, sending waves of hot air that hit you one after the other. Pieces of songs jump from open car windows, the Doppler effect playing with words and beats. Under an oak tree, you take a long drink from your water bottle, its overlapping stickers bumpy under your sweaty palms. You turn your back to the road, ignoring the sweat collecting along your spine. Movement in the trees catches your attention. The birds are drowned out by the thrum of tires, but they flit from branch to forest floor to sky, and you know they like to sing while they move.

The mirage from the road is in the forest, too. Strange—the conditions aren't right. A line from a Kalyn Fay song reaches out to you, a surprise in this place where there isn't a big Native population. The road noise recedes. Is that a creek down there? You step off the sidewalk, slip between the trees, follow the almost-path where other sets of feet have pressed the grass down before you. You walk toward the shimmering air, an arch of cedar boughs intertwined above it.

You reach the would-be mirage, but there's not even a puddle. Yet the space beneath the cedar branches shimmers. You put your hand up to the sparkling place, the echo of that Kalyn Fay song growing louder as you step through, the air a cool waterfall.

You blink in the sudden brightness, the shade trees gone. Jogging across an old highway with faded paint marking the lanes, you notice a worn sign straight ahead. The familiar song calls you closer.

Sandy June's Legendary Frybread Drive-In sits off the road, the parking lot more cracked asphalt than pavement, scents that feel like home stretching across it. Your mouth waters at the aroma of food you get only on special occasions like Cherokee National Holiday or Cherokee days at the Sequoyah Birthplace Museum.

But you don't have time for that now. The song—that's your priority. You pass the picnic tables, half-full of young families and Elders, move beyond the counter even though your stomach grumbles, the music pulling you toward the back of the building. An empty stage framed by trees is the epicenter of the song. You approach, stepping around people your age spread out on blankets or sitting on the grass. On the stage, a speaker plays the last of the notes that lead you here. A carpenter bee buzzes by, disappearing into the awning of the building.

You turn in a slow circle, taking in the washed-out yellow-and-green signs pointing to the camping showers. Across from the stage, a mural hints at what was once a brighter version of this place. In front of it, a girl about your age is singing along to the next song, spread out on a Heart Berry blanket staring at a canvas. She twirls a paintbrush in one hand, looks at her canvas with a twist of her lips, rinses her brush in a paper cup.

She looks up, catches you watching. "Siyo! Tohitsu?"

You smooth down your OsiyoTV shirt, close the distance between you. "Hawa. Nihina?"

"Osda! Always happy to find someone to practice Tsalagi with."

"I'm not— I'm only learning."

She raises an eyebrow. "I'm learning, too. It's not an *only* kind of thing."

"Fair. Mariah daquadoa." You're drawn to her half-done painting of the stage, surrounded by trees, fireflies dancing through the air and Cherokee syllabary sprinkled throughout.

"Lucy. You paint?" She motions to her painting, pats the blanket next to her. You sit, trace the floral design with your finger.

You answer with a half-shrug. "I've tried watercolor. But I'm not very good."

"Yet. You forgot to say *yet*." She winks. "Y'know, Levi is working on a documentary about artists. You should talk to him."

"I'm not an artist. Not like that, anyway. And I don't know Levi." You laugh to cover your discomfort.

"Hmmm. You give off major artist vibes."

The trapeze jumps into your mind from all those miles away. Practically a lifetime. "I don't know."

"But you paint."

You wrinkle your nose.

Waving you off, she continues, "Art isn't about the *product*. It's about the *process*."

"Sounds like *you* should be in the documentary."

"I am!"

"Oh. That . . . makes sense." There's a beat of awkwardness, then you both laugh. You nod to her canvas. "You're painting your version of the mural?"

"Willa—she's one of the legendary grandparents—invited me to freshen up the mural this summer. I wanted to do a small-scale one first." She gulps. "Then I have to start painting for real."

"You must be really good."

She reaches for her necklace, rubbing the sea turtle pendant. "Hope so. I don't want to let anyone down. Especially not Willa."

A voice calls around the corner, interrupting, "Luce! Honey or ani?"

"Both, duh!" she hollers back.

"You're impossible!"

"You're welcome!" she singsongs back. "My brother," she explains to you, dipping her paintbrush into the light green paint. The brush whirls on the canvas, the syllabary elegant and smooth. "You staying for the midnight movies?" she asks, but you're distracted by the scent of frybread and strawberries.

A guy emerges from around the corner, two plates clutched in one hand and a cardboard drink carrier in the other. He shakes his dark hair out of his eyes as he walks straight toward you. He carries himself with a flawless kind of confidence, the swagger of belonging.

"You could've at least helped me carry, you know." He nudges Lucy with his foot.

"Can't. Don't want to get paint on the goods." She wiggles her paint-free fingers at him. His stare says *for real* louder than any words could.

Lucy introduces you. "This is Mariah. She's new. And an artist. My brother, Levi."

"How'd you know I'm new?" you say at the same time as he says, "Osda! I need another interview."

"I'm probably not who you want."

"What's your medium?" His face is open, curious.

Lucy tears off a section of frybread with a strawberry slice on it, holds it out to you. "Want?"

"Wado," you say as you accept, the golden bread warm in your palm. You pop it into your mouth, the strawberry perfectly ripe, the bread melting against your tongue. You chew slowly, thinking of an answer. "Physics. Physics is my art."

"How?"

An embarrassed flush climbs your neck. "Oh, um, I don't know. It's stupid—sorry. I should go." You stand, smoothing out the blanket with the toe of your shoe.

Levi smiles around his straw. "No, wait. I'm just . . . I've never heard anyone describe science as art. Enlighten me. Please."

His unwavering attention makes you fidget. You clear your throat. "Most people just see physics as numbers and letters on paper. But I see how those formulas show limits, boundaries. Of movement, gravity. Knowing means working with it, instead of against it." You readjust your shirt, shuffle backward.

Levi leans forward, resting his elbows on his knees. "Tell me more."

Lucy rolls her eyes, bumps him with her shoulder. Raising her hand to shield her eyes from the sun, she looks up at you. "I think you scared her off, man. But maybe she'll come back tonight."

You throw her a grateful smile. "Maybe. Dodadagohvi."

"Midnight! Don't be late!" she calls after you.

You laugh as you walk back the way you came. A petite Black or Black Native, maybe your age or a year younger, stops walking to lean against the wall, wraps her arms around her stomach. You don't want to assume, but your own cramps ramp up. Definitely a sign you should say something, check in.

You step into her line of sight, give her an understanding smile. "Ugh, cramps are the worst. You okay? Need anything?" You're already unzipping your backpack, digging for your supplies.

She glances to the bathroom, back to you. "Do you . . . have an extra pad?"

"Yep." You hand her two, just in case.

She takes them and starts to speak, hesitates, then says, "Mvto."

You grin. You've always liked how *thank you* in Mvskoke and Tsalagi sound similar, like the words are cousins. "Anytime. I'm heading home to my heating pad. And chocolate. You good?"

She nods. You say bye, retracing your steps to the parking lot. On the way, you pass a tall, thin woman with short black hair and perfect red lipstick. Her legendary grandparent name tag has a beaded border, the name *Willa* written in oversize, loopy cursive. She winks as you pass. It makes you feel comfortable here, like maybe you could belong.

Your mom does *not* go for your solo trip back to Sandy June's for the midnight movies. But she offers to make it a family thing. Turns out she knows the place but doesn't explain how. She gives you an appraising look instead, like you finding this place reveals something about you.

A band is packing up when you get there. Two Elders are directing the band members to pull a movie screen down on the mural wall. Camping chairs form a semicircle farther back. Blankets are spread out between the screen and the chairs. Your mom picks a spot, and you lie out the blanket while she and Cassie order food. You search for Lucy and Levi, try not to look obvious about it. No sign of them.

Behind you, a projector whirs. Its beam highlights the dust motes dancing in the air.

"You came!" Lucy plops down next to you. "Do you want to sit with us?" She motions over her shoulder to several overlapped blankets.

"Sure." You signal to Cassie, then Lucy leads the way to their spot. Levi sits on the fringe of the group. You're usually self-conscious during introductions, but being back in a group of Native people is worth feeling awkward at first, and the feeling is temporary anyway.

After the Not Your Wild West Show song ends, a band member announces, "Tonight's movie is *Christmas in the Clouds*. Willa's trying to bring back Christmas in July." He stage-whispers, "No one tell her it's June."

"She just wants to swoon over Wes Studi!" comes a shout from the audience.

Willa calls back, "So?" Everyone laughs.

The band member groans, shakes his head, and goes on, "But first we have a short film: *udeyonv* O'Sɦ0ᴠ *What They've Been Taught*, directed by Cherokee citizen Brit Hensel."

The film begins, a camera moving from the sky through the trees. Your breath catches. You know that place, you lived near there for almost a year in middle school, the Smoky Mountains feeling close to home. An Elder's voice narrates, words in Tsalagi and talk of consequences.

Consequences. Newton's third law pops into your mind—actions and opposite reactions. What is the reaction, the consequence of losing trapeze? Do you lose that part of yourself? Do you lose the You-est you?

Levi leans toward you. "Nvneha is the focus of my doc. Where art comes from, how we make it from something."

It clicks, then, why he was asking about your art. "Who've you interviewed so far?"

He rests his elbow on his knee, surveys the crowd. He nods toward one of the band members. "Justin is a singer." His chin points at a girl. "Millie does pottery. Chitto and Harry are content creators. Willa— her art is food and helping people."

You notice Lucy, working on a sketch in the light from the movie. "That makes sense."

"Doesn't it? And Lucy, of course. She paints. Sometimes she even makes her own paint."

"Impressive."

"Yeah." He nods, sits back. You watch the film for a few minutes.

"Trapeze." You say it like a prayer. He looks at you, forehead crinkled. "That's my art. Trapeze."

"Like, circus, flying through the air stuff?" His hand mimes a flying trapeze.

"Circus, yes. Flying, no. The trapeze stays still. I move around it. It's just physics, really. But it lets me be . . . me."

Half his face is illuminated in the light from the movie. "That's how everyone has felt about their art, that it lets them be their truest self."

Their truest self. The You-est you.

It isn't just you.

The telltale flutter of trying a new trapeze skill stirs within you. Part challenge, part analysis, the thrill of adrenaline and focus. Conservation of angular momentum. Inertia changing velocity, energy output shifting. Your heart feels like when you do elbow circles, contracting and constricting, spinning faster and faster.

He looks at the movie. "You wanna be in the doc?"

"I don't have a trapeze here. I'm sorry." You face the screen, too, not wanting to see if he's disappointed or inconvenienced.

"But if you did?"

"Sure." You lean back on your elbows, the night sky reminding you of that last night on the trapeze.

The rest of the movie, you share snacks with Lucy, rolling your eyes together at a cringey line, whispering about sea turtles and climate change. You pretend like you aren't hyperaware of the heat from Levi's leg radiating toward you.

As the credits roll, he jogs over to talk with the guy running the projector. You help Lucy fold blankets, separate trash from recyclables, then sneak a glance his way.

Lucy elbows you, biting back a smile. "Levi, huh?"

"What do you mean?" You pretend to concentrate on straightening a blanket edge.

"Mm-hmm," she says as Levi rejoins you.

With a secretive smile, he asks, "Busy tomorrow?"

You shake your head no. "Come by here, nine a.m." He walks backward toward the folding chairs as he speaks before turning away. You watch him for a minute, noticing how he helps carry chairs, how he seems to know everyone.

You turn to Lucy. She shrugs. "Your guess is as good as mine."

The air is cooler the next morning, a light mist clinging to the trees and grass. The picnic tables sit empty. The dewy grass is slick under your sneakers. A postcard tacked to the corkboard grabs your attention:

> *Mariah—*
> *Meet me by the trees near the camping area sign.*
> *—Levi*

You tuck the postcard in your bag, follow the dirt path around the bend. Up ahead, sunlight glints off something in a tree.

You stop. Is this real life?

A trapeze is suspended from the tree. Levi sits on the branch, adjusting the ropes.

Siyo, the trapeze seems to say.

Welcome back.

Welcome home.

I LOVE YOU, GRANDSON

Brian Young

Jason Nez exhaustedly watched the wet ground blue corn mixture heat to a boil on the stove. This time it would cook. It had to. It was nearing seven in the morning and his mom's alarm would go off in about thirty minutes. He wanted her to wake up to a breakfast that Grandma used to make. Inside the stainless-steel pot, blue corn powder was amassing into tiny balls that grew into dense lumps.

Jason turned off the stove, frustrated that the mixture had curdled again. If it weren't for the fact that the water was near boiling, he would have thrown it across the small kitchen. He sat at the faux wooden table and his spine wilted. He pushed his palms against his eyes to fight his tears of disappointment and heartbreak.

It had been a week since they'd buried Grandma in Nazlini Cemetery. A week since the entire family gathered to honor that amazing woman. Uncles, aunties, cousins, other grandmas, other grandpas, his mom, and Jason shared stories and pictures of Grandma in the Nazlini Chapter House after the interment. The picture he shared was of his eighth-grade graduation. He was barely as tall as Grandma. He remembered how she smiled at him, with so much love and pride. And at the funeral luncheon, his mom ate a bowl of tóshchíín, blue corn mush. It was the last time Jason had seen her eat.

Over the next six days, his mom only slept and wept. They had subsisted on leftovers and the occasional McDonald's takeout from Window Rock. While Jason's own appetite was steady, his mom barely touched any food. Seeing her so sad and unable to leave the house scared him. By making her tóshchíín, he hoped she might be tempted to eat and regain her strength. He had seen both her and Grandma make it so many times before. So, why was it so hard to cook?

Jason poured the curdled blue corn into a bowl set aside for their two backyard dogs. It was filled with his previous two attempts. At least the dogs weren't in danger of starving.

He could make Pop-Tarts. He could fix bowls of cereal. He could scramble some eggs with Spam. But his heart had settled on tóshchíín. Not only had his mom eaten it before, Grandma had said that the Diné ancestors ate tóshchíín for strength to endure tough trials. And these days were full of tough trials.

Jason pulled his phone out and searched for DIY videos. There was this amazing collection by Bead Clan Kitchen that showed how to make many traditional Diné meals. The presenter, Jennifer, had labeled it taa'niil instead of tóshchíín. He had followed her directions as best he could, but she spoke only in Diné, and he knew just a few words here and there. He had added two parts of water to one part ground blue corn. He poured everything into the pot and turned on the stove. Hers came out smooth and velvety while his clumped up.

He was going to watch the clip another time when an ad began to play.

"Hankering for real tradish foods?" asked a thickly rez-accented voiceover. On the screen, "Sandy June's Legendary Frybread Drive-In" shone in bright neon-green letters. *Legendary* was in yellow, against a black background. A series of dishes flashed on his screen. Jason recognized Diné favorites like kneel-down bread and Diné tacos. There was even a sweet bread that he called "Pueblo Pop-Tarts" that he'd sometimes get at the flea market in Gallup. Some unfamiliar foods, probably from different tribal Nations, quickly appeared on his screen. Then he saw the most delicious-looking and velvety tóshchíín in the hands of an Elder woman. She wore glasses with bright turquoise rims.

The voiceover urged, "Hurry up, then, and come to Sandy June's, where your legendary grandparents prepare all the real good foods!" On-screen, seventeen Elders wearing aprons stood proudly next to one another. They all waved. "Our grandparents know what your spirit needs!" The word *grandparent* punctured his heart, but he powered through. "No need for EBT or tap to pay, just show up. All doors lead to Sandy June's, including your own fridge door!" the voice concluded. Then the strangest thing happened. An image of his refrigerator appeared on-screen! It even had the same magnets on it.

Jason dropped his phone and scanned the kitchen for a hidden camera.

After the ad ended, the video from Bead Clan Kitchen began to play.

Jason slowly turned to face his fridge door. He was fifteen. Too old to believe that his fridge was more than a fridge and some . . . portal? He remembered the smooth tóshchíín and how his mom ate it at the luncheon. If this was real . . .

He reached for the handle. It was absurd, but so was his own fridge appearing in the ad. Jason pulled the handle. Suddenly, he lost his balance and fell, hands forward. He closed his eyes and braced for impact with . . . the soft grass.

"What the?" Jason said, pushing to his feet, scanning the landscape. How did he get outside? To his right, an asphalt lot in desperate need of repair. To his left, a large neon sign that read "Sandy June's Legendary Frybread Drive-In." It was currently turned off, but the letters were green except for *Legendary*, which was yellow. The drive-in directly in front of him featured a large metallic awning—light brown and yellow with green trim. In its gentle shadow, multiple tables had been arranged. They could easily sit thirty people.

The air was fragranced by the late autumn scent of cornfields full of veggies ready for harvest, rivers swollen with sweet water, and gentle cedar from the nearby trees. The sun warmed his forearms and forehead. This was real.

His chest felt light. His head cleared. For the first time since Grandma was admitted to the hospital in Fort Defiance a month ago, he chuckled.

From the other side of the awning, framed by a service window, an Elder waved at him. "Txi̧'! Hágo!" She spoke Diné. Jason relaxed even more, comforted by the knowledge that there was another Diné person nearby. He took his time, walking past all the empty picnic tables. Another Elder was busy wiping the tables with a lemon-scented scour pad. She smiled at him. On her chest was a large, beaded tag with her name, Joyce.

"You're early." She stood up and dug her knuckles into her lower back. "We're not open until eleven."

"Oh, sorry. I can come back when you're open," Jason answered.

"It's fine. We're just doing prep work for the show tonight. If you're free, you should stop by. The Trixters, they're playing."

That sounded like fun, and any other time, he'd check it out. "No, thanks."

"That's fine, young one. Stop on by whenever you want. The drive-in is open seven days a week, thirteen moon cycles a year. But there's always a legendary grandparent or two around."

Jason forced a smile and continued to the Diné Elder by the awning. He recognized her bright, turquoise-rimmed glasses from the ad. When he got to the food counter, he noticed that there were already two plastic bowls ready to go. "So, this is a drive-in?" Jason asked her.

"'Aoo'! Sandy June's," she said. She was a little shorter than his late grandma. She also had more strands of black hair. Her face was rounder, but still filled with love. Her name tag read *Thomacita*.

The bowls had been filled with the smoothest tóshchíín Jason had ever seen. "How did you know I wanted this?"

She smiled. "T'áá kwe'é, we just know things."

"How did you make this?" Jason asked. "It clumps up every time I do it!"

"I can show you," she said. "Txị', come around to the employee door on the side."

Jason did as he was told. He entered and was surprised when he saw the kitchen. It was much larger than it appeared on the outside. There were twenty cook stations, each as big as his entire kitchen. One station had modern stainless-steel appliances that reflected light and sparkled like a still lake under stars. Another station had a big earthen firepit with charred metal grating and black cast-iron pots. Far in the back was a station that was made of crisscrossing beams, upon which were thin strips of meat being turned into jerky. At the moment, there were seven other Elders focused on prep work—dicing vegetables for stew, carving meat off carcasses. Laughter bloomed as they joked with one another.

"Over here," Thomacita said, and guided him to her station.

"Okay, Thomacita," Jason said.

"Call me Grandma," she said as she patted his shoulder.

Her words felt like a punch to the throat. He couldn't call her Grandma.

"Are you okay, Grandson?" she asked.

At least she hadn't called him "shiyáázh," like his own grandma. "I'm good." His words, like his backbone, trembled.

Thomacita stared at his eyes for a moment. She squinted, like she knew Jason was not telling the truth. "Txi', let's show you what to do." Thomacita's workstation had reclosable plastic bags filled with Diné delicacies like ground white corn, blue corn, dééh, and chiiłchin. There were also traditional cooking utensils like wooden stirring sticks and pots. To his side, a large pot sat on a foldable gas stove.

"Every family does it a little bit differently," Thomacita said. "But the deal is, you have to stir while it warms. I start by warming up one cup of water. Then, with the other cup of water, I pour in the ground blue corn and mix it with my sticks. Or a fork works. Just as the water is about to boil, that's when you pour the blue-corn mixture in. That way it doesn't curdle." Jason remembered watching the Bead Clan

Kitchen presenter constantly stirring the mixture. That's what he was doing wrong. Rather, what he wasn't doing. Thomacita said, "Your turn."

Jason used her long stirring sticks, and the tóshchíín came out smooth! Small curls of steam rose along with the delicious aroma of cooked corn. With strong, frybread-spotted hands, she patted his shoulder. "Nizhóníyee, shiyáázh."

That word. Only Grandma had called him that. His strength crumbled. Moisture dripped from his eyes and into the tóshchíín.

Thomacita wrapped him in her arms. She rubbed his shoulders in gentle circles. "Let it out, shiyáázh. It doesn't do any good to hold it in."

"I miss my grandma," Jason blurted out. "I want her back." He closed his eyes and remembered Grandma. The way she'd adjust her glasses with the back of her wrist when her fingers were caked with dough. Her white hair that she kept permed. The flower-print skirts she wore with Nike shoes.

"Shiyáázh," Thomacita whispered as the other Elders gathered near. "A grandparent's love for their grandkid is eternal. We never, ever stop loving you. We don't want you to hurt, but you must mourn, shiyáázh."

Jason felt a hand cup his shoulder; another rubbed the side of his head; another patted his lower back. More and more warm, gentle, loving hands comforted him. All the Elders had circled around, hugging and holding him.

"She's gone and not coming back," Jason said.

Thomacita frowned. "That is a part of life, shiyáázh. As much as we want, we can't change it. We also can't ignore it." Her calloused thumbs rubbed the tears off Jason's cheeks. She smiled and said, "But you're always going to have grandparents everywhere. You are the miracle of thousands of grandparents. We are here for you. 'Ayóó 'áníínísh'ni', shiyáázh.'"

His heart began to heal when he heard her say that she loved him and called him "grandson" in Diné. She let him go.

Then an Elder with a blue apron with pictures of blueberries and green ribbons stepped forward and hugged him. Her name tag read *Sarah*. She said, "Ecenokecyvyet os, osóswv."

Then a tall Elder with short black hair and red lipstick stepped forward and hugged him. Her name tag read *Willa*. She said, "ᎡᎳᎬᎢ, ᎣᏢᏏ ᎭᏧᏣ."

He didn't know any Indigenous languages besides Diné, but his grieving, healing heart understood. They were saying they loved him and were calling him grandson.

An Elder male with neat braids and a navy-blue bandana gave him a hug. "Gizhawenimin, noozhishenh."

By the time the last legendary grandparent had held him and loved him as a grandson, Jason's heartbreak felt soothed. It was still there, but he was no longer afraid of it.

With the support of his new grandparents, he allowed himself to finally start saying goodbye to Grandma, the first of many steps in a world, in a life, without her physical presence. But her love for him was eternal and would help him navigate his grief.

Once Jason had said his thank-yous and farewells, he opened the employee door to exit the building and found himself walking through his own front door.

The living room looked a little brighter than when he had left. From the kitchen, his mom popped her head around the corner. She was still in her pajamas. Her hair was up in a frizzy ponytail. "Where were you?" She spoke with her normal stern voice.

"Getting breakfast," Jason explained. He lifted his hand to show her the bowls but then realized he had forgotten them. "Oh man! They must still be at the drive-in. I'm sorry."

"What drive-in? This early? Where did you go?" She crossed her arms and examined him. The last time she had held this posture was when Jason had snuck out to hang with his friends on a school night. Even though she was mad at him, Jason was relieved to see some fragments of her usual fierce self. She wasn't just a motionless mound withering away under the blankets on her bed.

"I wanted to get you breakfast," he explained. "Actually, I think I can cook it for you now."

"Come sit at the table," Mom said firmly. She sounded almost normal.

In the kitchen, a big, steaming bowl of tóshchíín rested on the table. Mom had cooked a huge pot of the stuff. "I saw your earlier attempts in the dog food bowl. Were you craving this?"

"I wanted to make it for you," Jason admitted. "It was the last thing you were able to eat."

"Oh, sonny boy," she said. Her posture and expression softened. She pulled a chair out at the table and gestured for him to sit. "Is that what this is about? You're worried about me?" His mom squeezed his shoulder. She sat in the chair next to him. "I'll eat. I promise.

Everyone's grief takes a different form. Mine is kicking me to the ground. It's been rough. How are you holding up?"

Jason thought of the Elders at Sandy June's and the love they freely gave him, about how understanding they'd been, and how they reminded him of his grandma. "It hurts, Mom." He pushed against his chest.

"Yes, it does." Her eyes shone. "And it's going to, for a long while. But day by day, step by step, we'll carry on. She wouldn't want us to wallow. She'd want us to live and be happy." Then she grabbed a spoon and ate some tóshchíín. "Everything will be okay."

Everything will be okay, Jason thought. Day by day. Step by step. His mom's tóshchíín tasted just like how Grandma made it.

THE REST WILL COME
K. A. Cobell

I run my fingers over the medal. It's more bronze than gold. And the shoes on its front look more like loafers than track spikes, but it still means the same thing: first place. I shove it into my backpack as we lurch over another bump.

The late-afternoon sun is blaring through the wide windows of the school bus. Some of the other kids around me are wearing their brand-new invitational T-shirts, like me. Others are still in their sullied running jerseys. Nobody is talking too much. We're all quiet and gassed. The ride home from meets is always a snore compared to the ride in. There are no more buzzing nerves and churning energy. We already left it all out on the track.

Mom doesn't really see the point of these summer track invitationals. All I know is, every first place and new PR I get under my belt is one more thing to show colleges next year. Every meet is a stepping-stone to a personal best so good they'll never be able to look away.

I have to give myself every opportunity I can. I'm going places—that's what Mom raised me to do.

Me and my older brother, Calvin.

One of us has to actually make something of ourselves. Calvin sure hasn't.

The bus slows and takes an exit into some random town. The kid across the aisle from me pulls his earbuds out and tucks them into his duffel bag. "About time. I'm starving."

My own stomach growls as we take a few more turns. When we finally park in a small lot, Coach Wiley saunters to the front of the bus. "All right, guys, you've got thirty minutes. There are several fast-food places on this block. Go wherever you want—just get back here in thirty. Please. Don't make me go searching for any of you. Again." He glances down at me. "I'm looking at you, Trevor."

"That was *one* time." I pull my backpack on, laughing. "I got lost."

"Uh-huh." Coach folds his arms with a glare but smiles as I follow the other athletes off the bus. Everyone spills out and heads in different directions. There's a burger place with smoke pouring out of a pipe on the roof. A taco joint with a line out the door. A diner with pink trim. A dog sits in front of it. He looks just like the dog we had when we were little. Chuck.

He was some breed of mutt with ears too big and a mishmash of white-and-brown fur. He followed Calvin home from school one day. No collar. Skinny. Flea-bitten. Mom only let us keep him because Calvin said he'd already named him. Chuck—the first thing he thought of on the spot.

The Chuck look-alike turns and stares right at me. There's something odd about it, like he recognizes me the same way I recognize him. Maybe somewhere out here there's a Trevor look-alike that met this dog and made an impression.

The dog hops off the steps of the diner and sniffs my way before walking purposefully down the gravel road beside it.

I don't know why, but I follow him.

Maybe because this is the first time I've thought of Calvin without swearing under my breath. Or maybe because he reminds me of the good times before everything went down the crapper. It's not because I think the Chuck look-alike actually wants me to follow him. . . .

I'm not losing my mind.

The road passes between the fast-food joints and then cuts into a wooded area. The trees' crisscrossing branches stretch almost across the whole road, quieting the hum from the main street behind us. The dog looks back once and then disappears into the tangle of undergrowth.

The smoke from the burger place blurs the leaves above me until a breeze rustles through, clearing the air and exposing a huge black sign with neon-green-and-yellow lettering over the trees. Sandy June's Legendary Frybread Drive-In.

I take a few strides farther down the road and find an archway in the trees where the gravel road turns into a large parking lot.

A drive-in sits in the center of a huge clearing, the surrounding trees blocking out the town's bustling sounds and creating the illusion that we're far away. We could be up a mountain or at a lakeside campground.

The dog stops in the middle of the parking lot and barks, pulling me a few more steps over the worn asphalt. A sharp but warm aroma floats over. Something spicy and smoky. My stomach growls. I head toward the awning covering picnic tables where a family is eating . . . Indian tacos? The frybread is perfectly puffy and smothered in rich brown chili. The mom sees me staring and smiles, her quill earrings so long they almost dangle onto the plate.

What is this place?

A menu board near the order window is covered in scrawls of rainbow chalk. Milkshakes. Bison burgers. Indian/Navajo tacos. Elk stew and cornbread. The dog stops beside it at the order counter, where an older woman in a green apron tosses a gristly piece of meat into his mouth. She's got a beaded tag that says *Sandy June's Legendary Grandparent* and a massive beadwork medallion necklace that says *Cleo*.

I glance around the building. An old man in a cowboy hat with an eagle feather on it eases himself out of a truck. Grandpa wears a hat just like that. Farther down the sidewalk, a young girl is setting up a stand with an assortment of beaded key rings for sale.

I scratch my head. The people . . . the food . . . the collarless dog hanging around for handouts . . . It's like I just walked onto a rez somehow. Is there one around here? If we hadn't been driving for only one hour, I'd almost believe the bus took a wrong turn and ended up in Browning, Montana.

"Look what the cat dragged in."

I know that voice. I spin around.

"Or should I say dog." Calvin stands only feet away, hands in his jeans pockets. Here. Clean. Whole.

I yank him into a hug without thinking about it. It's a knee-jerk reaction, so fast I forget for a second that I'm furious at him. He's so still it brings me back to reality just as quick. I shove him away from me. "What are you doing here?"

He half smiles. "No more pleasantries for your big bro?"

"No."

I take a step back and bump into the dog, who lurches away and disappears around the corner of the building.

If Calvin noticed the dog looks just like Chuck, he doesn't say so. Instead, he pulls his hands out of his pockets and cracks his knuckles. "I hoped you'd be here."

Hoped I'd be here? I glance at the family eating Indian tacos and then at the legendary grandparent behind the counter pretending not to watch us. Where even is here? How would he know this is where my bus would stop? How would he know I'm leaving a track invitational? After being out of my life for the last three years, how would he know . . . anything?

"Yeah, right." I look over his shoulder, scanning for any of the deadbeat "friends" he left us for.

He shifts on his feet, restless. "Can we catch up?"

I laugh, breathless and sharp. He says it so casually. Like the talk we'd have would really be as simple as a *catchup*. He let us down, repeatedly. Stole our money, spit words that nearly killed Mom. Took for granted every sacrifice she made for us. He turned his whole life upside down and had us scrambling in the wake of it. Then he dipped out. . . . He left us, and I haven't seen or heard from him since. No goodbyes. No apologies. Nothing. "Catch up?"

"C'mon, Trevor. Huckleberry shakes? Like old times?"

I check the clock on my phone, avoiding his pleading gaze. We're supposed to roll out in twenty-five minutes. "I don't have long. The bus will be waiting."

"Yeah, no problem. I just . . ." He almost looks like he's missed me as much as I missed him, but I know better than to believe that. "I just really wanted to see you."

We step up to the order window and Calvin asks for two huckleberry shakes from the woman with the apron. Cleo. She has pin-back buttons all over her apron with various sayings.

Land Back

No More Stolen Sisters

You're on Native Land

I was told there would be frybread

"You're in for a treat," she says, rubbing her hands together. "I harvested these huckleberries myself, straight from Blackfeet Country."

"Oh yeah?" I motion between Calvin and me with my thumb. "We're harvested straight from Blackfeet Country, too." Once upon a time we were, at least. Then we moved to Washington.

"Aho. I thought I sensed something extra sacred about you two." She bends down with a laugh and pulls two tall glasses from below the counter. "This calls for the fancy cups."

Calvin and I sink onto a couple of stools that sit in front of the open counter.

"So, who's your family?"

"Lone Bull," I say.

"Oh yeah, I went to school with Kurt Lone Bull. He was a real knucklehead." Her voice tumbles out like gravel, but she says it with a genuine smile. "He your grandpa?"

I lean onto the counter. "Sure is." And that's about the best way you could describe him, too. A lovable knucklehead, but a knucklehead all the same.

"I'll get these going." She glances between us, probably sensing the weird tension, and then disappears into the depths of the kitchen.

Calvin watches me quietly.

"So what do you really want?"

"I messed up, Trevor. Big-time."

My thoughts should be racing, but instead they get all fogged up. Of course Calvin messed up. That's what he does. It's his thing. He made it his thing. "That's nothing new."

"You're not wrong. I just . . ." Something is different this time, though. There's shame in his eyes. Messing up may be his thing, but not caring usually is, too. "I don't know how to come back from this one."

Cleo returns and sets two huckleberry milkshakes in front of us, heaping swirls of whipped cream on top barely staying in place. She glances between our faces, then busies herself refilling the napkin holders on the counter, bracelets of silver and turquoise clinking against the metal. A flyer is taped to the side of the holders, advertising a Battle of the Bands coming up next weekend.

I tug the spoon out of the shake, sending a few purple drips to the counter, and take a huge bite. His words hang in the air.

"I know what you're thinking," he finally says.

I swallow the bite too fast and get a chest freeze. "Do you?"

"You're thinking I can't come back from *any* of the things I've done."

I yank a napkin from the holder beside us and wipe up the smears of purple.

"That I don't deserve to."

"No." I crumple the soiled napkin into my fist. "I'm thinking . . . do you even *want* to?"

His head cocks.

"You've been tearing down that road, hardly looking back. You know you've hurt us. Hurt me. Abandoned me. And it always seemed like you were fine with it."

He stares at me, whipped cream dripping down the side of his cup in the warm air. "I wasn't *fine* with it."

I shovel in another bite and shrug. "Fooled me."

He watches as more drops trail down the surface of his cup, jaw pulsing. "I don't blame you for hating me."

I should tell him I don't hate him. It's the truth. You can't hate your own brother—your own flesh and blood. But I've been so mad for so long—it's like I *want* him to hurt. Can that still be love? If we want to hurt each other?

All the ways he's let me down bubble up in my mind. All the resentment that I've held on to. It feels like he doesn't *deserve* to hear me refute him.

I keep scarfing down the milkshake instead of saying anything. Let him think I *do* hate him.

The pain that flashes across his face doesn't feel as satisfying as I expected though. He rakes his fingers through his hair. "That's what I thought. . . ."

Cleo leans onto the counter between us. "You two sound like you could use some old Indian wisdom."

I twist my spoon over the cup, watching the shake plop off in slow motion.

"Please." Calvin sounds as defeated as I've been the last few years.

"Take it from an old-timer," she says. "We hurt the ones we love the most. That's just the god-awful truth. You know why? Because we feel safest around the ones we love. Safe to be our true selves. Safe to feel our deepest emotions. Safe to lash out."

I feel Calvin's eyes on me.

"It looks to me like there's a lot of regret here. But there's a lot of love, too. You can get through anything when you've still got that."

I meet her gaze. Somehow, I think she knows the words on my mind. *What if that's not enough?*

"You need some good ol'-fashioned humility and honesty, too, nephew." She nods at Calvin. "Get yourself on that Red Road again. Turn your back on the things that damage yourself and others. Commit to positive change. And speak your truth—or whatever it is kids say these days."

"Speak my truth?" Calvin asks, shifting on the stool.

"If you're sorry, your brother deserves to hear that." She pushes off the counter. "Even if it makes you uncomfortable. You need to think of yourself less." She looks pointedly at me. "Both of you."

I want to tell her Calvin is the only one who needs to think of himself less, but she leaves me with a look that's so . . . *Auntie*, I know she's right. She eases over to the order window as a tall girl with a folding camping chair slung over her shoulder peruses the menu.

Calvin bounces his knee and looks at his wrist like he expects a watch to be there. "I know it's too late, but I *am* sorry, Trevor. I wasn't at first. It took me a while to see what I was doing. Once I did . . . I wanted to change things. I swear I wanted to. It just felt like I fell so far I couldn't claw my way out. I felt like . . . like the people I wanted to find my way back to weren't waiting for me anymore."

The twinge in my gut makes it hard to swallow another bite. He's right. I used to reach out all the time. Hoping he'd realize the path he was on wasn't as good as the one he turned from. I'd feel a spark of hope whenever Mom's phone rang. When a car pulled into the driveway. I always expected he'd come back.

I *was* waiting for him.

Then, somewhere along the way, I stopped hoping. Reality sank in. He had a new life. New people.

New priorities.

He didn't want to give those up.

And I stopped waiting for him to.

"I started feeling like I had nothing to come back to. So why bother?"

I shove the spoon back into the near-empty cup and turn to face him on the stool. "Hey, man, that's not true."

He runs a hand through his slick hair. "I just . . . got caught up. I never meant to burn all my bridges."

I've been angry. Mom's been brokenhearted. He ruined everything and then he missed everything. But still . . . "The bridges aren't burned. I'm *so* mad. Have been for a long time. But there's a big difference between giving up hope and not *being* here. We're still here, man."

He doesn't believe me. "You stopped reaching out."

"You could've reached out, too."

"I was in a bad place." He runs his fingertips along the shiny metal counter. "It felt impossible to."

"I wouldn't have stopped texting if I knew you liked hearing from me." But that's not entirely true. I probably would've still been mad enough to punish him. "I'm sorry, too. I should've kept after you. That's what brothers do."

He rakes his palms across his eyes. "You have nothing to apologize for."

"Well, I am."

"I just don't know if it's too late." He looks at his empty wrist again.

"It's not, but . . ." I glance at the time on my phone and groan. "I gotta hit the road."

He stands up. "Right. Yeah."

I swing my backpack on and stand. "Listen. I'm always here when you need me, Calvin." I pull him into a real hug. I'm taller than him now, but it still feels familiar. "And I need you, too. Okay? Do the work. Come home."

He releases me and nods. He doesn't quite smile, but I can tell he wants to. "I'll try."

"Don't try. Do." I walk backward a few steps before spinning on my heel and jogging across the parking lot toward the gravel road.

I glance back to see him sink onto the stool again and a familiar feeling seeps into my chest.

Hope.

Maybe he'll really change this time. Now that he knows we still want him to. That he hasn't severed all his ties.

I hope he believes I still have his back, the way he always had mine when we were younger. You can't erase that.

That's love. When you've torn each other up and somehow still have that unchanging bond. I think we can get back to that.

When I emerge from the gravel road, Coach Wiley is pacing outside the bus's open door with a clipboard. "There you are, Trevor. I thought you were going to make me go looking again! Let's get going." I stride past him and up the steps. I hop into my seat at the front of the bus as he starts yelling about the last two hours of our trek and to let our parents know now so they can coordinate pickups.

My phone buzzes with a call from Mom. I sink in my seat and answer.

"Can you hear me?" Her voice is choppy with static.

"Mostly."

"How much longer until you get here?"

I pull in my elbow as Coach sidesteps past me. "Two hours."

"Do you . . . do you think you can get the coach to allow you to be dropped off at the hospital on the way?"

"What? Why?"

"Something happened . . ." Her voice quakes. "I didn't . . . I'm sorry I didn't tell you earlier."

I sit up straighter as the bus rolls through the parking lot, brakes squeaking. "Tell me what?"

"I didn't want you to be distracted during your meet. I thought—"

"What happened?" I'm yelling into the phone now. The bus driver looks at me in his rearview mirror. The kid across the aisle leans over, brows pulling in concern.

Mom's silence on the other end of the line twists my stomach into knots. "It's . . . Calvin."

"What do you mean it's Calvin? Did he hurt someone?" I stand up, phone pressed to my ear, frozen. The bus stops, and I know there are voices around me, but I don't know what they're saying. Is that why Calvin seemed so out of sorts?

"He was in an accident. . . . We don't know all the details yet, but—"

"Who was?"

"Calvin. Are you hearing me?" She sucks in a breath. "Calvin is here, in the ICU."

"What?" It's the only word I can force out.

"He made it through surgery, but he wasn't waking up—"

"No." She's lying. Or confused. He's *here*. I take the phone from my ear. "Open the door." I'm breathless. Shaking. "Please!"

Coach stands up. "Did you forget something?"

"Yes!" I start down the steps and finally the door opens. I burst out, running across the street. Chuck's look-alike stares at me from the diner steps. I pass him, sprinting down the gravel road.

I don't see the archway in the trees.

Calvin said he messed up bad. He said he wasn't sure he could come back from it. Wasn't sure if we *wanted* him back.

My chest is heaving.

The dog appears at my side, nearly tripping me, but besides him, the gravel road is empty. Like I imagined the whole thing.

Like I'm losing my mind.

But it must be a trick of the light, because as I careen across the gravel, I see the tip of the Sandy June's sign. The tree branches seem to separate, and the arched roadway appears. I slow to a jog in the parking lot. There are still a few people sitting at the picnic tables under the awning, but the barstools in front of the counter are empty.

I grip my phone at my side and ease into a walk.

Cleo approaches the counter just as I freeze beside our empty stools. I scan the area, so sure I'm going to see Calvin, and somehow equally sure he was never here.

But our glasses still sit on the counter. Mine is empty, the purple remnants of huckleberry shake congealing on the silver spoon. Calvin's is untouched and a melted mess. The liquefied whipped cream pools on the counter around the streaked glass. The sludgy, light purple shake still hovers at the rim.

Cleo takes the glasses into the kitchen and returns with a rag, but her lips press into a frown when she sees my face. "Looking for Calvin?"

A spark of something besides dread lights in my chest. "Yeah."

"He already left."

"You saw him?" It should be a stupid question, but I don't know what's happening.

"I see him a lot here, you know."

"You do?"

"He was different this time. He's going to be okay."

I perch on the stool, finally remembering I'm still holding my phone. I stare at the minutes ticking by on the screen, the call still in progress, but when I hold it up to my ear there's only static. "I'm not so sure."

"He told me he's going to be okay. He said he was going to be okay for *you*."

I snap up to meet her gaze. "He said that?"

"I told him that wasn't good enough. I told him he needs to be okay for himself first. And the rest will come."

I nod, wanting to believe her.

"You'll be okay, too. I have a sense for these things." She smiles, lopsided and knowing, and disappears into the kitchen again.

I jog back toward the gravel road, phone pressed to my ear, and as soon as I'm through the archway, the static fizzles away. "Mom?"

"Trevor?"

"I hear you now. You're wrong; you don't—"

"Trevor." Mom's voice is sharp, the shaking in her voice gone now. "Let me finish."

I bite my tongue.

"I'm trying to tell you Calvin just woke up. He's going to be okay . . . and he's asking for *you*."

The dog watches as I stand frozen in the middle of the road. "Me?"

"He keeps saying he wants to tell you something. . . . He says he's ready to think of himself less."

LANGUAGE LESSON

Jen Ferguson

The language was hard. Really hard. Being immersed in it helped. Like, Berlin Chambers could now understand more than half of what was being said. As long as everyone involved talked slow, careful. But still she couldn't speak. Not more than greetings—taanishi, bonn swayrii, pishkapmisho—and an array of thank-yous. But she'd known those things before she got to Winnipeg. So was it really any big win?

The answer was plain as all get-out. In all the ways she could say it.

No.

Nada.

Nyet.

Non.

No.

The last one was in Michif. Berlin knew that word, too.

Tonight, all she wanted was to curl up in her shared room in the house in Inkster-Faraday and not use language at all. Maybe video-chat the impossible boy because he would get that she didn't want words; she wanted to lie under the granny square afghan the local Elders outfitted all the rooms here with and she wanted to just be in the same quiet, no-words space as him.

She missed the impossible boy.

Missed her home in the mountains, her own thrifted blankets, and Snapdragon—the three-legged rescue cat who ruled the Chambers house.

But no. The entire group, twelve teens from across colonial Canada, were headed out on a cultural excursion. To get fill-in-the-blank tacos. All day, it had been a replay of that old First Nations, Métis, and Inuit Student Association debate. Everyone in the house was Métis, but Berlin's roommates insisted on saying Navajo tacos because their stepdad was Diné, while Simon, the undisputed star of language camp, argued NDN was fairest. Now her roommates weren't talking to Simon.

Words were causing trouble again.

Berlin screamed into her pillow. She could play at being sick and stay here, but she was trying not to make cutting a habit—unless it was *really* important.

Some things were really important.

She'd video-call the impossible boy later. Maybe then she'd be up for more than silently staring at a screen.

"Wooooo-hooooo! NDN tacos!" Simon did a weird dance, all arms, no legs, as the group stopped at a streetlight.

Not quite a jig. Maybe the jig's backwoods cousin.

Simon continued: "I'm going to eat food by the boatload toniiii-ight!"

Even English hurt Berlin's ears.

They were supposed to speak Michif exclusively, but since Simon was good at the language, their program instructors let it slide.

This was deeply irritating.

They were walking east to St. John's Park, which bordered the Red River. It was a pretty park, when it got cleaned up. You had to watch the ground—but usually things were safe enough. The Bear Clan Patrol came this way. On Saturday afternoons, when they were freed from the language, Berlin and a few others joined the Youth Patrol. They mostly talked to the people of the North End, listened to stories, and took care of the land with assorted donated trash pickers in hand.

Tomorrow Berlin wouldn't be able to help because she'd be in a full-day intensive with a visiting Elder who was fluent in Southern Michif and Plains Cree, who had only enough English to get by. They'd be walking to the cultural center to meet her at eight a.m.

Simon fell in step next to Berlin. "Aren't you excited? We're eating out tonight!"

It was like someone had told the best language student to spend extra time with the worst language student.

Berlin's feet ached. She shrugged and continued walking. She didn't have the words to say what she was feeling, and unlike Simon, she wasn't offered free passes to speak English.

Simon got the hint. Without a single word.

It was part lesson about taking things slow, part budget issue, but their language camp walked a lot of places. At least walking was something Berlin was good at.

The park was green, full of summer flowers. A few people were picking through garbage cans, and someone was sleeping on a bench, curled up tight, and there was an enthusiastic game of basketball echoing over from the newly refinished court.

She heard the *thump, thump, thump* of the ball and then an exclamation when it hit the rim, bounced.

Voices carried.

"So close, man!"

"Close? There is no close, man. If it's not a basket, it's nothing."

Oof. Berlin got that philosophy.

Marcie, who didn't live with them at the house but ran the program from the cultural center, turned toward the southern boundary of the park. There was nothing in that direction but broken pavement, strewn with weeds and trash the Bear Clan Patrol didn't let the youths clean up. Some big company was fighting at the courthouse for use of the riverside property, but the land was winning out. One weed at a time.

Either you made the shot, or you missed. Either you got the words, or you didn't. Berlin followed her group, wondering if *that* was somehow the lesson and she'd have been better off faking a sore throat to video-chat with the impossible boy.

The air got tight. Like it was about to storm.

The trees almost blurred in the late-afternoon sun. She rubbed at her eyes. Like her feet, they ached, too. Something like summer allergies. It was the pollen, only the pollen.

One step, then two, over and out onto what should be busted-up pavement—instead, she found grass bordering black asphalt, run-down but sealed recently enough, and a big sign with neon-yellow-and-green letters: "Sandy June's Legendary Frybread Drive-In."

"Miitshootaak!" Marcie said, smiling wide, extending her arms as if she'd performed a magic trick.

The group cheered.

They were a cheery bunch.

And then as the others started to flit away, in English, to Berlin specifically, Marcie said: "Take a break, why don't you? Forget about learning for the night. Eat something, enjoy the band, the movie. Maybe even nap? You know? Relax?"

Berlin's cheeks got red. She nodded anyhow.

"Miina kaawaapamitin." Marcie offered parting words, but *see you later* came out like she was a bit disappointed.

Before Berlin could even try to formulate a response, Marcie left, after waving at someone parking their rough-idling Buick near the picnic tables under the big awning.

Stacked next to the main building, off to the side, were a bunch of folding camping chairs. A cardboard sign proclaimed "Not Your Wild West Show, FRIDAY 8 PM! The TRIXTERS, Saturday 8 PM!" At least Berlin could sit by the river, take in the music, and maybe she could forget about how much it was going to hurt, going home, when she would be going home a failure.

Even Marcie, who believed in everyone, didn't believe in Berlin.

Selecting a chair from the pile, she turned toward the river, or at least she thought she did. Berlin wasn't even hungry, was sick of Indian tacos—whatever you decided to call them—anyhow. She closed her eyes, absorbing the cool air, when she heard the impossible boy calling her name.

She let the chair drop to the asphalt and ran toward Cameron Sound.

"Oof," he said when she impacted. But Cam hugged her hard.

She spoke in English, her voice scratchy. "I completely, totally missed you."

With his hands, Cam framed her head, then leaned against her forehead, pushing her bright red glasses down her nose. "You smell really good."

She laughed the way she did around the impossible boy. "That's what you say to me?"

"Missed you, too, Bee." His words came out slow like molasses. Cam stared at her, nodding foolishly, as if it was that obvious. Then he exploded: "Missed you so much. I won't survive another month. Bring me back to Manitoba with you. I'll hide in your closet like a friendly ghost or a robot butler. No one will know I'm there! I'll just be a quiet ghost slash robot butler hanging out waiting for you to finish absorbing the language for the day."

She should ask questions. Berlin was good at questions.

But instead, a sharp whistle cut through the lot.

Berlin stepped back, but Cam held on.

"Yo, I'm not keeping your spot in this line, cousin, not if you're gonna—" Kiki cut herself off. "Bee! Get over here! I'm starved. Aren't you starved?"

Kiki pushed a stroller back and forth, back and forth, like if she stopped moving, something terrible would happen. The baby, Elora Greer, could crack plaster with her scream, it was true. But right now, EG was quiet, and Kiki was smiling in her neon pink, orange, and purple knee socks.

She looked happy.

Maybe Berlin was hungry. It had been a long time since break-fast, and she'd skipped lunch to get a break from the language. Maybe this was hunger brewing inside her and not a realization that all she wanted to do was quit the language camp and go on home. To accept she'd failed. To deal with the disappointment now, not later.

This wasn't depression. Bee knew what that felt like now. Plus, she was on her SSRI and, well, this was something else.

"You know what?" she said while Cam grabbed one of her hands, squishing it in his own. "Maybe I am."

A girl could hope.

It was the strangest thing. Two ordering lines, each with a handmade sign, written on lined notebook paper. One said "Coke," the other "Pepsi," in bold Sharpie.

Bee waved her free hand. "I've never seen a restaurant that sells both."

"Oh, crap," Kiki said. "We're in the Coke line. That just won't do."

"I can't believe we're related," Cam deadpanned.

"Come on, EG." Kiki pushed the stroller. "Your uncle led me here under false pretenses. Besides, the other line's shorter. Meet me by where the band is going to play. Bring chairs."

Cam nodded, then whispered so only Bee could hear: "We all know why that line's shorter."

And even if hope was still a hard thing to have, she laughed again. "You know I don't have a preference."

Cam sighed. Long and loud. "No one's perfect, eh."

It was true.

Hard as it was to accept.

Cam pulled her closer, so they stood side by side, his arm slung around her shoulder, one of her hands still clutched in his. The impossible boy's primary love language was not in doubt. Since the end of that week in February when they decided they didn't hate each other after all until she left for Winnipeg, Cameron Sound pretty much hadn't stopped touching her.

It was . . . nice.

To feel needed, grounded, by another person.

Still, there was a job to do. Berlin studied the menu. Because if she was hungry, she really ought to eat.

At the cash register she still didn't know what she wanted.

"You picked the right line," the woman behind the counter said, laughing. She scratched at a logo T-shirt weighed down over her right shoulder with a beaded pin that read *Sandy June's Legendary Grandparent*. Below the pin was a smaller name tag, this one Sharpie on plastic: *Joyce, she/her.* "So what's your heart asking for tonight? We've got all the meat you could want, and if you're into tofu, you know what, we've got that, too. L'aariyaanl, yeah. Some good lii bufloo. But you," Joyce said, looking right at Cam, "you look like you might want it tradish."

None of this was on the menu.

"Tradish sounds good to me," Cam agreed.

"With tots, right?"

Right now, Cam looked like he did when he was brainstorming

a new pizza recipe. "Yes, please."

"And for you?" Joyce asked, leaning out the window a ways.

Berlin hesitated.

Cam squeezed her hand. Not like *hurry up*. More like, *hey, it's okay, hey, I'm here, hey, you're doing fine*. Cam didn't hurry and didn't push anyone else to, either.

"Do you trust me to get it right, then?" Joyce asked, her smile sharpening, narrowing, when Bee still didn't say anything.

The words came out more like a question than Berlin would have liked. "Kinihtaawiteepon . . . ?"

She'd never go into another cook's space and question if they were good at it.

And yet, she just did. Or something like it. Never mind that she was terrible at the language and there was no sign that Joyce was Métis, just that she knew the names of some animals. Because of course, Berlin was wearing her program T-shirt and probably Marcie had called ahead.

This might be a test.

Berlin used to love a test. Not anymore.

Joyce only laughed. "Okay, okay, you're gonna wait over that way for your order and then you can tell me if I'm a good cook or not. Any allergies?"

Berlin shook her head.

Cam dropped her hand to pull some bills from his pocket.

"Save them for the band's fundraising effort and find that young one selling those beaded key rings. We'll call it what it is tonight: redistributing the wealth."

"Maarsii," Berlin said, meaning the word more because it was in Michif.

"Keep working on it," Joyce offered. Then she called into the building for someone to take over the cash. "Where's Sela with the good hair at? I said I'd do the cash for a few. Only now I've got a special order to put together."

Walking to where Kiki and EG were waiting, all Cam said was: "Told you Coke was better."

The food was good. Really good. Like Bee was pretty sure she hadn't had a better meal ever. Edamame and wild rice in a bowl with tender squash topped with lii pwayr—saskatoon berries—in a thick sauce, almost a gravy? And it wasn't because it was free.

Okay, free helped.

Everyone knew free food tasted better.

And it wasn't the company. Not exactly.

Even if Cam traced circles on her thigh or if Kiki was in full force, and already Bee had spit out her lemonade twice, laughing.

Or the music. It wasn't the music. Though the band was solid.

It certainly wasn't EG, who was already smiling, already seemed to have the world all figured out, though cuddling her was very good.

It wasn't thoughts of a Sandy June x Pink Mountain Pizza collab. Both places, here and Berlin and Cam's pizza shop back home in Canmore, were better exactly the way they were. Not everything needed to be about more customers, more money.

This night felt endless in the best way. No mosquitoes, no existing outside of the now.

Until that wasn't true.

All of a sudden it was late, and Berlin had to get up early, and though she couldn't spot anyone from her language camp in the crowd, they wouldn't leave her to walk home alone, and she hated keeping someone waiting, but also, no part of her wanted to leave.

Even after Kiki called it a night, holding a sleeping EG, catching a ride with a friend from her baby swim class, Berlin didn't push up from her camp chair and do the responsible thing: say good night to Cam, track down her group, and go off to bed.

"When do you have to leave?" the impossible boy asked like he was reading her mind.

"Soonish."

"The band's still playing and . . . there's what, one or two movies after, eh?"

"Right."

"So, until the end?"

It seemed fair. To get this break from something hard. Even if it was something worth doing, important and good, it was still right to get a break. "For sure until the band quits it."

Cam was smiling, yeah. But it was a sad smile. A not-ready-for-goodbye smile.

"I can stay until Simon finds me and says it's time to go. How's that?"

"You're making my night, Bee." Cameron finished his meal, cleaned his fingers with a napkin carefully. "He still top of the class?"

"Yes."

Cam turned so he wasn't as much facing the band as Berlin. "Do you hate it?"

For a second, Bee was sure he meant Simon being better at the language than she was. And then she thought maybe Cam meant not being at the top, like it wasn't about competition but her own personal standards. And then she laughed. Cameron wasn't trying to say anything more than he was saying.

"Yeah, I hate it. I miss home and it's hard and I want to be good and I'm not. I'm really, really awful at it. And I'm tired all the time. And you're not there. And I miss . . . Pink Mountain. And Snap, and Sandy, and I thought that this would be . . . different."

"Okay," Cam said. "It might not feel like it, but all of that is okay. To feel."

She missed this boy for lots of reasons. But, yeah, this was one of them.

The band finished another song and took a water break. That girl was still going round from chair to chair selling beadwork, her hair curly, messy, grunge, but her face all smiles.

"What about you? What's the thing you've been wanting to say but haven't said because you're not ready or because it's too weird to say on the phone?"

Cam laughed self-consciously, pulled a beaded key chain out of his pocket. "Promise not to punch me in the arm or make excuses and run away?"

"Have I ever punched you in the arm?"

"Does a door to the nose count?"

Berlin refused to smile. She refused. "Are you making me rethink whether I want to jab you in the arm with my fist?"

"A jab in the arm with a fist?" Cam spit out laughter. "That sounds awkward."

The key chain was Coke red, accented with shimmer. His finger made circles on the beadwork.

"And you're stalling."

"Ab-so-lutely." Cam pulled his chair closer, like he was creating a bubble here, like no others existed in this moment. "It's two things."

Bee put a finger up.

"So, it's great. It is. But . . . it's harder working with Joe than I thought. Or it's harder to get that monthly buyout payment than I thought. You know, I'm good at big plans. Me, a high school dropout thinking I'm gonna buy out ownership of Pink Mountain Pizza if I work really, really, really hard at it." Cam laughs at himself.

"Exactly how hard is it?"

"Fifty hours a week and one to two shifts driving Dad's taxi."

That was a lot of work. Too much.

Bee leaned closer. "Radical question: Have you talked to Joe about it?"

Cam shook his head, slow, back and forth, his hair brushing her cheek, her forehead. "See, I knew I was missing something. Only I didn't know what I was missing."

"Well, that was easy. Want to make it two for two?"

Cam pulled away just enough. "The second thing? The one I couldn't say on the phone? Yeaaaah." He started fidgeting, which was so unlike the impossible boy that it made Berlin suddenly nervous. He pressed the key chain into her hand but didn't let go of it or her.

All the calm she'd managed to take into herself cracked.

She wanted to do the thing he'd asked her not to do and run off.

And then Cam got brave, kept talking, maybe because he knew she needed specific words, these words, to ground her again. "I miss you in all the ways. As much as the video chats while I'm closing Pink Mountain Pizza are excellent and I text you more than I talk to my mom, dad, and sisters combined, I miss you. Being here. Where I can hold your hand or . . . And you promised not to laugh—"

"That was not part of your original list."

He pulled his hand away, leaving the key chain behind.

"A gift," he said awkwardly.

"Maarsii, Cam. Really, truly, in all the languages I know."

"Okay." He smiled big, as if refueled by a handful of words. "Permission to laugh at me is totally on the table . . . Um . . . I miss smelling you. And other things. Like that."

She didn't laugh. Instead, she got warm and, yes, that was happiness brewing inside her. But still, Bee played it cool. "You want to sit closer?"

"Yes," Cam said immediately. "I really, really do."

"That's easy enough to fix. And I was thinking . . ."

"I love when you think."

"Maybe . . ." she teased.

The impossible boy made a sound like puppies did when they got very excited.

"We could . . ."

"You're killing me. Like really pretty much stabbing me in the heart right now. I like it, don't get me wrong, but it hurts."

"We could . . . I guess . . . make out until the band quits it for the night and the credits run and they send us all home."

"Yes, please, and thank you, and Bee." Cam slowed. "I really miss you. I don't even have the words, eh? No words can explain the way I miss you."

She didn't have them, either. Not in any of the languages she knew.

But they didn't really need words right this second.

"Cam?"

"Yes?" He was sitting on the very edge of his camping chair now, his knees pressed against hers.

"Less talking. We're on the clock here."

Cam laughed—head-back, mouth-open laughter. And then they were too busy to laugh and the band kept playing and for a small while, it was real nice not to worry about the language or what tomorrow would bring or how it was pretty much impossible to be good at everything. And maybe that was really okay.

Or could be, if a girl tried hard enough to make it so.

HEARTS AFLUTTER

A. J. Eversole

When Ethan and I both reached for a french fry, our hands brushed. Nothing came of it. No fire. No spark. No tiny butterflies fluttering in my stomach to signal that *something* was clicking. Tonight's visit to Sandy June's Legendary Frybread Drive-In would go down with nothing but unmet expectations. Not the start of any fairy tale, but as a failed first-ever date.

Not that it was that awful. Almost everything about it was perfect. We sat at my favorite picnic table, the one where my grandparents had their own first date fifty years ago. Their initials were still carved into the edge of the table and stood out in the neon-pink light of the sunset. Ambient splashing and conversation from the lake made the perfect soundtrack to what I'd always imagined to be the best first date ever.

Everything *was* perfect, except for the boy across from me.

Listen, I'd always known exactly what I wanted, and it wasn't this. Or, well, it was exactly this but with a specific other person. I'd tried to force the fairy tale, but maybe it was time to admit I couldn't generate feelings for Ethan when I still had a massive crush on Trey.

At least I tried.

Honestly, Trey was a lot like Ethan—they'd probably get along great—but Ethan wasn't Trey. Ethan didn't read my favorite fantasy novel just because I told him I liked it. He didn't sit with me for hours after Haley Townsend told me I was too pale to be Native. He didn't console me on the shores of the lake by spooning homemade blackberry compote over a whole bucket of ice cream from the freezer at Sandy June's kitchen or join me in mourning my mom's decision to uproot us and move two hours away to her hometown. Trey had done all of those things and more because he was amazing and handsome . . . and I'd had to leave him behind.

I suppressed a sigh. Not only was my first-ever date a dud, but now I had to let Ethan down gently.

"Mia, it was humiliating. My mom made me get onstage and play my trumpet." Ethan gestured to the rear of the drive-in, where the stage faced the curve of the lake. "I was in beginner band, sixth grade, playing for a crowd of legendary grandparents. I sounded horrible. They gave me pity claps."

"What'd you play for them?" I asked.

"'Louie Louie,'" Ethan said, then after a beat, "and maybe the *SpongeBob SquarePants* theme song. But! That's when one of the grandparents brought up dancing and mentioned I should give it a try as another artistic outlet."

I took a drink so I didn't laugh. I'd watched videos of Ethan's dancing. His social media account, ChickaStomp, had tons of followers. It was probably for the best that he picked dance over music. Stomp dancing was popular in the southeastern tribes. His Chickasaw roots shared a lot in common with my Cherokee ones. Trey and I danced, too. It was a wonder we'd never crossed paths with Ethan, especially if he visited Sandy June's as regularly as he claimed.

Dressed in a nice polo (embroidered with our school logo), Ethan chattered on about dancing while I contemplated the best way to break the news to him.

It's not you, it's me. A classic.

The vibe's not there. Honest.

When I look at you, I feel nothing. Brutal.

"Around here, October is the best month for powwows," Ethan continued, taking a sip of his pop. "The weather is perfect, not too cold at night. Dancing in a gym just isn't the same. The drums echo differently. It messes up my rhythm."

I nodded, brushing my fingers over my grandparents' initials as my hands inched toward my phone. It would be rude to check it while he was talking, talking, talking, right? Maybe if I were rude, he would realize it was a bad date. Then he could be the one to say it hadn't worked out.

My foot bounced beneath the picnic table. I wanted to text my cousins for advice. Or do a quick web search for tips on letting someone down. Heck, an AI app might have a suggestion.

I decided to risk it. While Ethan went to fetch us refills, I scrolled through my message contacts. I'd just gotten to my cousin group chat (right below Trey's info) and selected it when Ethan set my Coke in front of me.

"You sure you don't want a milkshake? Sandy June's makes great milkshakes."

My chest tightened. This was *Sandy June's*. It was special.

During high school in the seventies, my grandparents' eyes met over the giant vat of vegetable oil (for frying up frybread) while

"Come and Get Your Love" played over the radio, and that was it—they lived happily ever after.

I longed for happily ever after, and, even more, I longed for it to start at Sandy June's. Every time Trey and I visited, my imagination begged for it. Once, we'd teamed up to teach a group of Red Lake rez kids how to play Cherokee marbles out on the dock, and Trey had given me this *look*. The sort of look that seemed obvious, even for me, who struggled to pick up on anything subtle. I'd thought he might kiss me, but it had been only a few days since we'd found out my mom and I were moving. I didn't respond fast enough, his face had shuttered, and the moment was gone.

"Sandy June makes them herself?" I pushed away my wandering agonies and shot Ethan a smile. "Or himself? You sure about that?"

"Well, Mia." He shrugged playfully. "It's what they say."

He was trying. He was really trying. I forced a laugh and shook my head.

Ethan plopped down on the picnic bench opposite mine. He glanced at my half-finished plate of fries and then at me. My chance to send an SOS text was gone. Or was it? I asked, "Could you tell me more about hunting with your cousins?"

While Ethan droned on about shooting ducks (it was all very fascinating), I snuck a peek at the keyboard toward the bottom of my phone screen and tapped out: **Hey, advice on how to let someone down after a bad date?**

I gave it a few seconds, but no dots appeared. Crap.

Suddenly, I realized Ethan had stopped talking and was waiting for me to finish.

"Um, do you need a second to reply to someone?" he asked, his expression pinched.

"Nope!" I put my phone facedown beside me on the table, right over my grandparents' initials. Ethan had been kind, polite, fine. None of this was his fault.

Stars shone above. The moon and neon sign glowed. Every time my grandparents came here, they sat at this table with two forks, one NDN taco, and the same moony expressions as all those years ago. Their story painted a sappy, romantic picture that I'd idolized. And if Trey had been with me instead of Ethan . . . *No, stop it!* I told myself. *What's the point of daydreaming about him, especially now?*

"You certainly seem distracted," Ethan pointed out.

I tilted my chin in a solemn nod. "Sorry, it's not . . ." I was being rude. Honest couldn't be worse than rude. "Back home, there's someone I've been into for a long time. It's one of those one-sided . . . Anyway, I thought I was over him. When you asked me out, I told myself, *Here's a nice guy.* . . . Seriously, thank you for showing me around and introducing me to the other section leaders during summer band. You noticed my discomfort when no one else did."

Ethan gave me a tight, flat smile. Right. Not amused.

I needed to get to the point. "I thought I could move on, but . . . Well, I can pay for myself."

"Nah, I've got it." Ethan stood and offered me a polite hand to help me up.

Many silent moments later, Ethan parked behind my mom's old SUV and said, "Good luck with . . . whoever."

I cringed at his tone, tinged with the tiniest bit of sarcasm, as I walked to my front door. He'd kept his feelings to himself until the final moment. That was noble of him. I could appreciate it. I waved and forced a pleasant expression before ducking inside. At least he waited for me to be safe before he left. Still a gentleman, albeit a disappointed one.

Rubbing my nose, I checked my phone.

Not many messages, which was surprising. I'd assumed that, after my question, the group chat would have blown up. Then I went numb, realizing why. I'd fumbled the text.

Instead of the group chat, I'd accidentally texted Trey. He'd tapped an exclamation point on my text and replied: **You went on a date???**

As soon as I replied to Trey that I'd made it home, he video-called me.

"You went out on a date?" Trey asked again. He held his phone above him on his bed. The blue comforter beneath him was covered with Star Wars ship schematics.

The last thing I wanted to do was talk about tonight's date. Sure, for about five seconds, I'd contemplated sending him outfit pics and asking which one made me look best. I fantasized that the conversation—and the sight of me modeling this pink floral sundress—would inspire Trey to reveal his own hidden romantic feelings and beg me not to go. But no. No way did I have the nerve for that. I collapsed into the pile of my stuffed animals on my bed and tugged my favorite (Rumble, the OKC Thunder bison mascot) into my arms.

"Tonight was my first. Date, that is. First date." Why did I say that? Trey should know that. Did he want me to elaborate? I didn't want to elaborate. "It didn't work out."

Was he hurt that I hadn't told him? We were still best friends, after all. He kind of looked put out. His lips were pinched and twisted.

"Well, then!" he exclaimed. "We need to go on a date, too!"

"What?" My heart skipped. "You mean, together?"

"For practice," Trey added, as if that made the idea any more reasonable. "If you've got experience, you need to share it with me."

Was this happening? How could this be happening?

"I know just where to take you." Trey flicked his wavy dark hair out of his face. "I'll dress up, go all out, and you can give me pointers."

"Pointers," I echoed. He did hear me say the date didn't work out, didn't he? What sort of pointers did he think I could give? "Where?" I asked, already knowing the answer.

"Sandy June's, of course," Trey said. "Logistically, it's the easiest place for us to meet. Plus, you've always said it's the perfect date destination."

I did always say that. Trey didn't drone on about duck hunting. Trey *listened* to me. He *heard* me. I liked him *so* much. I didn't want to settle for a fake date. I wanted to ask, *Who are you practicing for?* A fake date might be the closest we ever got to a real one.

"Mia?" he nudged. "You okay?"

No. No, I'm not. Over the summer, my mom moved me two hours away from Trey and my friends and from Owasso to Sallisaw. Yeah, I'm closer to Granny Mary and Grandpa Jimmy, which I love—don't get me wrong. Sure, it's all Cherokee Nation, but that's an hour and a half to two hours away from Trey, if you drive, which I don't. Now he wants us to go on a pretend date, which is ridiculous, and his calling it "practice" makes it perfectly, officially clear that he does not see me in the least bit romantically. Mortifying.

"Fine," I managed, kicking off my sandals. "Of course. Let's do that."

A whippoorwill called from the distance, bugs dive-bombed my ears, and I stood in the middle of Grandpa Jimmy's alfalfa field, stalks up to my elbows. I wondered, when they'd directed me this way, if my cousins had been joking. I'd known my way to Sandy June's from my house in Owasso. More than once, I'd opened the storm cellar to the beckon of neon and the scent of buffalo stew. Last weekend, Ethan had driven us there in his uncle's pickup. I wondered if he was always able to locate the drive-in on that same route or if it was more hit-and-miss.

Anyway, I didn't have access to wheels or a license.

"I need you to be patient with me," I told Trey, using my wireless headphones. Miraculously, I hadn't lost service yet, despite wandering deep into the Sequoyah County boonies. "I've gone sixty paces past the pond, and . . . I think my cousins are pranking me."

"Just keep going," he coached. "I checked, and my cousins told me the same thing." Both of us had family in the area—cousins and cousins and cousins. *Enough to create a hive mind and prank the both of us at once*, I thought. Cherokee Nation is one of the largest tribes. If you asked around enough, everyone knew someone in common. It had seemed awfully convenient that an entrance to the drive-in was at the edge of my grandpa's old allotment land.

My yellow Converse sank into an inch of flattened hay, and my sundress did nothing to protect my legs from it tickling my calves and ankles. I shifted my weight, and stalks broke with a satisfying crunch. Then I heard a mouse—a rat?—skitter off to my right.

"You know I wouldn't lead you wrong," Trey said.

I pushed aside alfalfa to reach the edge of the pasture. "What about your cousins?"

"No way," he said. "They know how I feel about you."

As I sucked in a breath, the line went dead. "Trey?" I fished my phone out of my pocket. The call had been dropped. *They know how I feel about you, how I feel about you, how I feel about you.* Trey's words flew around in my head like a trapped bird. *They know how I feel about you, how I feel about you, how I feel about you.* The tree line stood sentinel in front of a long-forgotten wooden fence. For a fleeting moment, I imagined the trees had the answers to all my troubles. I longed for a rabbit or robin to come sing me a song about true love. *They know how I feel about you, how I feel about you, how I feel about you.* But this wasn't a fairy tale.

Most likely, Trey had been referring to our close friendship. Our close, platonic friendship. Of course, that had to be it. The fact that I longed for a romantic spark didn't mean the feeling was mutual, and I had to be fine with that.

A cool breeze raised the hem of my dress, exposing my knees. I reached toward the intertwined branches, their leaves illuminated by the golden hue of the evening sun. Moving forward, I felt—the strange, humming vacuum between here and there.

"Osiyo, Mia." Glowing in the twilight, Trey stepped out from between two redbud trees. Normally, I would have launched myself toward him for a hug.

Would that be weird on a pretend date? Too enthusiastic, too aggressive, too desperate?

Trey wasn't super dressed up—he sported a nice pair of jeans and a crimson-red button-up with an *OU* embroidered on the pocket. "Mia?" he asked. "You okay? Ready to be wooed?"

A giggle slipped out. Our "date" had officially begun. Pretend or not, I felt giddy. Silly. Tempted to fully embrace the fantasy. I couldn't help it. I'd wanted him for so long. Pretending might be the closest I'd ever get. "Wooed?" Such an old-fashioned word. "Wooed how?"

"Like this." Trey caught my hand. He brought it to his lips.

My heart flipped. "Wasn't I supposed to be giving you pointers?"

He straightened and threaded our fingers. "Of course. What should I do next?"

I broke his gaze, pretending to be distracted by fireflies. "Be a gentleman. Escort me in."

Trey let go of my hand, offering me his elbow instead. Gesturing wide, he said, "My lady." Oh my gosh. Was he going to keep this up all night?

Ahead, an engine revved, an AC unit buzzed. Plastic clattered on concrete, and someone cursed in . . . was that Choctaw?

Trey pushed aside the brush, and Sandy June's Legendary Frybread Drive-In came into view. Trey led me to his elisi's vintage golden minivan, parked in one of the stalls, and pressed the button to open the trunk. "Best seat in the house." Inside, a bouquet of colorful flowers, wrapped in plastic (like he'd bought them from Walmart), rested on a neon Pendleton blanket from many a powwow. Trey picked up the flowers, and with an exaggerated bow, held them out.

"Beautiful flowers for, um, a beautiful girl."

Yep. He planned to keep the Prince Charming act up all night. Honestly? I loved it. I could definitely play along. "Wado."

But Trey was waving at someone waiting in line to order. "Be right back. I'm going to say hi. Then we'll figure out food."

Party foul! No ditching a date, especially right after arriving at your destination. Had he lost interest already? Was he off to say hi to whoever we wanted to date for real? As Trey jogged off, I called, "Sure! Meet you at the menu."

Burying my nose in the flowers, I sidestepped a legendary grandparent on roller skates and a couple of guys carrying guitar cases to reach the drive-in menu, posted at the service stall.

I wanted my usual order—an NDN taco, but it was a messy choice. I could say, "Hold the chili," but what was a taco without chili? Worst case, I'd spill it all over my sundress. Plus, my breath would be gross, full of spices and beans. Did it matter? I doubted pretend dates included kissing, and hey, Trey liked NDN tacos, too. We could split one the way my grandparents always did. I turned to look for him and . . .

Oh my God, he was talking to Ethan! Only steps from my grandparents' picnic table, it was duck-hunting Ethan of my failed first-ever date, wearing basketball shorts and a shirt that read *Chickasaw Pride*. As the roller-skating grandparent cruised by, I handed her my bouquet of flowers.

She brightened. "Mahalo, sweetie!"

Sidling up to the chuckling boys, I swallowed my nerves and locked eyes with Ethan. "Whatcha doin' here?" I didn't want him here. I didn't want them to know each other. Were they friends? Good friends? How did I not know one of Trey's good friends? Trey hadn't ever mentioned knowing Ethan when he would share ChickaStomp dance videos with me.

What's more, I didn't need reminders of my failed attempt at moving on.

Ethan was infuriatingly casual about seeing me. He even grinned, causing Trey's head to swivel between us in confusion.

"Hey, Mia," Ethan said. "I didn't realize one failed date would make me lose my Sandy June's privileges."

I tried to laugh with him, but could only focus on the way Trey's face had dropped at Ethan's words.

"Your date was with Ethan? Here?"

"Wait, how do you know her?" Ethan asked.

Trey ignored the question, addressing me. "You've already been on a date to Sandy June's? Mia, this is *our* place. It's been our place since . . . since forever."

Forever indeed. As long as I could remember we'd come here to get away from everyone. Sure, his siblings would tag along sometimes, but they were never a nuisance.

I tried to reassure Trey. "It wasn't the best date."

"Yeah, turns out she's into one of her guy best frien—" Ethan stopped abruptly and had the decency to wince when he caught my panicked expression. "Oh, I get it. He's . . ."

We both knew he'd figured me out. We both said, "Shit."

It took Trey another beat. "Shit."

He knew. Trey *knew*. And now everything would be weird between us, and maybe we wouldn't even be able to stay best friends anymore, which is exactly what I'd wanted to avoid. It's exactly why I'd never come out and told him about my feelings in the first place. My move hadn't come between us—not really—but my stupid heart had. Trey would never bring me his grandma's blackberry compote again.

It was too much. I took off, bolting past the restroom doors and past the mural, and wove between music fans on picnic blankets and in lawn chairs waiting for the concert to start.

My ridiculous daydreams about confessing my true feelings to Trey had always been sprinkled with puns or jokes, strategies for laughing it off without missing a beat, if he wasn't receptive. Nothing like this. Nothing so humiliating as another guy revealing what I felt. So undeniable. So unbearable. In the trees, near the lake, a loose thread dangled from the hem of my sundress. Picking at it, I wondered, how can I make peace with that?

I should leave, I decided. Would I be able to find my way back to my grandparents' house in the dark from the alfalfa field? Maybe there was a back exit. Sandy June's was pretty reliable about spitting you out where you were supposed to be.

What if I dived into the lake? Would that take me to the pond at Grandpa's? A midnight swim in the lake didn't sound bad right then.

One of the girls seated in front of me tilted her head as if to ask if I was all right. She was wearing neon socks that I would never be brave enough to wear myself. Beside her sat a giant Pepsi, and the teeniest, tiniest baby with the biggest, squishiest cheeks. She must have seen the sudden hearts in my eyes, because the girl laughed and grabbed one of the baby's feet to wiggle it in my direction. "I'm Kiki and this is Elora Greer—or EG because I loaded her up with a mouthful of a name. She gives great cuddles," Kiki said. "You need some?"

I did need cuddles. Very much. There weren't tears for me to wipe away, just pure mortification. I sat beside them and held my arms out so Kiki could place Elora Greer in my arms. As I bounced the baby on my lap, Kiki listened to me, patiently catching a dropped pacifier and offering it back to the baby. "And so then, Ethan just had to mention I was hung up on someone." I'm using a gentle voice so as not to agitate the baby. "Trey isn't clueless, he's not, so now he knows, and I'm not sure I can ever talk to him again. Goodbye, blackberry compote."

"Goodbye, blackberry compote," Kiki echoed, politely accepting my version of the story as fact. Her kindness and willingness to listen calmed me down. The sweet baby smell was like the cherry on top.

"His grandma makes it," I explained. "She sells it here. You should try it sometime."

"I'll do that. Would it go great on waffles?" Kiki asked.

I nodded.

We got quiet, only small baby noises between us.

"If you want some advice?" Kiki offered and waited until I signaled it was good. "It sounds like you've got some Disney-fied expectations of Sandy June's—and dating in general. Dreaming is important, but real life, the way it comes at you sideways, is always going to be a surprise." She gestured to Elora Greer. "I know this now. It's all about bending with the journey and not letting the surprises break you. You got this . . . um—"

"Mia." *I'm Mia, and I got this. I got this. I got this.* I was handing Elora Greer back to Kiki when a familiar voice shouted my name.

"Mia!" Having caught the attention of the concert crowd, Trey strode in a near straight line toward me, picnic blankets be damned, stumbling over the edge of the last one, shooting it a dirty look. "I brought you turkey feathers," he said. Then, as if this was a totally normal thing to do, Trey shoved a handful of feathers toward me like it was the bouquet of flowers.

"What?" As I reached to accept them, Trey brought up his other hand, capturing the hollow shafts of the feathers and my hand between both of his own.

My heartbeat thumped in my ears, thumping, thumping, telling me *he knows, he knows*. "They're . . . soft, velvety," I said cautiously, like he was a spooked animal.

Someone's hands were shaking. Not mine.

What was happening?

Trey pressed his lips together. "Bear with me. This is going to be the manliest thing you've ever heard." A couple of aunties to our left chuckled at that, and Trey shot them a dirty look, too. Then he swallowed thickly and refocused on me. "I hunted it myself. We used most of the feathers to make the bustles I wear for dancing . . . but there were some good feathers in the batch, and my mom mentioned, um, 'They'd make a lovely fan,' so I saved them. For you." Someone squealed, and someone else clapped. Elora Greer cooed, and Kiki breathed an *ohmygod*. Trey added, "I saved them to make you a fan. You know my mom beads and . . . We'd match when we dance at pow-wows. And it would be cool to match you. Because—because I—"

"You can do it!" called Ethan, who'd apparently joined our audience.

Again, Trey fumbled after "Because—"

I bit my lip and decided to meet him halfway. "I like you, too."

Trey relaxed like the newly released string of a bow. I tugged him into a familiar hug. His arms came up around me, palms searching awkwardly for a place to settle.

The crowd erupted in cheers and whistles, hoots and hollers, clapping hands and stomping feet. I buried my face in Trey's shoulder, and he rested his chin on top of my head.

Trey said, "I've liked you for a long time. I had a whole plan, your grandparents' picnic table, sharing a taco, I even bought a fake battery-operated candle, but then you said you had to move, and I was scared of what that would mean for us."

"Me, too," I confessed. "I thought things would be too complicated for us to ever get together. . . ."

"We're together now," he assured me. "*Together* together."

Together together. Of course. Trey ran a finger down my cheek before tilting my chin up and pressing his lips softly to mine. From now on, we could always find each other at the Legendary Frybread Drive-In.

LOVE BUZZ
Byron Graves

Dalton pats my back. "You ready, cuz?" He's wearing a T-shirt that his mom made with our band name—the Trixters—on it. The design on the shirt features the bunny from Trix cereal spray-painting the band name on the side of a church.

I nod and go back to practicing my guitar. We have our very first gig tonight and I'm a nervous wreck. What if I mess up the words? Or sing out of key? With my luck, I'll fall off the stage.

I'm having a hard time leaving my parents' garage; there's something comforting about this familiar blend of scents. Dust, motor oil, and boxed-up fishing nets. I strum a couple of chords from a tune I'm hoping to play tonight. It's an upbeat, radio-friendly jam, about the sweetest, coolest, most gorgeous girl I've ever met. Hannah.

I've had a crush on her since forever. She's the head of the student council, and a star volleyball player, and always doing something charitable. But it's usually the good-looking jocks who attract her attention.

Me? I'm a bit of a weirdo. I prefer geeking out on Nintendo or practicing guitar over spending a cold night at a football game. And even if I liked sports, I'd still look out of place. On the Red Lake Ojibwe rez, almost everyone at the high school dresses in Nike or Reebok sports apparel. I dress like I'm in a grunge band and wear distressed jeans and Nirvana or Pearl Jam band shirts, and I always rock a flannel.

That's not the worst part. Chris Cornell of Soundgarden dresses like that and he's a heartthrob. Not me though. I'm shorter than all of my guy classmates, and my black hair is a messy mop that I leave dangling in my face because it's less embarrassing than to show my never-ending array of zits. I'm the complete opposite of the guy that the popular, hot girl at school would ever date.

But hey, I sure can shred on the guitar.

Anyway, the chord progression goes like this: it starts with G major, on a couple of downstrokes. It's a comforting chord, a sound that you can exhale to. Next is D major—it's a chord that reminds me of happiness. I run my guitar pick up and down the strings.

Dalton lumbers by carrying a box of guitar and microphone cords. He ducks under the garage door, but his spiked-up hair gets smushed on the way out.

I strum the E minor chord, softer than the rest of the song. It adds a sound of longing, a brush of sadness.

Dalton walks back in and face-palms. "Please, no. This song again? Not—"

"'Your Valentine Card,'" I say.

"When are you going to give it up? It's too pop. We aren't that type of band."

One last strum through C major, the sound of everything being okay, and I sing the opening line: "This song is your Valentine card. In it are all the words I could never say."

Dalton puts his hands together in prayer and looks up. "Creator?

Please remind Charlie that we're not Duran Duran. We're a heavy rock band."

This is a new problem for us. The type of band we want to be. We've spent four years jamming out in this stinky, dusty garage. But it's only been this summer that we've mastered our instruments. We've played together for countless hours, so much so that we are always in sync.

Always.

Now?

We argue over the genre we want to be.

I put my guitar into the case and click it shut, then study our other bandmate, Awesiinh, who is air drumming. His real name is Ralph, but his parents nicknamed him in Ojibwe after Animal, from the Muppets, because he's been pounding and tapping everything in reach since he was born.

Come to think of it, it's been way more than four years since we've been a band. Well, sort of. When we were in fourth grade, there was a Halloween costume contest at school. But Dalton, Ralph, and I showed up that morning, all dressed as Gene Simmons from KISS. It was awkward and kind of embarrassing.

But Awesiinh had an idea.

At lunch, we switched our face makeup so that we were different members of KISS. We ended up winning the best group contest. So what if the grand prize was lukewarm cans of Pepsi and Snickers bars. To us, it felt like we were champions of the world.

We've been best friends ever since.

"Hey, Awesiinh, you got everything?" I ask. His drum set is

already loaded into the van, but that hasn't stopped him from air drumming, and right now, he's in the zone, apparently daydreaming that he's playing at a sold-out show. His long black hair swirls around him; his toned but rail-thin arms are a blur as he smacks drumsticks on a box of fish tackle, Dad's lawn mower, and the snowshoes I never finished making.

"Aww, seen!" Dalton shouts with a thunderclap like he's the Incredible Hulk.

Awesiinh jolts, dropping his sticks.

"Jeez." Awesiinh shakes his head and points at the dusty cement floor of my parents' garage. "Yeah, dude. It's not like I could forget the freaking drum set." His drum kit has left behind clean imprints.

Awesiinh picks up his drumsticks, twirls one in his hand, then taps my shoulder with it. "'Your Valentine Card' sounds a little too much like that Poison song 'Every Rose Has Its Thorn.' Did you really write that song for my cousin Hannah? You know I could just ask her if she likes you?"

I flash back to that time in seventh grade when I got to school early and slipped a poem I wrote into Hannah's desk, but she didn't show up that day. Her best friend found it while borrowing some markers. She announced her findings to the class, then read it aloud while everyone giggled. Hannah returned the next week, and everyone was still joking about it. Hannah didn't join in on the teasing, but she also never said anything about it.

I shudder. "Please don't ever ask Hannah if she likes me." I snatch Awesiinh's drumstick. "And for the last time, every rock band has its one pop hit to help propel them to superstardom."

"Let's not go there again," Dalton says.

I toss Awesiinh his drumstick back. "We have to play 'Your Valentine Card' tonight. The crowd will eat it up," I say.

"*We'll* probably get eaten up. By the bears and wolves in the woods. Sure as heck ain't going to be any people back there." Dalton grunts as he picks up his amp.

"Want to bet?" I ask.

Dalton sets the amp back down. "Bet what?"

"That Sandy June's *is* real."

"Okay. This is going to be an easy one." Dalton crosses his arms and grins. "I'm in. What are the stakes?"

Awesiinh throws his arms around us. "Aye, I might want in on this bet, too."

"If—I mean *when*—I prove that it's a real place, you guys have to play 'Your Valentine Card' as our opening song," I say.

Awesiinh and Dalton share a glance, and for a second, I think they're finally, for the first time, honestly considering playing my song. But then they bust out laughing. Like knee-slapping, bent-forward cackling and howling.

Between gasps, Dalton asks, "What do we win if it's not a real place?"

I look down at my beat-up Chuck Taylor high-tops. "I'll forget all about that song, and we'll only play heavy music."

Dalton shakes my hand and squeezes hard. "Deal."

"We better get going." I flick the light switch off, lead them to the open garage door, and pause. It's that time of year. It gets dark out so fast.

Mom, Dad, and their friends huddle around the firepit in the front yard. Dad kneels and turns up his radio. A Redbone song blasts so loud the whole rez can jam along.

I reach up and shut the garage door. "All right. You guys ready to go play our very first show or what, then?" Scrappy, my little mutt, spots us and runs over. I scratch the back of his ears.

Dalton adjusts the strap of his bass guitar slung over his shoulder. "At a place no one has ever heard of or seen."

"I've seen it." I stand and Scrappy joins me in mean mugging Dalton. "Not once, but twice."

Dalton shrugs. "Oh yeah. Just like the summer before seventh grade, when we took my grandpa's tents out to the shore, and you swore you saw a UFO skimming along the lake."

"I did see . . . something fast. If you two wouldn't have fallen asleep so early, you would have seen it, too."

"And there was the time you spotted Sabe," Awesiinh says, scratching the back of his head.

"I never said it was Sabe for sure. Just something big, furry, and walking on its hind legs by the creek."

"Sounds like Awesiinh's mom," Dalton says, and playfully punches his arm.

"Your mom," Awesiinh says with the weakest comeback we know.

We wave goodbye to my parents and their friends, and Dad whistles to Scrappy, who runs to join them. We hop in the family van, in all its rusted-out glory. I flick the tree-shaped air freshener, hoping it will fight the stench of the ashtray filled with Dad's cigarette butts, spilled soda, and forgotten fast-food wrappers that litter the floor. The engine coughs and barks, but it starts up. Ralph and Dalton wrestle over the front seat, with Dalton eventually muscling his way in.

We take off down the curvy dirt road that leads to the highway. The pine trees crowd the van, like they're trying to keep us from leaving. The moon is giant, bright, and a movie-theater-butter yellow. It looks magical—assuring me the portal to Sandy June's will be open tonight.

We head west to cruise along the highway, listening to Kurt Cobain sing and scream. A pack of rez dogs trot along a four-wheeler path in the ditch. Younger kids ride their bikes. Some play-fight with sticks or climb on broken-down swing sets.

Awesiinh leans over from the back seat and turns the music down. "So where in the heck is this place?"

"I told you. It's not always there." My hands get clammy. I can't imagine how much crap these guys are going to give me if we don't find Sandy June's. I can picture us being Elders at a powwow, me still hearing about it.

"So, it's like that really good lemonade stand at the powwows during the summer?" Awesiinh plays with some seat cushion stuffing that's poking out of a hole in the passenger seat. "Only on our rez for those magical couple of days?"

"Sort of. Except, when you get there, you've gone somewhere else. Somewhere that isn't here."

Awesiinh tries to push the stuffing back into the seat. "What did you say it was called?"

"Sandy June's Legendary Frybread Drive-In," I reply.

Dalton rolls his eyes. "Okay, *Indian* Jones." Dalton turns back and looks at Awesiinh. "This guy thinks he's going to lead us to the Holy Grail."

The ding of the gas-tank alert shuts us up. "Damn. My mom is always driving around on empty. Do you guys have any money?"

"Nope," Awesiinh and Dalton answer.

With one hand on the steering wheel, I pat down my pockets, hoping some cash will magically appear the way Sandy June's does. On the western edge of our rez, I pull into Beaulieu's Gas and Café and smack the dashboard of the van. "We're so close. We've worked too hard."

"Aye, look. It's your crush." Dalton nudges me and points at Hannah, walking out of the gas station with a backpack slung over her shoulder.

Hannah pauses as a couple of dudes on four-wheelers roar by her, slamming to a stop at the fuel pump.

"Shut up." I elbow Dalton.

Hannah spots us, waves, and starts walking over. She's wearing a frayed concert shirt and skintight blue jeans. Her once jet-black curly hair has been dyed blond.

"Let's see if my cuz can spot us some gas money," Awesiinh says.

"No way, dude. I don't want her to know that I'm a zitty loser *and* broke as hell," I say.

I mean, come on. Hannah is the most popular girl at school. And I'm in a band that no one has ever heard of.

"Here she comes. What's it going to be? Run out of gas on the way home or we ask to borrow a few bucks?" Dalton asks.

Dalton crushes me as he leans over and waves out my window. "Hey, Hannah."

Awesiinh peeks out from behind my seat. "What up, cuz?"

"Boozhoo." She nods at the guys. Her eyes settle on me, and my stomach churns. "Hey, Charlie."

"Hey, Hannah."

"What's up with the backpack?" Awesiinh asks.

Hannah unzips it and hands it to me through the van window. Inside are beautiful, beaded key chains.

"My mom and older sister made these. I'm in charge of selling them. We're raising money for the Elder care program. We want to get them stuff for arts and crafts and activity nights."

"You're the best," I say. The words spill out. Can't believe I said that, especially in front of the guys.

Hannah smiles and shrugs. "Nah, my mom and sis did all the hard work."

"You should roll with us. We're going to play a show. Natives from all over will be there, according to this guy," Awesiinh says as he pats my shoulder. "Bet you could sell all those there, cuz."

"Seriously? That would be great! I still have a lot of money to raise," Hannah says.

"Only one catch, though," Awesiinh adds. "This guy is too bashful to say anything, but in order for us to play this once-in-a-lifetime gig, we need your help."

With a knowing look on her face, Hannah gives me a smile. She's used to me being too shy to speak up. "Oh yeah, what's that?"

"Gas money. Could you spot us five bucks?" I ask as fast as I can, like ripping off a Band-Aid.

"Well, duh." Hannah hands over a five-dollar bill. As I'm putting gas in the van, Hannah demands shotgun and forces Dalton to the back.

Wow. That was easy. Wish I was as bold as she is.

We hit the road and are cruising again.

Hannah holds a Twizzlers candy stick up to my face. "Here. I owe you something actually yummy. The last candy I gave you was terrible, chalky-tasting."

I grab a Twizzlers stick and take a bite. "Miigwech. Oh, and I loved it. More than any candy I've ever had."

I steal a glance at Hannah. Red licorice dangles in one hand, her head is tilted to the side, and her eyes have sharpened. I smile and look back at the road. I'm guessing she didn't know if I meant that sarcastically or if it was something deeper.

Last February, when my grandpa moved on to the Happy Hunting Grounds, I was having a tough time. I wasn't eating or sleeping much and was even quieter than normal. Then one day in science class, I was sitting in the back row, totally zoned out. Hannah walked in and sat down next to me.

She didn't say anything.

But right before the bell, she dug into her backpack and handed over a Valentine card and a box of Sweethearts candy, the chalky kind with the messages on them. I opened the card, and she had written a note.

> *I'm sorry about your grandpa. I hope you feel better soon. Enjoy the candy.*

That was the day my puppy love, my silly crush for her, changed into something else. Something I don't quite understand. Like quantum physics, Einstein's theory of relativity, or how to flirt.

Hannah chomps on a Twizzlers stick. "So, where's this place? Like a basement party?"

"Nope. Way cooler than that. Tell her, Charlie," Awesiinh says.

Eyes on the road, I grip the steering wheel. "It's called Sandy June's."

Hannah gestures with the package to the back of the van, offering the guys some Twizzlers. "Never heard of it."

The van headlights shine on a deer grazing next to the dirt road that led to Sandy June's on my previous couple of visits.

I turn onto the road, and everyone is quiet. We cruise over branches, rocks, and large potholes. The van buoys like a boat on a stormy lake until we finally reach the spot. I park and turn off the engine.

"So where's this place?" Hannah asks.

"Over there." I point at an overgrown dirt path. I'm super grateful for the moonlight. It's so bright that it almost feels like daytime. We hop out of the van. Hannah offers to carry my guitar so I can help Awesiinh with his drum kit.

I lead the way, calling out when to duck, twist, and turn past sharp branches that reach out for us like zombie fingers. Dalton sighs. Awesiinh grunts. I check on Hannah. Trucking along, she smiles, showing those amazing dimples. Her green eyes shine with curiosity.

Finally, the path opens to a broad clearing. The moon is hanging along the edge of the tree line, just like the last two times. A few more steps, and we're through the brush. With the blink of an eye, the dirt path changes to worn-out asphalt.

There it is.

Ahead, in the distance, is Sandy June's. I can hear laughter and smell smoking meat. Hannah's, Dalton's, and Awesiinh's jaws drop; their eyes widen. I fight laughter. Knots in my stomach loosen up.

"May I present to you all . . . Sandy June's Legendary Frybread Drive-In!" I say with an over-the-top gesture and point to the lit-up neon sign. The word *Legendary* stands out in yellow; the rest of the words are green. "They don't call it Turtle Island's Best-Kept Secret for nothing." Yeah, after all the years of teasing about my imagination, I'd been saving that line for this very moment.

"What. Is. This. Place?" Hannah asks as we walk toward an awning. Underneath, people are seated at green wooden picnic tables, chowing down and chatting. Awesiinh stops walking, so we all stop. He sets down his kick drum and runs a hand across an old-fashioned muscle car, the way someone would lovingly pet their cat.

"Come on. We can buy some cars like that when we get our first big record deal," Dalton tells Awesiinh, and we continue walking.

We pass by the seating area and spot the front counter. There are two ordering lines and handmade signs hanging above each. In bold

Sharpie, one sign says "Coke," the other "Pepsi."

Dalton nearly drops his bass guitar. "Whoa . . ."

"It's an Indian taco stand," I say proudly, like I'm part owner. "Well, not just tacos—the menu changes up, but they serve different kinds of Indigenous foods and typical American stuff, too. This place, it's one of a kind."

A couple of kids race past us in hot pursuit of a rez dog with a piece of frybread in its mouth.

"I'm sorry, Charlie. Maybe there really are UFOs and Sabe, too," Awesiinh says.

A legendary grandparent approaches, wiping his hands on his apron. "Hey, are you guys the entertainment?"

"We're the Trixters," I announce.

Dalton points at his shirt. "With an *X*."

"You guys must really like cereal. Come on, I'll show you the stage."

We pick up our equipment and follow along past the building and to the stage. A crowd is already gathering, mostly on picnic blankets and lawn chairs, between the lake and the campgrounds.

"Aye, check this out. There's a Battle of the Bands next weekend. We should enter," Awesiinh says, pointing at a flyer.

"How about we play our *first* show first?" Dalton says.

A couple around my age are lounging on a neon-colored Pendleton blanket, sipping from milkshakes and staring at each other like they're hypnotized. I hear the cutie in the sundress call her boyfriend "Trey."

I daydream about being like that with someone, someday. Maybe Hannah, if I'm lucky. She's looking at them, too, longingly. Hannah catches me watching her, and we maintain eye contact longer than we ever have. She looks at me like she's trying to solve a puzzle.

A young Black woman with big, beaded earrings pushing a stroller stops right in front of us. The baby coos. There's a guy with them, skinny but tall, wearing a vest covered in patches, some beadwork, too. The guy looks at Hannah and clears his throat. "We heard you're selling beaded key chains. That is, if you're Hannah."

Hannah nods, unzipping her backpack and handing a couple of key chains to the guy. "I'm raising money for the Elder care program back on our rez. My mom and sister beaded those."

"I'm Cam. This is my cousin Kiki." Cam hands one of the key chains—it's red, orange, and yellow, fire colors—to his cousin.

"Your mom and sis have skills," Kiki says, rolling the key chain around in one hand while pushing the stroller back and forth.

"This little one right here is beautiful." Hannah leans over the stroller and makes baby sounds.

"That's Elora Greer. We call her EG."

"Hey, EG. You're adorable."

"Can I get four?" Cam laughs. "Key chains, I mean? Not babies."

"Four? Really? Yes, that's amazing. Thank you!" Hannah opens up her backpack, and Cam sorts through the key chains, searching for the four that call to him.

"Miigwech," Hannah says.

Cam hands over worn Canadian bills. "My sisters and my mom are going to love these. And . . ." He pauses. "Bee will, too."

Kiki laughs, dragging her cousin toward the food. "Lover boy, let's get something to eat. I'm starved."

They wave goodbye.

Hannah zips up her backpack and slings it over her shoulder. "That's a great start to the night."

I hold up a hand and she gives me a high five.

"Aye, there he is. The rock star." A familiar-looking legendary grandfather waves me over. He's wearing his same navy bandana and still has his black hair in neat braids. I set down a kick drum and step onto the wide, flat wooden stage that is about the height of a crate. He asks, "Ready to perform tonight? I'm feeling a buzz in the air about your music."

"We're ready," I say. "My band and I have been practicing non-stop. I even wrote a catchy song like you asked."

Amazing that we first met four years earlier. That evening at Sandy June's—talking to him while we listened to a Kickapoo blues band—inspired me to become a musician.

He starts setting up our mics. "That's great! I knew I saw something special in you. I've had this concert on the books ever since that day. Did you draft a rider?"

"A what?" I ask, sidestepping a cord.

He laughs like a shopping-mall Santa Claus. "Let your band know that you get free food and drinks tonight."

I don't recall paying for a meal on either of my previous visits, but why seem ungrateful by mentioning it? "They'll be stoked. I've been bragging about the frybread here for years."

"Good. Just don't ever tell your grandmothers, mom, or deadly aunties that it's better than theirs." He wags a finger at me. "They don't like that."

After introductions and a sound check, we are almost set up. Dalton tunes his bass guitar. "I didn't think there would be this many people here."

Awesiinh steadies his snare drum. "You also didn't think this place existed."

"This is so exciting. My nerves are running wild, and I'm not even performing." Hannah puts a hand on my shoulder. "I can't imagine how you feel."

"Super nervous. We've never played for anyone. Well, except for the neighbor's cat, oh, and my mom once. And she told me, 'Well, Charlie, it's not like Bob Dylan could really sing, either.'"

"Just find me in the crowd, okay. That might help. Look at someone you know, instead of strangers." Hannah grabs and holds up the cord to my guitar.

"Might want to plug this into the amp." She handles it herself, gives me a wink, and jumps off the front of the stage.

I adjust my guitar strap and do a mic check. A sound guy turns a couple of dials, then gives a thumbs-up.

I glance back at Dalton on my left, Awesiinh to the right and farther behind us. "You guys ready?"

With a grimace, Dalton says, "You were right, bro. You won the bet. Let's kick this off with your poppy song."

I laugh. "That looked like it hurt to admit."

"It hurt a little. Okay, a lottle," Dalton replies. It's an old joke from when we were little kids, and we all chuckle.

I clear my throat. My lungs feel empty. My palms, clammy.

"Boozhoo," I begin, my shaky voice ringing out. "We are . . .

the . . . Trixters." I freeze up and panic. Feels like I forgot everything. The words to the songs. How to play guitar. Oh no. Everyone is staring at me.

A waving hand in the crowd. Hannah. She smiles, gives me two thumbs-ups and a look that says, *you got this*. I mouth "Miigwech" to her, take a deep breath, stay focused. "Our friend Hannah right here is selling these beautiful beaded key chains to raise money for Elders back on our rez." I point to Hannah. "Stop and check them out when you get a chance."

Hannah gives me prayer hands with a smile and watery eyes.

I smile. And suddenly, I feel okay.

"This first song is called 'Your Valentine Card.'"

The crowd cheers and whistles, and a million little lightning bolts shoot through my body. Awesiinh taps his snare and I strum my guitar. Dalton claps in sync, beckoning the crowd to join him. Most of the audience climbs to their feet, and they all bring their hands together to the mid-tempo, steady beat. Dalton hits the first couple of bass chords, and everyone starts to sway. A couple of aunties in front slide their hips into each other and laugh.

Two more measures until my opening line. Music flows through me.

One measure to go.

My lungs fill with air and excitement. I find Hannah again, and sing to her, the words I've always been too afraid to say.

JILLY BEAN AND JESSA JEAN

Angeline Boulley

The way I heard it, I owe my very existence to Sandy June's Legendary Frybread Drive-In. Seriously! And I'm not the only one. There are multiple generations of rez kids whose parents met up at Sandy June's and, well, let's just say the frybread oil wasn't the only thing that was smoking hot.

"Eww, J. J.," Jillian says.

We carry wooden condiment baskets to place on the green picnic tables under the awning.

I shrug. "No diff than all dem Haskell Rascals running around."

"I beg your pardon?"

My cousin sounds like she's sixteen going on forty.

"Haskell Indian Nations University?" I watch for any sign of comprehension. "Tribal college in Kansas? Gramma Liz's best friend Barb went there?" Still nothing. "Nishnaabs from all over Turtle Island studying and hooking up."

Her perfectly groomed eyebrows rise quizzically.

I speak slowly. "Native Americans from across North America attending college and, ahem, engaging in extracurricular activities."

Jillian blinks. "Sex!" Her outburst draws attention from a car pulling into a parking spot. Our first customers of the day. The car of rowdies hoot and holler their approval.

"Shh," I whisper. "Yeah, and some named their binoojiins—their Haskell Rascals—after the buildings on campus: Winona, Sequoyah, Tommany."

"So, you're saying people who come to this drive-in on dates and end up pregnant, they name their kids after the menu items?" She glances at the handmade menu sign.

That's not at all what I was saying. I'm about to spout off until an echo of Gramma Liz's raspy voice reminds me to take it easy on my cousin. *Being here for the entire summer is different than visiting for a long weekend. And listen to what she has to say! You're such a chatterbox. You never listen, Jessa Jean.*

"I was pointing out that Sandy June's is a major hookup spot, and you haven't shown interest in anyone." Truthfully, I don't care, but Parker Kingfisher begged me to put in a good word for him. And it never hurts to have a line cook owe you a favor.

"But . . . why would I?" Jillian sounds genuinely perplexed. "I don't have anything in common with anyone here."

This is what you need to know about my cousin:

1. Our moms are sisters. Not twins, technically speaking, but eleven months apart is practically the same thing. Gramma Liz dressed them identically and even made their names rhyme. Jessa and Tessa. Auntie Jessa, who is Jillian's mom and my namesake, is the younger one. She left the rez after high school, went to college, met Uncle Bret, and now they live in Alexandria, Virginia. Auntie makes a point of saying, "*Old Town* Alexandria," so people will know it's the posh area with homes that are on the historic register.

They come back a few times each year for weddings, funerals, powwows, and other family gatherings.

2. We used to be as close as twins. Jilly Bean and Jessa Jean. Her middle name isn't Bean (it's Elizabeth), but our family likes rhyming names for dynamic duos. She and I were inseparable—literally—her golden brown beachy waves interwoven with my dark brown hair in one shared, thick braid. We spent one summer, our heads practically fused together, reading *Twilight* over and over. We'd recite Bella's and Edward's dialogue aloud, our throats hoarse from overuse.

3. Last summer, Jilly Bean insisted on being called Jillian. It was the start of her morphing into the same kind of snob that Mom accuses Auntie Jessa of being. Like, yesterday at work when a jumbo-sized Pepsi spilled all over her T-shirt, she refused my spare shirt because it was a cotton-poly blend instead of something called OEKO-TEX certified organic cotton.

4. Jillian is spending the summer with us because Mom knows how to win fights. Aunt Jessa had invited me to Old Town Alexandria but made the mistake of saying it was to show me the world beyond Munising, Michigan. Mom got ticked off at the implication that I was the rez equivalent of a country mouse getting to see the big city. So, she challenged Auntie to send the city mouse here instead and promised me for the next summer. The irony is that Jillian is the sheltered little mouse, not me.

5. Gramma Liz, who is one of the legendary grandparents (and has the beaded name tag to prove it), arranged for Jillian to work at the drive-in with me as carhops, which means that I am stuck 24/7

with my cousin, who is both snooty and weirdly naive about stuff. I assume the private school she attends in Old Town Alexandria is run by Lilly Pulitzer–clad nuns. When we were the dynamic duo of Jilly Bean and Jessa Jean, my cousin's visits flew by so quickly. More than once, our moms had to pull us apart in order to get Jilly Bean in the car for the drive to the airport. Now that we are Jillian and J. J.—and have nothing in common—time is dragging. The summer is half over, but it feels never-ending. It's like my cousin is tethered to me by an invisible braid that we cannot unravel until Labor Day.

Parker pesters me about Jillian each time I collect an order from the pass-through window.

"C'mon, J. J., you pinkie-promised you'd do it today."

"Sheesh, Parker. It's not even noon." I busy myself with rearranging the wrapped bison burgers on the tray. I sniff the wrappers. "You forget the onions? 'X' means extra."

He groans before motioning for the tray back through the window.

I've known Parker Kingfisher my entire life. Like everyone on our small reservation, we grew up calling each other cousin whether it was a blood fact or not.

When I turned thirteen, Gramma Liz started giving details on every boy. *That one's related to you. Him, too. Not him, different dads—don't repeat that.* When she pointed out Parker, it was with a warning. *He's not related. But that older brother of his is a troublemaker.*

Parker hands the tray back. He laughs when I sniff the rewrapped burgers. My eyes water. There's more onion than meat now.

"I said I'll mention you. Shift ends at seven. I'll do it by then." I turn to go.

He calls after me. "You pinkie-promised!"

As the afternoon flies by, Parker's expression goes from eager, hopeful puppy to sad, dejected old dog. Finally, I can't take it anymore. During the brief lull between the late-lunch rush and the early-bird dinner rush, I wait for Jillian outside the bathroom like a stalker.

"Battle of the Bands tonight, hey?" I say as soon as she opens the door.

She startles. "Battle of the Bands? Tonight? Here?"

Now her expression perfectly balances cluelessness and disinterest. How did she miss all the posters advertising the big event?

"Come back with me tonight after we clock out," I spell it out for her.

Jillian scrunches her nose like a rabbit. I snort a laugh. This prompts a raised eyebrow in addition to the nose twitching.

"What," she asks suspiciously.

"It's fun," I assure her. "Just listening to music. There are legendary grandparents who dance to anything bluegrass or old-school country music."

My cousin shakes her head as if she's been offered a plate of fish guts.

Sorry, Parker. I swear I tried.

Mom had first told me about our summer guest one night while I cleared the dinner table.

"Oh, goody. A summer of 'Jillian.'" I added air quotes around her name. A summer job at Sandy June's was already going to cut into my beach time. It wasn't fair that my formerly-fun-but-now-boring cousin would turn beach time into boring time. That was even before I found out that Jillian was going to work at the drive-in with me.

Gramma Liz started in on me. "Yous two used to be partners in crime."

"I'm not the one who turned into a snob," I muttered to the sink full of dirty dishes.

"You sure about that?" Gramma sassed back.

After we clock out and head home, I try again. I wait for Jillian to finish her after-work shower. She jumps back, startled yet again, when I practically pounce on her.

"Okay," I admit. "I want you to come to Battle of the Bands because Parker Kingfisher wants to hang with us."

"The cook who smells like onions?"

"He doesn't always smell like that." I laugh. "He's fun."

This time her wrinkled nose ticks me off.

"What?" I challenge. "You allergic to fun?"

Jillian recoils as if my tone was a slap. Something flashes in her eyes.

"Being at the drive-in with no pay?" She says it like an accusation. "Hanging out with the cook guy or anyone else we work with? Voluntarily listening to bad music while swatting at black flies?" She scoffs. "Not my idea of fun, J. J."

I think about how eager Parker was all day, hoping I'd come

through for him so he could talk to Jillian about things not pertaining to a food order.

"Well, what is your idea of fun, Jillian?" I drawl her fancy name. "Because acting superior to everybody and hibernating in my bedroom reading *Twilight* for the millionth time is only making your summer last an eternity."

I don't stick around for her response. Three seconds later I'm racing down the path behind my house. The trail through the woods leads to the edge of the parking lot at Sandy June's.

Back when we were the dynamic duo of Jilly Bean and Jessa Jean, we spent hours playing in these woods. As I run along the trail, I imagine us at different ages. At five, we carried lunch boxes filled with our Polly Pocket figurines, their tiny rubber outfits, and their shoes no bigger than a Tic Tac mint. We built their fairy homes out of birch-bark and flowers. At nine, we hauled a backpack filled with apples and books to read beneath pine trees that provided shelter from the summer heat. A few years later, we were obsessed with *Twilight* and debating whether we were Team Edward or Team Jacob.

Last summer Jilly Bean announced her preference to go by Jillian. I thought she was joking until she repeatedly corrected me. My cousin seemed so different. She talked about clothes. A lot. Everything about Old Town Alexandria was superior to the Upper Peninsula. It was a short ride on "the Metro" to Washington, DC—and all the museums, shops, theater, and coffee shops. My Jilly Bean was gone and in her place was Jillian, who griped about not being able to find any iced caramel macchiato lattes made with oat milk.

"Who even is she?" I grumbled to Gramma Liz.

Gramma shrugged. "She's just trying on different hats to see which ones fit."

Maybe Gramma Liz mentioned something to my cousin, the stranger, because Jillian started talking about *Twilight*. As if that was a way back to our friendship. But I had left the series behind after our Tribal Youth Council debated whether it was appropriate for a non-Native author to use elements of an actual tribe's cultural teachings without their permission. Our Tribal Youth Council adviser had pointed out that the real tribe named in the story hadn't received any compensation. Parker Kingfisher and I were on the same side of the debate that a tribe had the right to authorize the use of their name, like with copyright protections.

I told Jillian about the Tribal Youth Council debates and the research our adviser made us do to support whatever side we were on. I was surprised when Jillian hadn't automatically agreed with me, even after I repeated the information Parker and I had used in our winning argument. Surprised and angry. After all, I was right. Why wouldn't she agree with me?

Parker Kingfisher's face lights up when I emerge from the woods. He looks around, realizes it's just me, and becomes one sad puppy. I walk over to the colorful woven serape he's repurposed as a picnic blanket.

"Sorry, Park, I tried," I offer, before sitting next to him.

The first band finishes setting up. Parker's grandpa Ernie blows into the microphone.

"Testing. Testing. One, two, three," Ernie Kingfisher says.

"Boozhoo. Or as they say in my village, 'aaniin.' Welcome to Sandy June's. Me and my buddies, the Grand Island Boys, have the honor of kicking off tonight's battle. We won so many times we took ourselves out of the competition to give them young ones a chance."

With that, Ernie raises a fiddle to rest beneath his chin. The Grand Island Boys launch into the opening chords to "Walking the Floor Over You." A few Elders amble toward the dance floor in front of the stage.

Parker disappears sometime after the third band takes the stage. Gramma Liz finishes her shift early and walks over to me.

"Where's your partner in crime?" she asks, staring down at me.

I glance around. "Parker was here a minute ago."

"Not that boy," Gramma Liz says huffily. "Jillian."

I shrug. "I invited her, but . . ."

Gramma makes a *humph* sound.

"She doesn't want to do anything," I protest. "What am I supposed to do, babysit her?"

"You try talking? Or, better yet, listening?" Gramma scolds. When I don't answer, she scoffs again before joining her friends on the dance floor.

The next band is setting up when I sense someone next to me.

"I don't think I'm superior." Jillian's voice is small. "But I do feel . . . different."

There are at least a dozen ways she is different this summer compared to previous visits. But Gramma Liz's admonishment is still in the air, so I try the listening thing instead.

"It's just that I don't feel like I fit in here, around you and your friends."

"But I invited you tonight," I point out. "Parker, too."

"You both ganged up on me last time."

"What?" Now she's making stuff up. "That never happened, Jillian."

"Yes, it did. When I didn't agree with you and him about *Twilight*. You said I wasn't Native enough."

"I never said that!"

"You said that real Native people would understand why the *Twilight* author shouldn't have used that tribe's name in the book."

I try to remember the conversation from, like, a month ago.

"I said the author shouldn't have used the real tribe's name without their permission."

"You said that Native Americans who don't think anything is wrong with sports team mascots and books and movies that use Native imagery without permission, that those Natives are not as connected to their tribes."

"But I didn't mean you."

"Didn't you, J. J.? When I didn't agree, you ganged up on me."

I stare at Jillian. She remembered bits and pieces of a conversation and twisted things around. It's like we heard two very different conversations.

But the more I recall about the exchange, the more I remember being in full-blown debate mode. No one makes as many good points in the allotted debate time as I can. Parker once told me he'd rather be my debate partner even if he didn't agree with my position, just so he'd never have to go against me. I took his comment as a compliment. But was it?

"I didn't mean it as a judgment," I say, realizing that however I had intended my words at the time, it wasn't how Jillian received them.

Neither of us says anything. We remain seated on the makeshift blanket. The band begins their set, but I'm lost in my thoughts. I replay other conversations from earlier this summer. Maybe I wasn't as welcoming to Jillian as I thought I'd been.

"Isn't that your friend Parker?" Jillian asks.

I follow her gaze to the stage.

What the . . .

Parker Kingfisher sings into a microphone. He stands next to a taller guy who plays lead guitar. They sway in unison.

"Did you know he was in the band?" Jillian sounds impressed.

"No," I admit. "I didn't know." When did Parker join a band? Is that why he kept badgering me to get Jillian here tonight?

Parker leans toward the lead guitarist, who joins him on the chorus. The guitarist has long hair pulled into a thick braid that swishes a beat after he strums the guitar. He resembles Parker but is more muscular than my slender friend. The guy wears tight, faded jeans and a billowy white shirt with the front lacing partially undone to reveal bronze skin sans any chest hair. My stomach flips in the most delightful way. It takes me a hot minute to place this Ojibwe pirate rock star.

Parker's brother, Navarre. I hadn't seen him since before he went to college downstate. He seems much older than the three years that separates him from Parker and me.

Gramma Liz comes over. "Why aren't you girls dancing?"

Jillian gazes at Parker. She looks as if she's seeing him for the first time.

"C'mon." I nudge my cousin. "Gramma is challenging us to a dance-off."

Jillian and I follow Gramma to the dance floor.

"Don't think I didn't catch the way you're staring at the brother," Gramma Liz tells me. She motions toward Navarre Kingfisher with her lips.

"You said he was a troublemaker," I remind Gramma.

"I didn't say he was a troublemaker," she corrects me. "I said he was trouble and a heartbreaker." She shakes her head. "You never listen, Jessa Jean."

As we dance with Gramma, Jillian and I catch each other's eyes and smile. It's a familiar, almost shy smile, like when my cousin would first arrive for a visit. It would take us a minute to fall back into our friendship, but then we'd once again be the dynamic duo.

Tonight, Jillian sees Parker as a surprisingly decent singer who dances in a bouncy and carefree way that is distinctly different from his older brother's sexy moves. The same Parker, who is also a line cook who smells like onions sometimes, and the second-best debater in Munising, Michigan.

Maybe Jillian isn't the only one seeing people with fresh eyes and realizing that people can be more than one thing. Posh, well-dressed Jillian who will probably be Team Edward for the next hundred years. My cousin, who keeps urging me to add a hydrating serum with hyaluronic acid and vitamin C to my skincare regime. Next summer I'll be in Old Town Alexandria, seeing everything Jillian wants to share with me. And listening, too.

We've been Jilly Bean and Jessa Jean, and now we are Jillian and J. J. Maybe someday we'll be college roommates, or bride and bridesmaid, or auntie to each other's kids. That's the thing about being a dynamic duo. The dynamic part means always changing. But, at its core, the duo remains braided together: past, present, and future.

KATHY'S POEM
David A. Robertson

On Saturday morning, Kathy woke up feeling depressed. Depression was a complex emotion to describe, but how she would have summed it up was that she didn't feel like she could get out of bed, that she couldn't imagine wanting to get out of bed, and so she was relatively sure that she would not get out of bed. Her moshom had told her the night before that she would only be upset for the evening, and when she woke up, she'd feel better.

"Time has a way of easing those feelings," he told her.

Kathy didn't believe him at the time. She was so upset when she got home from school that she was sure, 100 percent, that she would never feel better ever again in her entire life. She didn't think that sleeping it off was a magic remedy, and it turned out that she was right. Sometimes, even moshoms were wrong, she decided.

Of course, in his defense, Kathy didn't think that her moshom had been in quite the same situation she had found herself in. It had started in English class, midway through the afternoon, her last class of the day. Last week, she and the entire class had been given a creative writing assignment. There were two parts to it, and the first one was simple. The students had to write a poem—no big deal. Kathy loved writing, and she wrote poetry all the time. At her desk in her bedroom on a little metal shelving unit, she had a stack of notebooks that had all been filled with journal entries and poetry, and sometimes journal entries that were done in verse. Kathy loved it whenever they got any writing assignment. She even loved it when they were assigned essays because it still involved writing, and she thought she was so talented that she could get a high mark on an essay even if she didn't know much about the topic.

The second part of the assignment had turned out to be the problem. Writing was all well and fine. She'd written a good poem. She'd written a *great* poem. She'd written such a monumentally excellent poem that she was sure she would get an A+. However, part of the mark was on their performance of their poem when they recited it in front of the class, which changed everything. Yes, Kathy loved writing poetry. Yes, she had been writing poetry since she was in grade two. But she had never once read any of her poems out loud. She had never once read *anything* that she had written out loud. Only once had any of her writing been read out loud, and that was when her little brother stole her journal and shouted every word he could while she chased him around the house until she tackled him onto the couch and retrieved her notebook; since then her parents had agreed to put a lock on her door so the incident with her brother wouldn't be repeated. Kathy Chubb. Her last name started with a *C*. The students recited their work alphabetically, and before she knew it, she was up in front of all her classmates with her poem, handwritten on lined paper, clutched in her hands.

Her heart was pounding. Her breath was short. Her hands were sweating so badly that she was worried her poem would suffer water damage. It was deadly quiet. Everybody was leaning forward in anticipation, waiting for Kathy to start. The person who went before her had nailed it. He'd written a mediocre poem but had performed like a trained actor, which made his mediocre poem sound excellent. But after moments in front of the class that felt more like years, Kathy clumsily folded up her unread poem, stuffed it into her pocket, and ran home almost halfway through the rez.

Kathy spent most of Saturday in her room. Her parents or moshom brought her meals and left them outside her door as if she were a prisoner, but she wasn't. Well, maybe a prisoner to her embarrassment. She didn't eat much. She didn't go on her phone much. All she did was lie on her bed and stare at the ceiling or at the poem she couldn't bring herself to recite in front of her classmates. The day wore on, unconcerned with her depression, and as evening approached, daylight faded into more fantastic colors, and Kathy turned onto her side and closed her eyes, letting the poem fall like an autumn leaf to the floor. Maybe her moshom was just off by one day. Perhaps she would open her eyes tomorrow and feel as good as new. She doubted it, but it was the only hope she could muster.

There was a knock on her door immediately after she closed her eyes, as if whoever was on the other side of the door somehow knew to wait until just that moment like she had a concussion and shouldn't be sleeping. Standing awkwardly in front of the class and saying nothing felt like getting hit in the head.

"Come in," Kathy said sullenly, ensuring that her voice matched her mood so everybody in the house knew she was still a massive ball of gloom and shame.

The door creaked open, and her moshom walked in. He sat on the edge of her bed and placed a gentle, weathered hand on her blanketed leg.

"Not feeling any better, my girl?" he said.

"You're right about that, at least," Kathy said.

Instantly, the sadness and embarrassment welcomed guilt to the party. She'd snapped at her moshom, and she'd never snapped at him before. When you're grumpy, it's hard to un-grumpy yourself, but she sighed and calmed the burning in her chest long enough to apologize for her tone of voice.

He patted her leg and chuckled. "Don't even worry about it," he said. "I've been spoken to far worse than that in my life, trust me."

"It's just that," Kathy said, snapping up into a sitting position and just as quickly resting her chin on her forearms, which were, in turn, resting on her knees, "I got up to the front of the class, and I felt like a deer in headlights. I know that's a cliché, but it's an accurate, fully true cliché because I've seen a deer in headlights, and that's exactly how I looked." She clutched her hair in her hands for a moment. "One of my friends even showed me a picture, and if you glanced at it, you couldn't tell the difference between me and a deer!"

"First of all," her moshom said, "don't forget to breathe."

"Breathe. Right." Kathy took a deep breath, which did help. It made her feel calm. She wondered if she'd forgotten to breathe in front of the class. That was entirely possible. When she swam in the lake and tried to hold her breath, she felt the same kind of nervousness that she felt when she was supposed to have read her poem. Her moshom didn't expand on his advice, but she decided that he meant it applied to both situations. Don't forget to breathe when you feel nervous, and don't forget to breathe when you're freaking out like she was doing now.

"Any advice for reading my poetry in front of a big crowd?" she asked.

He chuckled again. Not in a way that was making fun of her. Instead, in a way that indicated understanding. That's what she decided he'd meant.

"I've never been in front of a big crowd reading poetry," he said, getting up from the bed and standing beside her. "But I've told stories in front of people. That's kind of what Elders do well."

"And your sage guidance?" she asked.

"I could tell you, Kathy, but I think I'd rather show you," he said, then turned away and walked toward the door before stopping in the doorway and facing her again. "That is, if you aren't busy at the moment."

She knew he was teasing in the gentlest way possible. Of course she wasn't doing anything—she'd been in bed the whole day. And no matter how upset she felt, she knew that denying herself an opportunity to learn from her moshom was never productive.

"I don't currently have any plans," she said.

"Then why don't you get dressed? I'm going to take you somewhere," he said. "Be outside in five minutes."

"Take me where?" she asked.

But her moshom just walked into the hallway and disappeared, and she listened while his truck keys jangled, while he put on his shoes as the stool in the front hallway creaked when he sat on it, and while he opened the front door, where his faint footsteps led toward his vehicle parked in the gravel driveway.

"Take me where?" she repeated.

By then, though, he couldn't have heard her. She took one of those deep breaths he'd suggested she take, forced herself out of bed, threw on jeans and a hooded sweatshirt, and followed him out the front door, where she was confronted with headlights shining on her like a spotlight.

Kathy and her moshom drove through the rez. Kathy knew the rez like the back of her hand. Everybody in the community did. They knew every rock at the shore, every ripple in the lake, every house in every little pocket nestled within the trees, every family that lived in those houses, the way the northern lights looked like ribbons in the wind, the way that you were familiar to everybody and everything. And so, as they drove, Kathy couldn't even guess where they were going. She didn't know what her moshom could've been showing her when she'd already seen everything there was to see. But on he drove, ignoring or not bothering to worry about the looks she threw at him filled with confusion and curiosity. He leaned against the steering wheel, whistling, listening to the local radio as it called out bingo numbers—he was one of the few band members who didn't play often. They were near the college, which sat across the road from the hospital, and facing an empty parking lot where there used to be a hockey rink when he abruptly turned into that old parking lot and kept driving through it, toward the trees, without slowing down much at all.

"Ummmm, Moshom?" Kathy said as they got closer and closer to the trees. Was the lesson that she shouldn't worry about poetry reading in front of people because you never know when you might drive into the forest?

"Yes, my girl?" her moshom said, sounding rather pleased with himself.

"We're kind of driving straight toward the . . ."

But before she could panic or even finish her warning, a road appeared before them. The road, indicated by a distinct set of tire tracks, wound through the trees before disappearing to the right.

"I've never seen this path before," Kathy said.

"It's there when it needs to be there, for whoever needs to follow it," her moshom said.

"I don't even know what that means," Kathy said, but was intrigued enough not to question it further, so she just watched as Moshom expertly navigated the truck through the trees until they banked right and came to an end. The road opened to a clearing and a place, like the road, she had not been aware existed. The truck bumped over a cracked and uneven asphalt lot, lit by a sign to the left that read "Sandy June's Legendary Frybread Drive-In." The word *Legendary* was in bright yellow, while the rest of the words were green on a midnight-black background that blended into the darkening sky. The ride smoothed out when they drove back onto the grass before coming to a stop under a large awning where there were other parked cars to the side, all mainly of the rez variety, which meant old boxy sedans and trucks, and wooden picnic tables with peeling green paint lined up down the middle. Moshom brought the truck to a stop beside one of the sedans, an old Buick idling, coughing as though it had caught a cold.

"Well, here we are," her moshom said.

Kathy looked around and tried to take it all in. What she could see of it. But the only thing she could see beyond what they'd already driven through or into was a food counter at the end of the awning, where there was a lineup of other Neechies patiently waiting for their turn to order. Kathy rolled down the window and was instantly hit with the best-smelling food she thought she'd ever had the privilege of smelling. Homemade, old-school, real tradish rez food. Her mouth watered.

"Where is here?" she asked.

Her moshom got out of the truck, walked around to the passenger side, and, like a true gentleman, opened the door for Kathy. She stepped out, planted her feet on the grass, and felt instantly at home. So much so that she didn't even need to be told much else, but he told her anyway.

"This is Sandy June's Legendary Frybread Drive-In," he announced.

"What?" Kathy said.

"It's a place that has been created for Indigenous people across Turtle Island," her moshom said. "It's there for every one of us, wherever we are. A gathering place."

"And that'll help me with my public reading problem?" she asked.

Maybe she should have been too stunned to speak. After all, had they not just gone through a magic portal? But she wasn't. She knew that Indigenous people all over the place had stories that, to others, may have seemed magical but were not. They were real, like stories of the Memekwesewak. Hearing that story might seem like fantasy fiction to the uninformed, but she knew that her moshom had seen them when he was younger. They weren't a fantasy at all. So, something inside her took the presence of the Legendary Frybread Drive-In as fact (she was there, wasn't she?), and she wondered more about how it would help her not have a panic attack the next time she got up to read her poem, which she had to do, or else she might fail her assignment.

"I think it'll do just that," he said, leading her away from the truck, through the awning, toward the counter where people were ordering food.

On their way, she passed all the full picnic tables occupied by who she guessed were people from different reserves or urban locations heavy with an Indigenous population. On one table was a group of teenagers playing what looked like a DnD session. They had all their stuff spread out on the table and looked intense, as if they were in another world while sitting somewhere otherworldly. One had black, tousled hair with jeans and a T-shirt; another had bleached hair with dark roots growing in; another had braids and a dress; and the final kid, who looked to be leading the game, had long, straight hair, with leggings underneath her dress and a beanie. For a moment, Kathy wanted to stop what she was doing and join in on the game, but she knew her moshom had plans for her, so she dutifully followed him to the back of the line, and they waited their turn like everybody else.

Kathy and Moshom inched forward. There were a lot of people waiting to order food, and Kathy could understand why. She had smelled why already. She would have been quite happy to sit around the counter and catch the scent of every plate of food passed out to customers all night if it weren't for her stomach grumbling. She caught a glimpse of the menu as they drew closer. There were milkshakes, lemonade, sweetgrass tea, NDN tacos, bison burgers, elk stew and cornbread, fries, veggie roast, edamame with wild rice, and so much more. Of course, there was frybread, the namesake of the drive-in.

"How am I ever going to pick one thing?" Kathy asked as they were now second in line.

"You don't have to," her moshom said. "We can always come back for more." He rubbed his stomach; it must've been growling, too. "And I'll help you finish whatever you can't."

After what felt like an eternity, it was finally their turn to order, and greeting them at the counter was a woman Kathy heard being called SJ. She was short, pushing five feet if she were lucky, but looked strong with working hands and black hair tied back into a braid, a hairnet covering the top of her head.

"What'll it be?" she asked, not beating around the bush.

Kathy understood that. She glanced back, and even though they'd made it to the front, the line seemed to have grown even longer. More people were arriving all the time. She felt terrible being indecisive. She felt something worse than bad after she'd scanned up and down the menu several times, feeling as if everybody behind her was impatient, even though nobody was yelling at her to move. Panic rose, and suddenly, she was back in front of the class; everybody was staring at her, and she was tongue-tied. She remembered her moshom's advice to breathe and took a few moments to inhale and exhale slowly.

"What do you suggest?" she asked. "Honestly, I'll eat anything. I'm pretty hungry."

"My girl, when anybody asks that, I tell 'em the same thing," SJ said. "You have to try the frybread, of course. Isn't that right, Dulas?"

She winked at Kathy's moshom.

"Ehe," Moshom said. "Right as rain."

"Well then," SJ said. "Coming right up." She turned back to the other staff in the kitchen, busily putting plates together for patrons waiting for their orders. "Two frybreads!"

Moshom and Kathy sat down to wait for their frybread beside the group playing DnD. A few minutes later, SJ brought over two plates, one in each hand, and set them down in front of them. Then the short woman with the big smile sat with them, cozying up beside Kathy. Moshom seemed unfazed, but Kathy just sat there with the plate in front of her, wondering what was happening.

"Well, go on," SJ said. "Try it out."

Kathy glanced at SJ and then at the line of people eager to order from the menu.

"Don't you have a million people to make stuff for?" she asked.

"My staff can take care of that," she said. She met eyes with her moshom, then returned her attention to Kathy. "Your moshom told me that you might need some encouragement."

"When did you tell her that?" Kathy asked her moshom, who shrugged in response. "When did he tell you that?" she asked SJ.

"I talk to all the grandparents," SJ said. "Kind of comes with the job, you know."

Kathy leaned back, though there was nothing to lean back into, and she crossed her arms skeptically.

"And just what did my moshom tell you?" she asked, eyeing her moshom simultaneously.

"He said that you were having trouble speaking in front of your classmates for an assignment," SJ told her.

"Oh," Kathy said, leaning forward, elbows against the picnic table's peeled green paint. "That's pretty much exactly what's wrong."

"What scares you about it?" SJ asked.

"I don't know," Kathy said, and searched her feelings to articulate the issue. She imagined herself in front of everybody, a poem in hand, and felt anxious again. "I'm just not used to talking in public. I'm scared I'll screw up, and everybody laughs at me."

SJ sized up Kathy for a minute, then pointed at the frybread with her lips. "I think it's time you try my food."

Kathy, unsure of what else to do and not wanting to relive the moment in school again, picked up the frybread and took a bite. It was the best thing she had ever tasted. It melted in her mouth. She took another, bigger bite, almost finishing the whole thing, then placed the remnants back on the plate.

"That's deadly," Kathy said. "Holy."

"Now," SJ said, "do you think my frybread was *always* that good?"

"I'm guessing that question is rhetorical," Kathy said.

SJ chuckled. "Clever girl." SJ then picked up the frybread, the last of it, and placed it into her mouth, then made an "mmmmm" sound while closing her eyes. Back to reality, she met eyes with Kathy. "When I first tried to make frybread, it was awful. I wouldn't have fed it to a rez dog. But I tried again and again and again and again and again and again and again and again and again and even more, and each time, I got better. Eventually, I made the best frybread on Turtle Island." She shrugged. "Or so I've been told." She clapped her hands together, and flour particles exploded into the air in a cloud. "It's an art form. Like poetry. You see what I'm saying?"

"If I don't try, I'll always be scared," Kathy said.

"Exactly, my girl," SJ said.

"I used to suck at DnD," said the girl with the beanie, who'd over-heard Kathy's troubles. "Now I'm the dungeon master, dude."

"Thank you very much," Kathy called over to the girl.

"No problem!"

"Well," SJ said. "After all that"—she inspected the line, which had grown—"I better get back."

"Thanks, SJ," Kathy's moshom said.

"Anytime, Dulas."

SJ gave Kathy a reassuring pat on the shoulder, held her hand there momentarily, and then disappeared into the drive-in. Kathy heard her instantly directing her staff to make this or that.

"So?" her moshom said.

"This is great, but now I have to wait until next week to face my fears, right?" Kathy said.

"Not necessarily," her moshom said, getting up from the picnic table.

He held out his hand to her.

"How many places are you going to lead me today?" Kathy asked with a smile and took her moshom's hand. He guided her around the building to the back, where a bunch of chairs were set up, and people were sitting on the grass facing what looked like nothing. At the front of the crowd, a microphone was on a stand at the back of the build-ing. Stacked up on either side of the microphone was equipment that looked like it could be made into a stage, and hanging from the top of the building was a projector screen that hadn't been pulled down. "What's all this?" she asked, but she had an idea, and the panic started to bubble.

Her moshom explained that tonight, there was a schedule of performances. Soon, the stage would be set up, and there would be a musical performance, and then later, there would be a movie screening.

"But before all that," her moshom said, "it's an open mic. Anybody can get up and read a story, or . . ."

Kathy instinctively placed her hand against her jeans pocket, where she'd thrust her poem earlier. By now, the paper was probably crumpled up and hard to read.

"Or read poetry," Kathy said unconvincingly.

"So, to answer your question of what this all is," her moshom said, "everyone is waiting for you to read your poem, my girl."

"Now?" she said.

"Whenever you're ready," her moshom said, then backed away, leaving her pretty much in front of the crowd, standing near the mic.

But her moshom hadn't abandoned her. Standing near her, he looked at her encouragingly, as if to say, *You can do it*. Kathy's heart started to pound, her palms were sweaty, and her breath was short, but she kept her eyes on her moshom, and what SJ had said echoed in her mind. The only way to get better was to have the courage to do it in the first place. The more she did it, the better she would get. She wanted to get better. She wanted that more than getting a good mark. She closed her eyes and took many deep breaths until her breath evened out, and then she walked in front of all those people and stopped in front of the stand, her mouth inches away from the microphone. She cleared her throat, and it sounded like a thunderbird. The noise was followed by feedback before the mic settled down.

"Ummm," Kathy said, focusing primarily on her moshom. She noticed the gamers she'd passed earlier, led by the dungeon master, taking a spot at the side of the crowd. It was nice to see kids her age. She imagined they were her classmates. This was perfect practice for school on Monday when she'd have a second chance to recite her poem. This would help her not stand there in silence but speak loudly and share the story she'd written in her poem. "This is something I wrote for school. It's about a caterpillar."

She waited for somebody to laugh, but nobody did. She didn't expect that. She reached into her pocket, pulled out the paper, and busily straightened it until it was legible to her. (She didn't think anybody else would have been able to read it, and maybe she wouldn't have been either if she were being honest, but she'd worked so hard on it that she'd committed it to memory anyway.) She cleared her throat again and then recited her poem to the people before her, sitting politely and expectantly.

This is the dream of a cylindrical lad
Crawling amidst the weeds and the dirt
Making castles from clouds, grinning a tad
Then pinching itself and returning to work

What work! Weaving comforters, cozy indeed
More cozy than campfires in winter's duress

To sleep softly and lie in the bed it has made
Longing for something to beat in its chest

The longing, the wanting, the spit in one's mouth
The hunger for shadows with no means of light
The clearest blue sky in this seasonal drought
The deadness of air, the dusty green kite

Then a crack from the comforter warming a sleep
The awakening hope rubs its greedy black eyes
In a rainbow-sweet blur, tickled ribs know a beat
And the lad so long wanting takes leave for the sky

These wings! They bleed the blackest tears
Which streak the trails pronounced against
The purest orange, so pure it tastes
These wings flutter soft as silky lace

There was silence after she'd recited her poem until one student started to clap. This opened the floodgates, and soon, every classmate of hers was clapping. Standing at the front of her class on Monday morning, she remembered her time at Sandy June's Legendary Frybread Drive-In and felt thankful for what she had learned there. Her performance hadn't been perfect. She'd messed up a few words, her hands were a little shaky, and she was sure her voice had also been shaky. She'd lost her place once. And she didn't know what grade she'd get when eventually the class's grades would be handed back. But it was only her first time. Well, second time. Next time it would be better, and the time after that. She smiled and dramatically bowed, which caused the laughter she'd been afraid of in the first place, but this time, she'd asked for it. As she smiled, she tasted the distinct warm, soft sweetness of SJ's frybread and couldn't wait to return so that she could get more practice, company, and, of course, more food.

OPEN MIC AT THE DRIVE-IN

Cynthia Leitich Smith

Run-down, neon,
legendary drive-in.
Good medicine
on the menu,
stories on the side.

Blankets in summertime,
first blush to first kiss.
Rez dogs jammin' to Redbone.
Uncles tunin' sharp fiddles.
Cousins, clan, come as I am.

Sisters safe and shining,
with grad-cap feathers flying,
rock your beads and rock your vote.
Wind croons of brothers
from the red-dirt plains.

Should we still *fry* bread?
Should we still fry *bread*?

Teach family recipes,
reclaim tradish ways,
and surf into tomorrow.

Island aunties sing of blue.
Future Elders hum along.
Turtle Island forever.
Come to my protest, my party.
Pass the sweetgrass tea.

A NOTE FROM CYNTHIA LEITICH SMITH, AUTHOR-CURATOR OF HEARTDRUM

Dear Reader,

At Sandy June's Legendary Frybread Drive-In, young Indigenous heroes navigate a bounty of emotions, from the sweet joy of a long-awaited first kiss to the healing comfort of loving reassurances. In weighty moments and sparkly ones, throughout the slipstream of time, these characters share good food, good company, good humor, and mutual support in an intertribal community, with legendary grandparents and of course with one another.

If you're feeling bookish, you might think of the fictional drive-in as a utopia, meaning an imaginary, extra-positive vision of a rezzy drive-in experience. While our setting's official status is "fictional," I prefer to think of it as a collective dream.

The authors collaborated, creating winks, nods, and overlaps in their writing, through emails, phone calls, in-person meetups, and an online message board. We talked about big topics like nutrition—"eat traditional," "frybread in moderation!"—and what the passage of time does and doesn't mean to us. We talked about fun topics such as our picks for an Indigenous movie night and what to title this anthology. Collaboration is a layered process, but community is a lot of what this book is about, both on the page and behind the bylines.

Have you read many books by and about Indigenous people of what's currently called North America and the Hawaiian Islands? After finishing *Legendary Frybread Drive-In*, I hope you'll reach for more. This anthology is published by Heartdrum, an award-winning, Native-focused imprint of HarperCollins Children's Books.

Finally, I want to encourage you to honor the loving Elders in your own life. They have wisdom to share, and someday, you may become a legendary grandparent, too.

Mvto,

Cynthia Leitich Smith

GLOSSARY

"Maybe It Starts" by Kate Hart

Chickasaw Glossary

Chikashanompa (Chi-kash-sha-nom-pa'): Chickasaw language.
In the words of our language revitalization committee, "There
is no 'right' or 'wrong' way to spell Chickasaw. It is an oral
language, so ultimately it is up to each Chickasaw person to
determine how they want to spell (and speak) their language."

pashofa (pi-sho-fa): traditional dish of pork and hominy

"Mvskoke Joy" by Marcella Bell

Mvskoke Glossary

hesci (hens-jay): hello

mvto (muh-dō): thank you

"Game Night" by Darcie Little Badger

Lipan Apache Glossary

solé flowers: spiderwort

"Braving the Storm" by Kaua Māhoe Adams

Hawaiian Glossary

ʻaʻā (AH-AH): sharp, jagged lava rock

lanai (la-nai): porch

laulau (lau-lau): meat and fish wrapped in lu'au and ti leaves, then
steamed

lu'au leaf (loo-OW leaf): taro leaves

mo'o (mo-O): gecko

'ono (oh-no): delicious, tasty

ti leaf (tee leaf): a type of shiny, green leaf

'uala (OO-ah-la): sweet potato

"You Had One Job" by Andrea L. Rogers

Cherokee Glossary

dagsi/ᏖᏍᏏ (dah-gah-see): box turtle

donadagohvi/ᎥᏡᎯᏕᎪᎥᎢ (doe-nah-dah-go-huh-e): until we
meet again (to one person)

hawa/ᎣᏩᎦ (hah-wah): okay

osiyo/ᎤᏍᏫ (oh-SEE-yo, shortened to SEE-yo for informality):
hello/hi/hey/greetings

saloli/ᏡᎦᏟ (saw-low-li): squirrel

wado/ᎦᎥ (wah-DOE): thank you

Chickasaw Glossary

ho'mi (ho-mi): okay

"Heart Berry" by Cheryl Isaacs

Mohawk Glossary

ihstá (EEH-sta): auntie

Kanyen'kéha (gah-NYEN-geh-hah): Mohawk language

Konorónkhwa (Guh-no-ROONG-kwah): I love you

"Momentum" by Christine Hartman Derr

Cherokee Glossary

ani/ᎠᏂ (ah-nee): strawberry

Daquadoa/ᏓᏆᏙᎠ (dah-gwah-doe-ah): My name is / I have a name

dodadagohvi/ᏙᏓᏓᎪᎲᎢ (doe-dah-dah-go-huh-e): until we meet again (to two or more people)

Galiheliga/ᎦᎵᎮᎵᎦ (ga-lee-hey-lee-gah): I'm grateful

hawa/ᎭᏩ (hah-wah): okay

Nihina/ᏂᎯᎾ (nee-hee-nah): And you?

nvneha/ᏅᏁᎭ (nuh-neh-huh): art (you are making it into a thing)

osda/ᎣᏍᏓ (oh-s-dah): good

osiyo/ᎣᏏᏲ (oh-see-yo, shortened to siyo [see-yo] for informality): hello/hi/hey/greetings

Tohitsu/ᏙᎯᏧ (toe-he-juh): How are you?

Tsalagi/ᏣᎳᎩ (jah-lah-ghee): Cherokee

wado/ᏩᏙ (wah-doe): thank you

Mvskoke Glossary

mvto (muh-do): thank you

"I Love You, Grandson" by Brian Young

Navajo Glossary

'aoo' (oa): yes

'Ayóó 'ánííníshʼni' (Ah-yo ah-knee-nihsh-nih): I love you

chiiłchin (chiihl-chin): sumac berries

dééh (dei): tea, greenthread plant

Diné (Din-eh): people, Navajo

Hágo (ha-goh): Come here

Nizhóníyee (nih-zhoh-nih-yeeh): It is beautiful (literal meaning). Good work (conversational meaning).

shiyáázh (shee-yahzh): my son (mom to son), widely used by females to young children

t'áá kwe'é (t-aah kweh-eh): right here

taa'niil (taw-kneel): ground blue corn, or thin blue corn mush

tóshchíín (tohsh-cheen): blue corn mush

Txı̨' (Tyih): Let's go

Mvskoke Glossary

Ecenokecyvyet os, osóswv (Ee-gee-niv-geh-jay-say-dose, oh-soh-swuh): I love you, Grandson.

Cherokee Glossary

Gvgeyui, ulisi atsutsa / ᎬᎥᎨᏯᎢ, ᎤᎵᏏ ᎠᏧᏣ (guh-gay-you-ee, oo-lee-si a-choo-jah): I love you, Grandson.

Ojibwe Glossary

Gizhawenimin, noozhishenh (Gih-zha-way-nah-min, nooh-zhi-shih): I love you, Grandson.

"Language Lesson" by Jen Ferguson

Southern Heritage Michif Glossary. Compiled with acknowledgments to the Amelia Douglas Institute, the Gabriel Dumont Institute, itwêwina Plains Cree Dictionary, all the language keepers who worked on these excellent resources, and Samson LaMontagne.

bonn swayrii (bunn swayrrr-ee): good evening

kinihtaawiteepon (ki-neh-taa-wi-tee-poon): you are good at cooking / you are an expert cook

l'aariyaanl (la-ree-yanll): moose

lii bufloo (lee buff-low): buffalo

lii pwayr (lee pw-air): saskatoon berries

maarsii (maar-see): thank you

miina kaawaapamitin (mee-na ka-waa-pa-mittin): see you later

miitshootaak (mit-show-taak): let's eat

pishkapmisho (pish-kap-mi-shoo): take care

taanishi (tawn-sheh): hello (fun fact! this also means "how")

"Hearts Aflutter" by A. J. Eversole

Cherokee Glossary

elisi/ᏪᏟᏏ (eh-LEE-see): grandmother

osiyo/ᎣᏏᏲ (oh-SEE-yo, shortened to SEE-yo for informality): hello/hi/hey/greetings

wado/ᎦᏪ (wah-DOE): thank you

Hawaiian Glossary

mahalo (ma-hall-oh): to express gratitude

"Love Buzz" by Byron Graves

Ojibwe Glossary

awesiinh (aww-seen): animal

boozhoo (boo-jhew): greetings, hello

miigwech (mee-gwech): thanks

"Jilly Bean and Jessa Jean" by Angeline Boulley

Ojibwe Glossary

> **aaniin** (ah-NEE): hello
>
> **binoojiins** (bih-NEW-jeez): babies
>
> **boozhoo** (boo-ZHEW): hello

"Kathy's Poem" by David A. Robertson

Swampy Cree Glossary

> **ehe** (eh-hey): yes
>
> **Memekwesewak** (Meh-meh-gwee-see-wack): Little People
>
> **moshom** (mush-um): grandfather
>
> **Neechies** (nee-chees): Indigenous people (slang)

NOTES AND ACKNOWLEDGMENTS

"Maybe It Starts" by Kate Hart

Yakoke to Lokosh (Joshua D. Hinson), Executive Officer of Chickasaw Nation Division of Language Preservation, and Jacquelyn Sparks, Citizen of Cherokee Nation of Oklahoma and Chickasaw Cultural Center Senior Collections Manager, for their help with fact-checking and vocabulary as well as for their general radness. Any mistakes are mine.

"House of Stray Cats" by Eric Gansworth

When you step inside someone else's narrative universe, you have to play by that person's rules. The real world makes us do that all the time. In high school, you have a ton of outside parameters inflicted upon you, and you're expected to stay within their bounds. I've never had this rule-following skill in abundance and was often foolish enough to ask for clarification as to why arbitrary rules existed. This trait did not win me much favor. Yet, for all the negative feedback, I haven't changed much. What I have learned to do is accept the costs of my disposition.

Tuscarora Nation, where I was born and raised, has been a place with a very strong communal identity, though that doesn't mean everyone agrees with the leadership's decisions. Members of the

Nation recognize these decisions are made for the unknowable future, not necessarily for the present moment, but if they have strong, differing opinions, they may voice them. It's a cultural philosophy, and the people who live in the community accept this trait as a signature, sometimes at great personal cost.

I live a few miles from Nation Territory, and one rule I've had to accept is that I've largely given up any right to share an opinion on community matters, no matter how much I personally dislike a decision. While it's quite possible no opinion of mine would have mattered anyway on many concerns, when you are truly committed to a community's identity, you understand that it means accepting the bad with the good in equal measure. Sometimes you have to acknowledge that the situation you hope might be over once you graduate is really just the beginning. This story is partly about the process of awakening and all the ripple effects that occur when your eyes flutter open.

"Mvskoke Joy" by Marcella Bell

Mvto, *thank you*, is the first Mvskoke word I ever learned and it is the last word of "Mvskoke Joy." That's because, of all the sentiments I know, I think gratitude is at the root of the strongest connections. I am thankful to Cynthia Leitich Smith, who responded to my tentative reach-out with the warm embrace of a relative, who encouraged and supported my participation in the We Need Diverse Books Native Writing Intensive, and who always makes sure to include everyone. Everyone. This story also could not exist without my grandpa (who made sure I knew I was Mvskoke), my mom (who brought me to Native spaces throughout my whole life), my dad (who is the closest to knowing what it has been like to be Black like me), my partner (who I couldn't do any of it without), my children (who inspire me to be an example of a person who follows their heart), and my late dog, Tiller (who, even in death, made sure to take care of me). Thank you to you, and so many more, from the bottom of my heart.

"Game Night" by Darcie Little Badger

This story is dedicated to the bards, GMs, and other dreamers; to those who find themselves and community in worlds of imagination.

"Look Away" by Karina Iceberg

Thank you so much for reading Mary's story! A million years ago, when I was a teenager trying to navigate the world of first dates, I remember many "rules" being touted as the right way to do this or that. It took me a while to figure out that the only rules you need are the ones that feel right to you! My deepest, most heartfelt thank-you to Cynthia Leitich Smith and Rosemary Brosnan, who continue to teach and inspire me in my writing. I am so lucky to have such wonderful mentors! And to the kind group of writers I've had the pleasure to work with and learn from in this anthology—thank you all!

"Patent Red" by Cynthia Leitich Smith

When I was your age, I was blessed by the wisdom, guidance, good food, and robust humor of Elders like those at the drive-in. I am forever grateful for those relationships.

We could split hairs over what it means to be an Elder or your Elder. Opinions and interpretations abound. As for me, I hope that your interactions with Elders are positive—that they're good medicine flowing across generations. After all, our Elders have much to teach us. But they are also people, real human beings. They're not magical creatures or all-knowing Jedi masters. An unfortunate few are what my grandpa would've called "real stinkers" and best avoided. But none of them are finished people.

They're still maturing, still learning, and may make an occasional mistake they later regret. So, sometimes you teach them, too.

I wrote "Patent Red" in part to honor the messier aspects of people of all ages and for those at any stage of life who are fierce enough to admit their mistakes and do better.

"Braving the Storm" by Kaua Māhoe Adams

Thank you to Cynthia Leitich Smith, for your unwavering support of my writing. And for always encouraging me to celebrate myself.

Thank you to my editor, Rosemary Brosnan, for her sharp eye and for truly seeing the heart and soul of this story.

Thank you to Melanie Crowder, for reminding me that I am a poet.

Thank you to Caroline Cullinane, for being the first person to read this story. Friends like you are one in a million.

Thank you to Ty, Alexis, Mckenna, Mary, and Caroline (again), for always cheering me on. It is a gift to be loved by such brilliant writers and friends.

Thank you to Charlie, the love of my life.

This story was inspired by my own grandfather, James Ka'ohu Kauhanehonakawailani Adams, for whom I would drive through every downpour, every raging storm, to hug just one more time.

Finally, this story is for all the scared kids, the anxious kids, the "what if . . . ?" kids.

I see you, and you are brave.

"You Had One Job" by Andrea L. Rogers

Wado, Rosemary and Cynthia, for letting me hang out with Maggie once more. Wado, Lokosh, for sharing your language expertise. I wrote this story in honor of my daughter, Ana, and her friend Elise, who is Osage. I was inspired by their friendship and the annual Osage dances. To me, the dances were a beautiful reminder of the importance of history, tradition, tribal identity, and community. Thanks to Christine Derr for letting Lucy befriend Maggie, and Kate Hart for bringing Auntie Bernadette to the party. Wado to Kirby Brown for sharing his research and work with me and writing about Ruth Muskrat Bronson in *Stoking the Fire: Nationhood in Cherokee Writing, 1907–1970*. Wado to her relatives Jen Loren and Rebecca Kunz for teaching me more about Ruth. What an amazing woman. She was an activist, teacher, advocate, writer, and so much more. Her work is fire!

"Heart Berry" by Cheryl Isaacs

For the lucky among us, community is close and accessible every day. For others, community is, at best, something we have to work hard to find, and at worst, just a dream. The community we're a part of or not affects how we see and feel about ourselves. For Dawn, its absence leads her to believe that she's lacking somehow, that she needs to be more like someone else to measure up. But meeting Mystery Auntie sets up an interaction that convinces Dawn that not only is she enough as she is, but she's worthy of the love of her harshest critic—the one in the mirror.

The drive-in as a place of refuge, where people can go when they're in need of support or love—or just a laugh—is a beautiful idea that is maybe more feasible than we think. We just have to listen and follow our own paths there. We all belong. We're all worthy.

"Momentum" by Christine Hartman Derr

Finding what, where, or who makes you feel the most at home with yourself is a lifelong journey. Maybe, like Mariah, you already know your "thing." Not knowing is okay, too. You may find yourself through a hobby, an exploration of your identity, or by spending time in your community. If you aren't sure where you fit yet, take heart and have hope. One day, you'll know. You'll find your way home, to your You-est you.

Wado, Cynthia Leitich Smith, for dreaming up Sandy June's and inviting me to visit. Wado, Rosemary Brosnan and the Heartdrum team, for all their work on this collection. Gratitude to all the contributors—it's an honor to be in this anthology alongside your brilliant work.

Thank you to my family and friends for their support and endless patience. Archer and Alex, I'm beyond delighted that you are growing up in a world with books like this one. Gvgeyui. James, thank you for listening to all the words I haven't written yet. Jamie Roberts, thanks for being the world's best sister, for sharing your books and your time. Mom, thank you for reading to me and for teaching me to follow my heart and art. Dad, you never got to see this. I hope you can feel my gratitude for all you taught me. Special thanks to friends old and new who celebrate with and for me—your belief in me means the world. I'm thankful to Laura Shovan, VFCA faculty, for shepherding me through the semester in which I was writing this story and my critical thesis. Critical and creative work feed one another, and Laura's feedback was insightful and heartful.

Wado, Ed Fields ale Meli. Cherokee Nation's online language classes are such a gift, as are your teachings. I am also a Cherokee language learner; any mistakes are my own. Wado to Cherokee Nation for language revitalization initiatives and keeping at-large citizens connected. Galiheliga. Wado!

"I Love You, Grandson" by Brian Young

I want to thank Marcella Bell, K. A. Cobell, Christine Hartman Derr, A. J. Eversole, Byron Graves, Andrea L. Rogers, and Cynthia Leitich Smith for their help in providing translations for the phrase "I love you, Grandson" in their respective Indigenous languages. My vision of having multiple Indigenous languages on the same page became a reality because of your help!

I want to give a special and individual huge thank-you to Jennifer Wheel of the YouTube video channel Bead Clan Kitchen, which is an actual page with actual videos that depict how to make some traditional Diné delicacies. You should totally check out the videos!

'Ahxéhee', Jennifer, for giving me permission to reference you and your amazing YouTube videos in my short story!

Lastly, I want to thank my late grandparents—John Williams Sr. and Jessie Williams of Sawmill, Arizona—who I love and miss every day.

"The Rest Will Come" by K. A. Cobell

There's something special about sibling relationships. Having three brothers and one sister of my own, this is something I've always felt. I try to draw from these unique bonds in every story I write, and I hope Trevor and Calvin show that. I'd like to dedicate this story to each of my siblings—I have looked up to them my whole life.

I also want to give a huge thank-you to Cynthia Leitich Smith and Rosemary Brosnan for including me in this anthology and working so hard to uplift Indigenous voices. It's an honor to write stories with such brilliant authors. Many thanks to each of the contributors for their inspiring creativity, craft, and culture.

"Language Lesson" by Jen Ferguson

If you want more of Berlin, Cam, and Kiki, you can find out how they got here by picking up my novel *Those Pink Mountain Nights*. And whatever you do in life, friends and foes, remember that you're allowed to suck at something, you're allowed to take breaks, and perfection is impossible.

I am learning Southern Heritage Michif as an adult, and one thing my language teacher keeps telling my class is how important it is to try! That practice matters more than perfection. That listening to recordings of Elders and repeating what they say and how they say it is key, even if you don't get it right immediately. The other thing my language teacher keeps saying is how important it is for all of us to learn our languages—especially because with Southern Heritage Michif, like many other Indigenous languages, our Elders and language keepers will not be with us forever. The task is an urgent one. It's on all of us to learn our languages and to use them in our lives.

But that doesn't mean language learning can't be fun, too. Maybe that's what Berlin still has to learn. Maybe our girl has another language lesson coming her way. <3 Jen

"Hearts Aflutter" by A. J. Eversole

Romance, a little pining, turkey feathers, and frybread: these were the ingredients chosen to make this story come to life, and I hope you, dear readers, find some joy in the secondhand embarrassment the way I do.

This story wouldn't have been written without those who work tirelessly to advocate for Native voices, so thank you to Cynthia and Rosemary for being the heartbeat of Heartdrum. The biggest thanks to the Native children's literature community, especially the ones who started when there wasn't even a road for us and have since established and widened the path. I hope its future is well traveled. And lastly, my critique partner, Sarah LeFebvre, you're the best, and my husband, Zach, for always supporting my artistic endeavors and believing in me at every step.

"Hearts Aflutter" is dedicated to my momma, the Lorelai to my Rory . . . or, depending on the day, the Emily to my Lorelai.

"Love Buzz" by Byron Graves

My story is dedicated to two of my best friends, Derrik and Junior Jourdain, for introducing me to so much of my favorite music, for all the last-second road trips driving to concerts, and especially for all of the late-night jam sessions. You guys were always super supportive of me even though I was singing off pitch and out of key. I didn't know it at the time, but writing song lyrics back then was the beginning of my creative writing journey. For that, I'm forever grateful. Miigwech.

"Jilly Bean and Jessa Jean" by Angeline Boulley

My story is dedicated to my daughter Sarah Jaye and her cousin Joselynn. One summer they giggled nonstop and were literally insep- arable, conjoined by a blended braid. Miigwech to Cynthia Leitich Smith and Rosemary Brosnan for inviting me to be part of this project.

"Kathy's Poem" by David A. Robertson

I had an intention to write a simple story that had a profound mean- ing. Profound but also simple. Community helps us overcome fear. I've learned that in my own life. When we share our stories, we never know when it will help somebody. In this case, not to give away a spoiler, but one person telling their story helps another tell their story, and that impact can be immeasurable. I'm very honored to be a part of this collection of stories by authors who I respect and admire. These stories are a reflection of community, and I hope that they welcome you, the reader, to be a part of that community, too. Ekosani to Cynthia, Rosemary, and everybody involved with this project. It was magic from the start, seeing it all come together, and that magic is now on the page for everybody.

"Open Mic at the Drive-In" by Cynthia Leitich Smith

Mvto to the authors and their literary agents, including my own agent (Ginger Knowlton of Curtis Brown, Ltd.), to Heartdrum editor and guiding (neon) light Rosemary Brosnan, and to my author assistant, Gayleen Rabakukk. Mvto also to editorial assistant Carter Wilken, production editor Mikayla Lawrence, agent James Farrell, cover designer Molly Fehr, and cover artist Paula TopSky Houtz. A shout-out to Native educators, librarians, and booksellers, and to our allied friends! You have all been instrumental in nurturing and supporting Indigenous authors who hail from what the publishing industry calls "the North American market." And a shout-out to young readers! We write for you because we respect and value you as an audience. We're all rooting for you!

You are loved. You are loved. You will always be loved.

ABOUT THE CONTRIBUTORS

Kaua Māhoe Adams is a mixed Kanaka Maoli (Native Hawaiian) author originally from Seattle, Washington. She received her bachelor of arts in English literature and creative writing from the University of Washington and her master of fine arts in Writing for Children and Young Adults at the Vermont College of Fine Arts. She writes stories about Kanaka kids looking for a way home.

Kaua lives in sunny Southern California on a bird sanctuary, with her partner and their very, very lazy dog, Guava.

Darcie Little Badger is a Lipan Apache writer with a PhD in oceanography. Her critically acclaimed debut novel, *Elatsoe*, was featured in *Time* as one of the 100 Best Fantasy Books of All Time. *Elatsoe* also won the Locus Award for Best First Novel and is a Nebula, Ignyte, and Lodestar finalist. Her second fantasy novel, *A Snake Falls to Earth*, received a Nebula Award, an Ignyte Award, and a Newbery Honor Award and was on the National Book Award long list. Her third book, *Sheine Lende*, continues the adventures of the Elatsoe universe. Darcie is married to a veterinarian named Taran.

A writer's life is forged by a kaleidoscope of experiences, and ***Marcella Bell***'s (she/her, Muscogee Freedmen, Black,

European-American) is no exception—from gracing newsrooms and theater stages to wild encounters with raven bites and pelican lice. Prophetically voted "Most Likely to Write a Bestselling Novel" in high school, she may not have conquered the bestseller lists yet, but she's made good on the rest with seven published novels under her belt so far, including her sizzling Closed Circuit romance duology, *The Wildest Ride* and *The Rodeo Queen*. Whether crafting captivating romances for adults or developing uplifting stories for young readers, her narratives reflect her intimate understanding of intersectional identities, buried histories, and undertold tales. When not writing, you might find Marcella chasing after her children like a Regency-era butler, nerding out over anime and corvids, getting tattooed, exploring the outdoors with her beloved, eating, reading, or otherwise feeding her insatiable curiosity and a hunger for understanding the world through diverse lenses and experiences. Marcella earned a master's in public administration as well as a bachelor of arts from Portland State University and remains grateful to learn new things each and every day.

Angeline Boulley, an enrolled member of the Sault Ste. Marie Tribe of Chippewa Indians, is a storyteller who writes about her Ojibwe community in Michigan's Upper Peninsula. She is a former director of the Office of Indian Education at the US Department of Education.

Firekeeper's Daughter is her debut novel and was an instant #1 *New York Times* bestseller. A Reese's YA Book Club selection, it won both the Michael L. Printz Award for Excellence in Young Adult Literature and the William C. Morris YA Debut Award from the American

Library Association. *Time* named it one of the 100 Best YA Books of All Time. *Warrior Girl Unearthed*, her second novel, was a *New York Times* bestseller, won the Boston Globe–Horn Book Award, and was named a Youth Literature Award Honor Book by the American Indian Library Association.

Angeline lives in southwest Michigan, but her home will always be on Sugar Island.

K. A. Cobell, Staa'tssipisstaakii, is an enrolled member of the Blackfeet Nation and the author of *Looking for Smoke*. She currently lives in the Pacific Northwest, where she spends her time writing books, chasing her kids through the never-ending rain, and scouring the inlet beaches for sand dollars and hermit crabs.

Christine Hartman Derr is a citizen of the Cherokee Nation of Oklahoma. She's a graduate of Vermont College of Fine Arts' Writing for Children and Young Adults MFA program. Originally from Broken Arrow, Oklahoma, Christine lives in East Tennessee with her spouse, children, and a rambunctious crew of lovable pets with themed names. She runs the blog *Paw Prints in the Sink* and has written articles for regional publications. Her picture book, *Until We Meet Again: Donadagohvi*, and her debut novel, *The Witches of Bear Creek Falls*, are forthcoming from Heartdrum.

A. J. Eversole grew up in rural Oklahoma, a place removed from city life and full of opportunities to grow the imagination, which she did through intense games of make-believe. She is an author who writes across all age groups, currently living in Fort Worth, Texas, with her husband and children. As an enrolled citizen of the Cherokee Nation, she is incredibly passionate about supporting Native and Indigenous voices and works as a Native Voices Reporter at Cynthia Leitich Smith's *Cynsations*, which celebrates children's and YA literature.

Jen Ferguson (she/her) is a queer woman with Métis/Michif and white settler ancestry. She is also an activist, a feminist, an auntie, and an accomplice armed with a PhD in English and creative writing. She believes that writing, teaching, and beading are political acts. Her debut YA novel, *The Summer of Bitter and Sweet*, received seven starred reviews, won the Governor General's Literary Award for Young People's Literature—Text, is a Stonewall Honor Book, an NPR Best Book of the Year, a *School Library Journal* Best Young Adult Book of the year, a Chicago Public Library Best Teen Fiction, a *Horn Book* FanFare Book, a *Kirkus* Best Young Adult Book, a White Pine Award Nominee, a Young Adult Golden Poppy Finalist, and a William C. Morris YA Debut Award Finalist, among other honors. Jen's other YA novels are *Those Pink Mountain Nights* and *A Constellation of Minor Bears*.

Eric Gansworth, S·ha-weñ na-sae? (Onondaga, Eel Clan), is a writer and visual artist from Tuscarora Nation. He has been widely published and exhibited. Lowery Writer-in-Residence at Canisius University, he has also been an NEH Distinguished Visiting Professor at Colgate University. His work has received a Michael L. Printz Honor, was long-listed for the National Book Award, and has received an American Indian Youth Literature Award, PEN Oakland Award, and American Book Award. *Apple (Skin to the Core)* was chosen for *Time*'s 10 Best YA and Children's Books of the year.

Byron Graves is Ojibwe and Lakota. He was born and raised on the Red Lake Indian Reservation in Minnesota, where he played high school basketball. When he isn't writing, he can be found playing video games, cleaning up after his cats, or skateboarding. His debut novel, *Rez Ball*, won the American Indian Youth Literature Award for Best Young Adult Book and the William C. Morris YA Debut Award.

Kate Hart is the author of *After the Fall* and a contributor to the young adult anthologies *Out Now: Queer We Go Again!*, *Toil & Trouble*, *Body Talk: 37 Voices Explore Our Radical Anatomy*, and *Hope Nation*, as well as the adult Indigenous horror collection *Never Whistle at Night*. A former teacher and grant writer with degrees in history and Spanish, Kate has appeared at literature festivals across the country and helped run YA Highway, a three-time pick for *Writer's Digest*'s "101 Best Websites for Writers." Born in Oklahoma and raised in Arkansas, she is a citizen of the Chickasaw Nation with Choctaw heritage and a member of the Tulsa chapter of Matriarch. She lives with her family on an Ozark mountainside, where she co-owns Natural State Treehouses and sells woodworking, beading, and fiber arts as Kate Hart Studio.

Karina Iceberg lives in New England with her husband, their two wild children, and a nearly tame cat. Otherwise, you can find her in her first and forever home, Alaska. From Alaska, she learned to find inspiration from the world all around her, and also from her heritage (Aleut/Alutiiq). She has an MFA in Writing for Children and Young Adults from Vermont College of Fine Arts. She has two forthcoming picture books with Heartdrum, *Free to Fly* and *A Good Hide*.

Cheryl Isaacs is a Mohawk/white writer from southern Ontario and the author of *The Unfinished*. She believes that outdoors is the best place to be and that sweet potato fries should be a food group.

David A. Robertson is a two-time winner of the Governor General's Literary Award and has won the TD Canadian Children's Literature Award and the Writers' Union of Canada Freedom to Read Award. He has received several other accolades for his work as a writer for children and adults, podcaster, public speaker, and social advocate. He was honored with a Doctor of Letters by the University of Manitoba in 2023 for outstanding contributions to the arts and distinguished achievements. He is a member of Norway House Cree Nation and lives in Winnipeg.

Andrea L. Rogers is a citizen of the Cherokee Nation and writes fiction and nonfiction for young people and adults. She grew up in Tulsa, Oklahoma, but currently lives in Artists Point, Arkansas. Andrea graduated with an MFA from the Institute for American Indian Arts. Andrea taught both art (all grades) and English (high school) in public schools in Dallas–Fort Worth for fourteen years. Her books include *The Art Thieves*; *Man Made Monsters*, winner of the Walter Dean

Myers Award for Outstanding Children's Literature; *Mary and the Trail of Tears: A Cherokee Removal Story Survivor Story*; and the short stories "Hellhound in No Man's Land" in *HOWL*, "My Oklahoma History" in *You Too?*, and "The Ballad of Maggie Wilson" in *Ancestor Approved: Intertribal Stories for Kids*. She has published two picture books, *When We Gather (Ostadahlisiha): A Cherokee Tribal Feast* and *Chooch Helped*.

Muscogee citizen *Cynthia Leitich Smith* is a highly acclaimed, *New York Times* bestselling author, Southern Mississippi Medallion Winner, and an NSK Neustadt Laureate.

Her debut novel, *Rain Is Not My Indian Name*, was named one of the 30 Most Influential Children's Books of All Time by Book Riot, which also listed her among 10 Must-Read Native American Authors. Cynthia's young adult titles include *Hearts Unbroken*, winner of an American Indian Youth Literature Award, and the YA ghost mystery *Harvest House*, a Bram Stoker Award Nominee for Superior Achievement in a Young Adult Novel. Her award-winning books for children include *Jingle Dancer*, *Indian Shoes*, *Sisters of the Neversea*, *On a Wing and a Tear*, and the Blue Stars graphic novel series. She also edited the groundbreaking anthology *Ancestor Approved: Intertribal Stories for Kids*. Cynthia is the author-curator of Heartdrum, a Native-focused imprint of HarperCollins Children's Books, and was the inaugural Katherine Paterson Endowed Chair at the Vermont College of Fine Arts MFA program. She is a graduate of the White School of Journalism at the University of Kansas and the University of Michigan Law School. Cynthia lives in Austin and Denton, Texas.

Author and filmmaker *Brian Young* is a graduate of both Yale University with a bachelor's in film studies and Columbia University with a master's in creative writing fiction. An enrolled member of the Navajo Nation, he grew up on the Navajo Reservation but now lives in Brooklyn, New York. As an undergraduate, Brian won a fellowship with the prestigious Sundance Ford Foundation with one of his feature-length scripts. He has worked on several short films, including *Tsídii Nááts'íílid—Rainbow Bird* and *A Conversation on Race with Native Americans* for the short documentary series produced by the *New York Times*. He was a participant of the sixth-annual Native American TV Writers Lab with the Native American Media Alliance, where he learned to write television scripts. Brian's books for young readers include *Healer of the Water Monster*, which was an American Library Association Notable Book and winner of an American Indian Youth Literature Award, and *Heroes of the Water Monster*, which was an American Indian Youth Literature Award Honor Book and Junior Library Guild Gold Medal selection.

In 2014, We Need Diverse Books (WNDB) began as a simple hashtag on Twitter. The social media campaign soon grew into a 501(c)(3) nonprofit with a team that spans the globe. WNDB is supported by a network of writers, illustrators, agents, editors, teachers, librarians, and book lovers, all united under the same goal—to create a world where every child can see themselves in the pages of a book. You can learn more about WNDB programs at www.diversebooks.org.